IT'S
A WRAP

The Waiting For Callback Series

PERDITA & HONOR CARGILL

IT'S A WRAP

SIMON & SCHUSTER

First published in Great Britain in 2018 by Simon and Schuster UK Ltd
A CBS COMPANY

Copyright © 2018 Perdita and Honor Cargill
Quotes used by kind permission of Guardian News & Media Ltd and
News UK and Ireland Ltd. Full details for individual quotes
are listed at the back of this novel.

The right of Perdita and Honor Cargill to be identified as the authors
of this work has been asserted by them in accordance with sections
77 and 78 of the Copyright, Design and Patents Act, 1988.

1 3 5 7 9 10 8 6 4 2

Simon & Schuster UK Ltd
1st Floor, 222 Gray's Inn Road
London WC1X 8HB

www.simonandschuster.co.uk

Simon & Schuster Australia, Sydney
Simon & Schuster India, New Delhi

A CIP catalogue record for this book
is available from the British Library.

PB ISBN 978-1-4711-6615-0
eBook ISBN 978-1-4711-6616-7

This book is a work of fiction. Names, characters, places and
incidents are either the product of the author's imagination or are
used fictitiously. Any resemblance to actual people living or
dead, events or locales is entirely coincidental.

Typeset in Caecilia by M Rules
Printed and bound by CPI Group (UK) Ltd, Croydon, CR0 4YY

Simon & Schuster UK Ltd are committed to sourcing paper
that is made from wood grown in sustainable forests and supports
the Forest Stewardship Council, the leading international forest
certification organisation. Our books displaying the
FSC logo are printed on FSC certified paper.

To Geila, who will like this
dedication more than she'll ever admit.
With our love xx

Main Characters – the story so far . . .

Elektra James: almost sixteen. Failed at all extra-curriculars except acting. Break-out agent-getting role? Performing carrot. Finally – after a long and painful year when her biggest role was the voice of the second-most-important squirrel in a local nuts commercial – landed a role, as Straker, teen lead and action hero in Raw, world's most dystopian film. Great times (shame Elektra runs like a wonky chicken and Straker got killed off early in the rewrites . . .).

Moss Sato: Elektra's best friend. Spiky, funny and far too good to be being messed around by sort-of-boyfriend Torr.

Archie Mortimer: practically perfect. Also Elektra's boyfriend ♥ . . . well, until she broke up with him (due to toxic combo of stupidity, misinformation and rampant insecurity). Currently filming vampire-slaying teen hero Tibor Snolosky in *The Curse of Peter Plogojowitz in Transylvania*, supported by a cast of maidens of outstanding beauty and a horse called Angelina Jolie.

Elektra's family: **Julia**, her mum, world-class worrier, **Bertie**, her dad, hates colour and mess, but otherwise most rational member of family, **Eulalie**, her adored French step-grandmother (life-loving, bit of a fantasist). Also, **Digby** (RIP), recently deceased favoured sibling – OK, Dalmatian & **Plog** (short for Plogojowitz, see above) new dotty, four-legged arrival.

Acting: Elektra's agents are **Stella** and **Charlie** at the **Haden Agency** (child actors' agency handily located above the dentist).

The long-suffering **cast and crew of Raw**. The Hunger Games meets Planet of the Apes meets Avatar meets Romeo & Juliet meets etc. etc., production on this post-apocalyptic action movie has been dogged by delays and disasters and rewrites. Even before filming is over the critics and trolls are gathering ☹ ☹ ☹ ☹ ☹ ☹. The Terra Tribe (inc. Elektra) is fighting it out with the Warri Tribe (who have better costumes). There are floods, there are scary wolf-like creatures, there isn't much more to eat than bugs and it's hard to say more because the plot keeps changing . . .

Carlo Winn: plays Jan, the only other teen in the cast, Elektra's on-set unreliable friend. Committed flirt, gossip, way more likeable than he probably should be.

The A-Listers. Sam Gross, nurse-punching, ex-rehab, action hero — drinks too much whisky (his own brand) and has a pet pig back in LA. **Amber Leigh**, glowing matcha-drinking, Yoga-honed, screen goddess rarely separated from hard-to-love pet pooch, Pomeranian **Kale**. S-Amber have a long-running complicated on-off on-screen, off-screen love-thing going on.

Sergei Havelski: Director, has fallen hard for Eulalie ♥. Hungarian, ~~mildly~~ terrifying, drinks too much coffee. Plagued by the producers, the suits at **Panda Productions** and ever-changing roster of screenwriters. Assisted by **Ahmed** the first AD. Also, **Eddie**, an assistant with a thing about schedules, abs and ABBA (usually at the same time), **Sound Dan** (i.e. Dan the guy who's in charge of sound) and **Naomi**, the on-set tutor.

School: Tragically, Elektra still spends a lot of her waking hours dodging detentions at all-girls' Berkeley Academy. It's Year Eleven so it's basically a cesspit of stress. Head of year **Mrs Green:** is also least pastoral head of pastoral care in history. Thank God for **Moss** (see above) and **Jenny**. Others are **Flissy and Talia:** unavoidable power couple of meanness & (annoyingly) hotness.

It's the night of Elektra's sixteenth birthday party and ...

★
CHAPTER 1

'Everyone's tried to have a perfect career. No one in the history of Hollywood's succeeded.'

Anna Kendrick

'Nothing says "guilty" like gifting a puppy,' said Carlo.

Great. My ex-boyfriend turns up unannounced with a tiny Dalmatian snuggled into his jacket – which is probably the most romantic thing that will ever happen to me – and my ex-co-actor fresh from the *Raw* set has to turn up too to share the limelight.

'Archie, meet Carlo. Carlo, meet Archie,' I said resignedly. They sort of nodded at each other. 'What are you even doing here, Carlo?'

'It's a party.' He shrugged like it was obvious. It was. The house was *pulsating*.

'I didn't invite you.' But then I hadn't invited at least half the people who'd turned up.

'Why not? We can't have worked together for months on the world's most dystopian movie without me earning an invite. Come on, E, we saved the world together.' Put like that, it did sound bad.

'No, I died while the world was still under threat.' Strictly speaking it was Straker (my character) who had died but they were *my* lines that had been cut so it counted as a personal tragedy.

Plog – because for better or worse that was the puppy's name – made a weird noise that would probably grow into a bark; another male to fight for the limelight.

'It's not going to work,' said Carlo.

'What's not going to work?' asked Archie, pulling me closer. I'd forgotten how nice that was. I tried to relax but Carlo was still talking.

'The puppy gesture.' Carlo tickled him under the chin (Plog not Archie). 'Nice try, mate, better than flowers – but she's not going to fall for it. Are you, E?'

'Yes,' I said simply. 'I am.' I wanted Carlo to go away. It was a bit crowded in this conversation. Archie was *back*. Couldn't I just enjoy that for a bit without Carlo materializing to remind me of all the complicated stuff?

'It's not an apology,' said Archie. 'Also, Plog's not exactly a gift.'

'He's not?' I asked. 'God ... no, I hadn't assumed ...' I tailed off. I *had* assumed. *Why* had I assumed? If anyone else had turned up on my doorstep with a puppy I wouldn't have jumped to the conclusion they were going to hand it over. This was awkward.

Archie laughed. 'Obviously he's your dog ... if you want him.' I did. 'But it's more of a delivery than a gift. I mean ... whatever, Plog's not an apology.'

'But you're hoping he's going to get you out of some difficult conversations,' Carlo said. 'That Elektra's going to be too busy with your little fur baby to ask you too many questions about life on-set in Dracula country?'

I wished, not for the first time, that I'd never told Carlo that Archie was filming a vampire-slaying-teen-hero in Transylvania surrounded by a supporting cast of maidens of outstanding beauty. In my defence, it's quite a hard fact to ignore and we'd had a lot of time hanging around on-set together to fill with gossip. 'He doesn't have anything to apologize for,' I said. Definitely not the full-on-cheating-with-hot-leading-lady thing that I'd recently and wrongly accused him of. *Complicated.* And now my phone was barking – *Mum wants FaceTime.* Oddly enough I *really* didn't, but the stream of angry texts complaining about the noise (why, oh why had she stayed in the neighbourhood?) were becoming harder to ignore. I was in deep trouble. The last one simply read: **You've had your last warning. I'm coming home RIGHT NOW**.

'Don't panic,' said Archie when I held out the screen. Of course I was panicking, I had fifteen minutes, tops, before Mum got here and my life was over. 'We've got this.' He sounded like the hot guy in war movies who singlehandedly restores peace and order to an entire geo-political region while getting the girl. I wasted a precious minute just gazing at him before harsh reality kicked in again. 'We'll just go in and get everyone out.'

'*How?*' I wailed. 'There are still people trying to get *in*.'

'Nobody'll want to stay when they find out your mum's on the way,' said Carlo. For someone that hadn't met my mum that was a weirdly accurate prediction.

'*Archie!* You came!' Moss emerged from the crush in the hall and flung herself on him, narrowly avoiding being the second person to risk squashing Plog to death on his first night in his new home.

'Where's Torr? It was the worst question he could have asked but then Archie wasn't up to date with the recent ups and mostly downs of Moss's love life. She broke off from giving Plog little besotted pats and looked at us like she was about to cry.

'Who's Torr? Weird name.' Carlo had stopped trying to get people out and was staring at Moss.

'Moss's sort of boyf . . .' I tailed off. This wasn't the moment to try and explain the intricacies of that relationship. Torr had flaked on my party to go to a cool-year-above-party and rumour had it he was having a very good time. Moss had briefly tried to have a 'good time' too with a guy with excellent arm game but no conversation; judging by the mascara'd tear tracks it hadn't gone well.

'The . . . *kitchen*. Oh, God, Elektra, wait till you see the kitchen.' Moss looked at her phone and did a sob-hiccup.

'You're not crying about the kitchen, are you?' Carlo was getting in touch with his sensitive side.

This probably wasn't the *perfect* time for my hot reliable best friend to meet my hot, unreliable friend from filming but I gave in to the inevitable. 'Carlo, Moss. Be nice, Carlo, but not too nice.' Moss wiped her tears and stuck out her hand, Carlo went in for a double kiss. Only the deepest loyalty stopped me from laughing.

'I'm always nice, E.' He turned to Moss. 'I don't know why she hasn't introduced us before.'

'Carlo just stop. Moss is my best friend. I tell her everything. It's way too late to make a good first impression. Anyway, there's no time for small talk.' I squashed back against the wall to let people get

5

out. The word that there was a parent on the way was getting around but not fast enough.

'You and Dracula Boy have got this. Lend me the puppy, I'll cheer her up.' Carlo snaffled Plog, grabbed a startled Moss by the other hand, and headed back out of the door.

'Might work?' said Archie.

That was what I was worried about – Moss had probably had enough drama for one night – but there was no time to waste. I clung onto Archie and we faced the kitchen together like Jack and Rose in the final scene of *Titanic*.

Wow.

There were shards of glass on the floor; an open drawer was full of popcorn and for some inexplicable reason all the carrot sticks my mother had insisted on supplying had been spiked on cocktail sticks and lined up neatly along on our kitchen counter.

The humans were less ordered.

'Party's over,' yelled Archie. No one heard him. I turned off the music; he roared again. Not enough happened. 'We can't sort this out in ten minutes.' Ten hours wouldn't have been long enough. Plan B.

'Here's the thing,' I said to Mum, stalling her at the door some painful minutes later. 'It's quite bad but it's not a *disaster*.' This time I felt like the captain of the Titanic.

'I. Am. Not. Happy.' She didn't look happy. 'There must be a hundred people in there.'

'Definitely not a hundred,' I said, employing a strange dance-y manoeuvre to let people out without her getting in.

'There are at least twenty just hanging out of the windows,' she spluttered.

'No—' It was unfortunate that at that exact moment a shoe fell to the ground from the second floor. 'Er ... it's just that ... everyone's on this side of the building?'

'And why would that be, Elektra? Is there a fire in the kitchen? A body in the hall? What exactly should I be prepared for before I walk through that door?'

'I think the best thing is if you *don't* walk through that door right now. Just give us a bit more time for ... a little tidy up.' OK, Plan B was weak. How long could I hold her off?

'I'll help,' said Archie.

'We'll help too,' said Moss, who had reappeared with Carlo to join our human barricade. She wasn't crying anymore, which was good, but Carlo was looking smug, which was ... troubling.

'No,' said Mum without even saying hello. 'This needs an adult.' There was the unmistakable sound of breaking glass. 'Possibly one in uniform.'

'Have you seen the puppy, Mrs James?' Archie

reclaimed Plog from Carlo and held him out like a peace offering to a vengeful god. 'Aaaaaw, he likes you.'

'He's good,' whispered Carlo. 'Don't trust him, E.' I ignored him. This wasn't the moment to fill him in on the real facts surrounding Archie's alleged straying.

Plog's spell couldn't hold for ever, or apparently even for very long. 'Everyone still has to leave,' Mum said grimly.

'But Archie's just got here,' I protested.

'I've just got here too,' said Carlo, looking at Moss, who blushed.

'Archie's crossed seas and brought me a puppy,' I added. Archie shrugged like it was all in a day's work.

'I don't care if he's slain dragons for you,' said Mum.

'That'll be his next trick.' I had a suspicion Carlo didn't like anyone else playing the action hero.

'If you ever want Archie, or anyone else, to come over to this house again, they leave now.' Mum wasn't lightening up.

'Is it not still OK for me to stay over?' asked Moss.

'I'll walk you home,' offered Carlo, inching ever closer to her. She looked panicked, as well she might.

'Everyone leaves except Moss,' said Mum.

It was hard to say goodbye to Archie with her giving it the full Medusa.

After an hour so grim I will be reliving it in therapy in twenty years' time, the house was empty – of 'guests', anyway – and Moss and I had finally managed to steer Mum upstairs (clutching *my* puppy like a comfort blanket) on the promise that we'd clean the kitchen. 'It's really *bad*.'

'I know. *Messy*.'

'Everything's sticky,' I said, looking for a cloth under the sink and finding only empty crisp packets and a hoody that wasn't mine.

'I wasn't talking about the kitchen,' said Moss.

'Ah, yes ... *Carlo*?! What was going on there?'

'Nothing.' She looked sheepish. 'He was comforting me.' I raised an eyebrow. 'He was sweet to me. I *cried* on him.' Moss squirmed.

'Sweet?' Carlo and I had shared a lot – we'd eaten (fake) bugs, we'd climbed (fake) cliffs, we'd fought off (fake/green-scene) scary-wolf-like-creatures together. That made for a weird bond but I wouldn't describe him as 'sweet'. 'What did he say to you?'

'*Nothing.* I just went on and on about Torr and he made sympathetic noises and let me cry on his shoulder. She slumped down at the table, her head in her hands. '*What was I doing?* So cringe. And he's probably still into you if he bothered to turn up.'

'He was never into me.' As I'd told her a billion times. 'He just likes parties.' Now she was scrolling her phone, muttering Torr-related curses and looking seriously stressed. 'And the other guy?'

'I am a terrible person.'

'No, you're honestly not. You just needed a *distraction*.' I was going with that because the dodgy alternative was that she'd been trying to get Torr's attention. I abandoned tidying and started to make us toast.

Her phone buzzed. *'Torr is calling,'* she read out. Spooky timing. 'Do you think he knows?'

'Nooooo.' Of course he did. It had been at least two hours, news spread fast. 'And so what if he does?'

'I feel so bad.' Double standards right there. The phone beeped with a text and she chucked it into an open drawer. Under less painful circumstances, I'd have congratulated her on her aim.

'Um ... Mossy?' I ventured. 'What did it say?'

'I have no idea. That's why I placed my phone in the drawer.' Placed? More beeping, Moss stared at the drawer as if she was hearing muffled scratching from inside a coffin.

'You haven't done anything wrong.' Torr was too up himself for basic boyfriend commitment. I put a plate of uneven buttery rounds in front of her.

'I got with some random guy.' She munched and despaired. 'Oh, yes, and then I cried on a hot-breakthrough-actor's shoulder. Mustn't forget that smooth move.' Her phone rang again. She tensed. 'I should pick it up.' She stayed where she was. The drawer stopped beeping and started buzzing. 'What am I going to do?' Another text. 'Shall I just put it on silent? Yes, I'll put it on silent, and then I'll ... leave. I could move to Stockholm. Apparently, the guys there are hot and respect women.'

'What? All of them? Are you sure?'

'Positive – everyone knows that. It's probably in Wikipedia.'

I would have laughed except that she was struggling not to cry. I plonked myself right in front of her. 'Torr's behaved really badly.' Possibly *really*, really badly. 'No way does he get to make you feel guilty about anything.'

'Can we just talk about you?' She forced a smile. 'At least one of us had a successful evening. I knew Archie would show.'

'No, you didn't!'

'OK, no, I didn't. But I'm so happy he did.'

'Me too, Mossy. But ...'

'What? Come on. It was like the most romantic thing ever.'

'It was *mad*. In a good way. But ... Archie and me, we still need to talk. We can't just pretend the last couple of months didn't happen. I need to say sorry.'

'Puppies speak louder than words.'

'I wish.' We looked at each other for a moment and then, as one, reached for more toast.

CHAPTER 2

'But at sixteen your brain isn't fully formed yet, is it?'

Ryan Gosling

It was eight in the morning (which, given that we'd crashed four hours earlier, was the crack of dawn) and Mum was already in the kitchen wearing Marigolds and an ominous expression when Moss and I came downstairs. 'You promised me the kitchen would be perfect by the time I saw it.'

'I'm *really* sorry, Mum,' I said, ineffectually wiping toast crumbs off the counter with my dressing-gown sleeve. 'We didn't think you'd be up yet.'

'Well, unfortunately for you, I am. And I think this is yours?' She held up a big bedraggled piece of paper scrawled all over with gold marker pen.

Goals
(for Elektra on turning 16 – feel free to add ...)

1.
Become less uggers.

I was pretty sure that was Moss's writing. I hoped it was Moss's writing. If it was Moss it was funny. If it was anyone else it was mildly soul destroying.

2.
Become world's most unlikely big screen action hero and DON'T FORGET ME. Then get a part in something/anything I'd pay to see. Mean Girls 3???

Same handwriting.

3.
Throw more parties.

I was up for that but I'd probably need to rethink the venue.

4.
Get ...

And then some letters ... I think they were letters. I tried about 12 different combinations on Urban Dictionary. Nope, it would forever remain a mystery – probably for the best.

5.
Move to Arizona and become a cactus.

That was rude. You don't turn up to someone's party and tell them to move to a remote part of America and become an inanimate object.

6.

~~Stop breaking up with boyfriend~~

7.

~~Have boyfriend gift you a dog.~~

I had a suspicion numbers six and seven were Archie.

8.

Break up with boyfriend and get with hot co-star (call me) ;) ;) ;)

I wonder who that could have been.

9.

^^LOL Jokes. Give me the phone number of your hot friend – the one that was crying.

Nope, no idea, none.

10.

Survive release of what critics are already calling the world's worst dystopian movie.

11

PASS YOUR GCSES!!

The ink was barely dry on this one.

'Where did you find it?' I asked nervously.

'On the watermelon. Impaled with a chopstick. If you'd tidied the kitchen properly – if you'd tidied the kitchen *at all* – you couldn't have missed it.'

I took it from her and read.

'Thanks, Mum, for reminding me that this is the year of my imminent death and destruction,' I said, although for her that was restrained (she usually specified minimum grades).

My phone barked. **How was being last night?** A text from my party-loving step-grandmother Eulalie.

So good I'm now in deep disgrace

Bravo, cherie! I loved Eulalie. We understood each other.

Also, LOOK. I attached some pics of Plog.

I am being in love already. Archie brought him? Non?

You knew?

Bien sûr

'Was I the only person in this family that wasn't expecting Plog to turn up?' I asked my mum.

'Yep,' said Dad, wandering in looking crumpled. 'Good surprise?' He yawned and set about making coffee.

'The best.' I yawned too. It was catching. 'Good time at your work party?' I asked. He'd failed in basic parenting duties by avoiding my party and sloping off to some 'unmissable' work thing.

'Judging by all this,' he waved his arm around the kitchen (which I thought was looking *fine* now), 'it wasn't as fun as yours. Do you need coffee?' He waved the pot at us.

'You know I don't drink coffee,' I said at the same time as Moss nodded desperately.

'I didn't ask if you wanted it, I asked if you *needed* it.' He filled Moss's mug and then his own. 'Did you have fun, Moss?'

'Sort of,' she said, her eyes welling.

'Ah,' he said, leaving well alone.

'Oh, Moss!' said Mum, beetling over. 'Boyfriend problems?' She never left well alone. 'Will it help to talk about it?'

'Er . . .'

'I think we need to take Plog outside,' I said, mostly to allow Moss to escape, but also because he was enthusiastically sniffing out a potential wee spot in the corner. 'If I were you, I'd go home,' I said when we were safely in the garden. 'It's not going to be chill around here for a bit.' We watched my mum through the windows. She was brandishing a mop like a light sabre.

'I feel bad abandoning you.'

'Just go. It's OK, they won't actually kill me.' I paused, 'Although could you phone in a couple of hours just to be sure?'

'If the worst happens, can I inherit Plog?'

'Yes, but I don't want Torr to be his step-father.' He would be a poor influence on my dog. 'Don't message him.'

'I'm not going to,' she said, cuddling Plog goodbye and not looking at me.

It took another hour of heavy-duty sweeping and scrubbing after Moss had gone before I was allowed to sit down and have breakfast. 'See, I told you we'd get it back to perfect,' I said.

'When you said "we" I hadn't realized you meant mostly "me",' said Mum. 'But, yes, it's almost back to normal. Do you think it still smells?'

'Only of bleach,' I said, covering Plog's little nose with my hand before he could be poisoned by all this cleanliness.

'Oh, well, let's put it behind us,' she said, and I breathed a big sigh of relief. 'Of course there'll be consequences.' I sucked my breath right in again. 'What do you think,' she looked at Dad. 'We could ground her?'

He nodded, 'That could work.'

My phone barked and Plog startled (I needed to explain ring tones to him before he got attachment issues); a text from Carlo. **That girl from your party with the face – THE FACE – can I have her number?**

That's not narrowing it down. I knew exactly who he meant.

THE FACE ELEKTRA. Hot but crying. Oh Carlo. I

think she had a fringe? Jeans? Some kind of top???
Stunning powers of observation.

'Elektra? Can you explain why there is a shoe in this plant pot?'

'Hang on, I just need to reply to Carlo.'

'Carlo? There aren't any *complications* there, are there?'

I was getting a bit bored of reassuring people that there wasn't some dark, surprising hidden attraction between me and my ex co-actor. 'No.'

'Good, I like Archie,' said Mum, as though that was the most important consideration. 'And it would be unsettling for Plog.' Sorry? 'We don't want you to suffer from a broken home do we?' she cooed to the tiny dog. Plainly the thin thread connecting her to reality had finally snapped.

That girl has a name. I texted. **I think you should maybe know that before her number**

Something weird. Carlo texted back. **Grass? Weed? Algae?**

MOSS . . . **but she's really nice**

And?

Too nice for you

I was SO nice.

You mean you creeped on her when her defences were down

He didn't bother to contradict me. **Does she have a boy?**

19

A boy? What, like a pet? Possibly. Send her a friend request. Put in the work

Text would be better

And again, creepy . . .

My phone barked again. **Seriously. I liked her**

You barely spoke to her

She was cool. She had something

What?

How would I know? I'm not that in touch with my emotions. He was hopeless. My phone barked again. **But I did like her.**

Interesting. I put down the phone and grabbed more toast. 'Please don't ground me. Nobody gets grounded at sixteen.'

'We could go for something more imaginative,' said Dad.

'What are you thinking?' asked Mum merrily, as if they were discussing holiday options. 'Ooooh, her phone?' She picked it up off the table.

'Anything but my phone,' I pleaded. 'I would literally die. I would have no life.'

'I'm sure your social life would survive,' said Mum. 'There's always real-life communications.'

'No. I might *actually* die. I could be, like, attacked or abducted or ... there could be an alien invasion?' These were real concerns for my mum. 'How could I summon help? How could I let *you* know?'

'You'd survive.'

What? This was not a good moment for her to turn rational. Was she going to be one of those mums that ties their kids' shoelaces for them until they're sixteen and then sends them on a solo trip to Colombia with an out-of-date Rough Guide?

My phone barked. Mum looked at the screen and read aloud, '"I'm literally five mins from your house."'

If there was one thing worse than not having my phone it was my mum having my phone, especially when – if my guess was right – Archie was texting. I lunged for the phone but not fast enough.

'"How's the industrial clean-up going?"' she read out. '"Did you get the stains out of the curtains? Do you think they'll let me come round or are they being too cray? I've got a bad feeling I blotted my perfect bf rep last night.' Make. It. Stop. 'How intuitive of him.' Mum commented dryly.

'*Please*, I am literally *begging* you, give me back my phone. You can ground me for as long as you like if you give me back my phone. Dad?' How come he wasn't in trouble? He'd got home super late. 'Show some mercy. I'll be an actual slave. I'll do *extra* revision.' Mum slowly lowered the phone. 'I'll ... wash the curtains?' I probably wouldn't. I was desperate. 'And you'll let Archie come?' The phone was back on the table. I made a grab for it. 'He's got to go back to Transylvania on Tuesday.' I didn't just *want* to see him; I *needed* to see him.

'All the more reason for him to spend time with his own family.'

'*Muu-u-mmm.*'

'OK, OK, stop looking at me like that. Archie can still come but that's it. Then you're looking at convent-like seclusion till the end of the month.' And off she went to inspect the curtains.

Archie flicked a cigarette butt off a low wall in our garden and we sat down. It was a serious contribution to the tidying-up efforts. I shivered. He shrugged off his jacket and – as I waited smugly for another rom-com moment – wrapped it around Plog. So, that would be the famous rom-com where the hero prioritizes the dog above the love interest.

'What?' Archie shifted so that there was no space between us. That was better. 'He looked cold.'

'Didn't I look cold?'

'He's a lot smaller than you.'

'But he has *fur.*' Given that it was October and my legs were safe in jeans, I had a fair amount of fur too but Archie didn't need to know that.

'Are you really getting jealous of the dog?' Archie laughed.

And then it was quiet. 'I'm so sorry,' I blurted.

'You *are* jealous of Plog?' It was a half-hearted joke. We were both tense.

'We need to talk.' Oh God, I'd said it out loud. I sounded like my mum. It wasn't that I wanted to have a heavy conversation – I *hated* heavy conversations – but *not* having this one was starting to feel worse.

'Don't say it like you want to break up with me ... again.' Plog was getting all his attention. 'Unless you do?'

'No, I don't.' I really didn't. 'I want to explain.'

'You don't need to.' He stopped stroking Plog and laced his fingers through mine. 'I get why you reacted like you did.' He did? 'I was really crap.' No, he didn't get it. This was going to be even worse than I'd thought. 'You had a lot going on. The rewrites on *Raw* and your character getting killed off and ... Digby. I feel really bad that I wasn't there. I'm sorry, Elektra.'

'You couldn't be there.' Nobody got to walk off a set just because their girlfriend's dog died. Even a dog as legendary as Digby. It would be touch and go if the girlfriend had died. Archie/Tibor Snolosky had been needed in Transylvania – still was. There were vampires to slay and the BBC were paying him to slay them.

'I should have phoned more and texted more and—'

'No.' I interrupted. 'That wasn't why.'

'What wasn't? Why? What?'

'I didn't break up with you because I thought you weren't paying me enough attention. I thought . . . I thought you'd cheated on me.' I said it very quietly but he heard me. He was going to be angry. Or upset. Angry and upset. He drew away and turned and stared at me. There was a long pause. I tried to read what he was thinking.

'You *what?*' At a wild guess I'd say he wasn't happy.

'I thought—'

'You *idiot*.' Under the circumstances I'd let that go. 'Who with?'

'Poppy Leadley,' I said, very much in the direction of the paving stones. Poppy Leadley, the beautiful maiden that captures Archie's heart. But only his on-screen heart as I'd belatedly worked out.

'*What the* . . . *Why?* What made you think *that?*'

I could run away or I could try and explain. It was a tough call. 'It was in *The Bizz*. They said you and Poppy made "*one fit vampire-fighting couple*".' I could have quoted the whole post.

'*The Bizz?*' he smiled but it was more of a grimace. 'You believed *The Bizz?*'

'They said it quite a few times in quite a few ways . . . It was *persuasive*. And there were pictures of you together . . . having fun.'

He looked at me like I was mad. '*So?* We're mates. And she's dating Izzy from Costume.'

'I know that now. *The Bizz* finally got it right.'

'So you stopped being paranoid because you read on the same crappy online gossip site that Poppy was gay?' I hung my head. 'That's quite ...' He tailed off.

'If she had a girlfriend she probably wasn't ...having a thing with you.' I spelled it out in a very small voice.

'*Come on,* Elektra, you didn't need to worry whether Poppy was dating anyone or not. I was dating *you*. I am dating you. I am, right?' I nodded nervously, hopefully. 'Why didn't you ask me if it was true?'

That was the obvious question and I didn't have a good answer. 'I didn't know how to and everyone was telling me something must be going on. And ... I felt *insecure*.' That was putting it mildly.

'Everyone who? Carlo?'

'Sam and Amber, too.'

'You were discussing my alleged cheating with *Sam Gross* and *Amber Leigh*?'

And most of the rest of the cast of *Raw* and all of the crew. 'It came up,' was all I said.

'I don't know whether to be horrified or flattered. So, two A-list actors told you to break up with me because ...?'

'There's always stuff going on on-set and long-distance stuff doesn't work out. Well, that's what they said and I thought they probably knew what they were talking about.' Sam and Amber had both been drawing on a lot of real-life experience – not least their own on-off on-set off-set relationship. 'And I didn't *exactly* break up with you – I said we should leave it till you got back to London—'

'You broke up with me, Elektra.'

'You let me.' I still couldn't look at him.

'I messaged you so many times. And I texted you. You didn't get back to me. I even *called* you.' Real voice conversations were hard.

'Because I thought you'd *cheated*.' And because I'd watched Moss *not* breaking up with Torr for months when she should have. 'And I was upset ... more about Digby than anything else.'

'More upset about Digby than breaking up?'

'That sounds bad?' He didn't answer. 'It's just, we hadn't been together that much – well, not real, actual together-in-the-same-place. And me and Diggers were pretty much inseparable. I should stop now, right?'

'There's not much chance of my ego getting out of control while I'm going out with you.' But now he smiled for real. 'I'm going to have to work harder at being your Digby substitute.'

'Except *Plog*. I've fallen for Plog.'

Archie sighed dramatically. 'OK, I accept my lowly position in your life as third to Digby R.I.P. and Plog. Anyone else?'

'Well, Moss?'

'And Moss.' He was leaning in. 'But you should definitely stop talking now.'

I was one hundred per cent good with the no-more-talking plan but first I had to say it again, so he knew I meant it. 'I really am sorry, Archie.'

Sweet ♥ Pop!

Libra Sept 23 - Oct 22

Work
One tricky project is almost over (but don't think you're safe from it yet) and there are yet more daunting challenges ahead. Questions are being asked of you – there are right answers, you just might not know them. Don't try and bluff it out, you won't get away with it. Trust yourself.

Relationships
You've had a tumultuous time recently with Venus, your planetary ruler, connecting with Neptune, the planet of fantasy. You are dreaming big and could find it easy to fall in love. Don't get in your own way . . .

If it's your birthday today
This is a potentially life-changing year. The stars will not always be aligned; you will seek balance and not always find it. Challenges will come from the known, the unknown, the real, the not-so-real and the super-real. You can't foresee or control the future. Resilience will be your greatest asset.

This Week's Celebrity Horoscope!
Amber Leigh (35)
Currently loved up again with Sam Gross, her co-star in Raw, this is going to be an exciting year for Amber. We asked the stars in the sky whether this would be the year these two stars of the screen would wed and the answer was Definitely Maybe . . . ♥ ♥ ♥

This Week's Celebrity Uncovered Georgie Dunn (currently filming costume drama Fortuneswell)

- ♥ She loves Cronuts and has a MASSIVE crush on Sam Gross (we feel ya G!)
- ♥ She's **never** cheated . . .at games
- ♥ She prefers Pretty Little Liars to Poldark
- ♥ Her fave make-up brand is Glow Box (check out sponsored giveaway on back page!)

This Week's Ex-Celebrity Spotting is Maisie Moon (17), who, just two years ago, stole our hearts as tearaway-teen on huge hit drama Hopeless, spotted punching movie trickets in our local O2. Good to see you're still in The Business, Masie!

From: Stella at Haden Agency
Date: 16 October 12.11
To: Elektra James
Cc: Julia James, Charlie at Haden Agency
Subject: *Raw*: release date and production meeting

Dear Elektra,

I've just had confirmation on the release date for *Raw*! ***25 March***.
I know it seems ages away – next year – but it'll come sooner
than you think!

There are going to be lots of exciting things going on in the run-
up and the producers have set up a meeting with some of the
lead actors and other key players on *Raw* to talk about plans for
promotion. Because they're still filming (!) the meeting will take
place at the Fairmount Studios on Saturday 24 October at 11 a.m.

Stella x

P.S. Belated Happy Birthday! I'll try and find you a lovely casting
as a late present, I know it's been a bit of a dry spell ...

162

Days to Go . . .

TheBizz.com

Bringing you the all the Best
Backstabbing in the Bizz . . .

22 October

Roll up, roll up, our spies are telling us that the sets are finally coming down on Fairmount Studio's Sound Stage A as filming on *Raw* makes way for the next Bond film, *Skeleton Island.* Come on, souvenir hunters! Polystyrene cave, anyone? Weird wood-carvings that are probably cultural appropriation? No? No. Final scenes and any reshoots — and on this *painful* production there'll be lot of those — are going to be filmed on one of the smaller stages but post-production has already begun. It's end days now — maybe in more ways than one — is Havelski heading for his first big flop? And how bad is bad? BAD? We've even heard a few *direct-to-digital* whispers 😵 😵 😵 😵 😵 😵.

We're pretty sure most of the cast and crew are *desperate* to be released to new projects *buuuut* for some, parting will be such sweet sorrow — what now, for everyone's favourite dystopian couple, Sam Gross and Amber Leigh? Will true love keep (start? *cynical journo-face) running smoothly when the cameras stop rolling? Well, for now the signs are good. S-Amber were spotted working up a sweat in London's most fashionable and expensive gym yesterday and they say that the couple that works out together stays together. Or maybe we should say the *family* that works out together stays together? We definitely heard the patter of tiny feet — all four of them. Kale, Amber's pet pooch was working hard on his own mini-treadmill.

Aaaaawwww or should that be Paaaaaaaaaawww!

★

CHAPTER 3

'The threat of egomania and narcissism are always looming.'

Colin Firth

'Elektra James, I've missed you!'

Eddie, one of the production assistants, met me at the security gate of the studios. 'I've missed you too!' I disengaged myself from his hug because his clipboard was sticking into my shoulder. 'It's so nice to be back!' I stood and sniffed the Fairmount air. Some might have said it smelled much the same as all the other Greater London air but I'd swear I was getting a whiff of Hollywood. I zoned out into a little fantasy that they'd resurrected Straker (it wouldn't be the maddest thing in the plot) and that I was going to get whisked into hair and make-up and fed biscuits and gossip (happy sigh) and then into Costume and then onto set (happy sigh) and then—

'Elektra?' Eddie snapped his fingers to get my attention. 'I've checked today's schedule.' I was pretty sure he'd *memorized* the schedule. 'We need to get to the production offices at A Stage by precisely 10.53 a.m.' He was a slave to precision timing. 'The meeting starts *promptly* at 11.00 a.m.' I wasn't back to do any acting, I was here for a meeting about 'pre-release publicity' whatever, exactly, that was. 'We should take a buggy.' Eddie was already walking over to the little line of neatly parked Fairmount-Studio-branded golf-cart thingies parked by the security hut.

'Can we go fast?' I asked like a five-year old. I had good memories of illicit buggy racing with Carlo and a couple of speed-crazed Grips up and down Godzilla Avenue. I missed the buggies. I missed the stupid races. I even missed the street names.

'I don't think we should break the speed limit.' The speed limit was five miles an hour. Eddie was reminding me painfully of my mum.

'Stop!' I yelled minutes after we'd set off and Eddie gave a little nervy swerve and stalled. 'Sorry, but it's Dan.' I jumped out and went to hug my favourite sound man. I'd *missed* him.

'Elektra James! Have you come up to see the Cliff of Dreams tumbling down?' A.k.a. the largest built part of the *Raw* set. Climbing up that cliff (OK, a metre of it, with a safety harness and a net underneath) was one of my proudest achievements.

'What? Why? Plot twist? Another natural disaster?'

Dan laughed. 'No – it's getting dismantled today. There's only about half of *Raw* world left in there.' He gestured to the huge doors of Sound Stage A. 'Come and have a look?'

'Definitely.' I'd had some of the maddest, most terrifying and utterly brilliant times of my life in there. They'd built a whole world on that set, with 'cliffs' and 'forests' and 'rivers' and 'caves' (which was just as well because none of the rumoured location shoots had ever happened). I *missed* that world. I needed to get a grip.

'Sorry, no time, no time,' said Eddie. 'We're going to be late.' He waved away Dan and started up the buggy's 'engine' – it was like being carted around by a really angry sewing machine. 'We'll need to go faster.'

'Let's go mad,' I said, watching the speedometer go past the seven-miles-an-hour point. Mad.

'Hey, E, I got here before you.' Carlo was still filming; he'd had a five-minute stagger to this meeting room. Even before my little buggy tour, I'd had an hour and a half in a minicab that smelled of vomit and dangly fir-tree air freshener. I looked at Carlo's 'blood'-stained face. 'Skirmish with the Terras?'

'No, the wolf-like creatures. Your old favourites.'

'You look gross.' Despite repeated exposure, I hadn't got over my fake-gore squeamishness.

Carlo shrugged. 'If I wipe it off I'll be another hour in Make-Up and I've read all the mags. I know everything there is to know about the *Love Island* contestants *and* the crisis in North Korea.' You got a well-rounded education on-set. 'So, what's up? Are you out of the post-party dog-house?'

'Nope. Still grounded.' He laughed but it wasn't funny. And when I wasn't being grounded I was at school. Even if Archie hadn't been back in Transylvania, I wouldn't have been allowed to see him. Dark days. 'I'm so jealous that you're still filming.'

'It's got to finish soon, though. My agent's got some really good stuff lined up.' Oh. My agent didn't. All I'd had since they'd killed off Straker was a failed casting to play a Tudor maidservant and an offer of a two-minute appearance in a speculative crime drama that was made, then unmade for reasons undisclosed. 'By the way, your mate Moss hasn't accepted my friend request.'

I wasn't surprised. Moss was too busy poking over the still-twitching corpse of her thing with Torr to think or talk about anything else. It wasn't healthy. 'Un-request and request again?'

'I'm trying to hold onto some dignity here. Also ... I tried that.' He looked baffled. 'I'm not used to being ignored.'

I shrugged. 'It's good for you.' If Moss had been trying to get Carlo keen she couldn't have played it better. 'I looked around at all the strangers in suits talking in low voices to each other in the corners of the room. It was set out for a meeting with rows of chairs. I don't know what I'd been expecting (it's not like I went to a lot of meetings) but it was all very serious. I heard snatches of conversation, 'Early warning signs ...', 'disappointing predictions ...'. It wasn't an upbeat vibe. 'Carlo?' I whispered. 'Did you read *The Bizz* today?' But before he could answer me, Havelski and Ahmed (the first Assistant Director) and Sam and Amber (with Kale, her turbo-charged miniature Pomeranian, under her arm) burst through the door together. S-Amber had duvet coats over their costumes and fake mud all over their faces. This was more like it. Everyone talking at once and lots of hugging. I hadn't seen them since my last day on-set – except for Havelski, who I kept glimpsing in the background when I FaceTimed Eulalie (I took one hundred per cent credit for that unlikely romance).

A man I vaguely recognized from the first-ever

meeting we'd had with the Panda Production people went up to the front of the room and cleared his throat aggressively. I grabbed the nearest seat and found myself between Amber and someone who whisper-introduced himself to me as 'Bob-the-Attorney' in a strong American accent. I wasn't sure why a lawyer was there but it wasn't reassuring. 'Can someone bring that flipchart up front?' Someone duly did. 'And some water? And a Sharpie? No, no, not the pink one ...' There was more flapping around before he was good to go. 'So. I'm Pete. And our executive producer, Jonathan Martin, is here today too.' He gestured at a tall guy in the front row. 'And some of the key people from Personality PR who'll be helping us – especially the cast – with publicity.' He pointed out a woman who was wearing more colours than I'd known existed and a small nervy-looking guy in top to toe corduroy. 'And of course, we've got so much talent in the room.' He waved his arms around generally.

'And they all know each other,' interrupted Jonathan, pointedly looking at his watch. 'Before we kick off.' He looked around and waited until everyone was paying attention. '*No scandal.* Anyone. Or we'll *erase* you.' There was a collective shudder. 'And we can. Right up until the last minute.' He sat down to utter silence.

'Right. Absolutely.' Pete regrouped. 'Let's talk

about promotion.' **#RawTheMovie** *'Pushing Audiences Over the Edge'* he wrote on the chart in enormous (purple) writing.

Silence.

'That tagline might need rethinking,' said Havelski finally. 'Although, to be fair, it's pushed *me* over the edge.'

'Hahahaha.' Pete didn't seem to notice that he was the only person laughing. 'Such a funny guy, Sergei! Hahahaha.' He was writing again.

Pride in the Art! Confidence in the content! 'This is important.' Pete enthusiastically rapped his marker along every word and the flipboard wobbled. 'You guys have made a *great movie*.' We had? You could feel the nerves in the room. 'You guys have made *a whole movie*.' Ahmed coughed and Pete corrected himself. 'OK, you guys have made *nearly a whole movie*. You should all give yourselves a round of applause.' He left a gap. Kale bark-yelped enthusiastically but even he subsided when no one else joined in. 'Come on, *back yourselves*! What do you say, Sergei?'

'So . . .' began Havelski in his strong accent, 'what I say is that you need to speed this up because I've got a *lot* of work left to do. Anyway, it doesn't matter what I think. And right now it doesn't matter what anyone on the internet or anywhere else thinks. This movie *will* open and all that matters is what the guy who pays for his ticket thinks.' Had they given up on the female vote? Never a good sign. 'So. We wait. The future is an uncertain land.' He was getting carried away with the inscrutable sphinx thing. 'And then *Raw* will not need me any more and I will fly away – far away – on a long and luxurious holiday with the woman of my dreams.' He winked at me and I sensed Bob-the-Attorney jerk to nervous attention. 'A beach holiday. Bikinis, cocktails . . .' Bob was clutching his chest now and breathing raggedly. I made a mental note to take Eulalie bikini shopping.

Pete had out his marker again. '*Harnessing the Buzz,*' he wrote and underlined it three times.

'Sorry, sorry, sorry.' A burly crew member in cargo pants with a *massive* 'stone' (polystyrene) foot under his arm was standing in the doorway. I couldn't remember his name but I recognized him so I waved happily at him until I remembered where I was. 'Sorry to interrupt,' he grinned at me and kept talking, 'but we need to borrow Ahmed for a second. We've accidentally crushed the Warri God statue that was meant to be in the background of the reshoot of scene thirty-seven . . .'

Ahmed got up and started apologizing his way across the row to the door. He didn't look happy. Havelski didn't look happy either.

'Harnessing the buzz.' Pete sighed, he was running out of steam. 'Fiona, you're probably the best person to tell us how we're going to *make* people watch the movie.'

A woman weaved her way to the front. 'Hey!' She gave a little upbeat-rally-the-troops wave, statement necklaces swinging. 'I'm Fionaaaa. I work at Personality PRrrr in Sohhooo. We, at PPR, work on designing the sort of publicity that will rrrreallly connect on a conscious and subconscious level with the target consumerrr. Yah?' Sam pulled out a hipflask (possibly not the original reason for the deep pockets in his silvery-grey, feather-trimmed, gore-stained and ripped Warri-tribe-leader cloak). 'The aim here is to create a campaign that really touches the hearts of the consumerrrrrrrs, that taps into the moral and social issuessssss of modern society.' Sam took a slug and passed the flask along to Havelski. 'In eighty years' time, as the curtain falls on the twenty-first century, centenarians tucked into their little blankets, in their little rocking chairs by their little fires, will sit and remember, remember this movie moment—'

'Basically we need to make money.' Jonathan-the-Producer interrupted. 'You've spent it all and we just have to make it back.' He smiled venomously at Havelski who took another swig before he passed the flask back to Sam – only for it to be confiscated en route by Amber who glared at them both. 'The trailer's dropping soon and hopefully that will earn us some positive online chatter and we can get this campaign on track – *back* on track. And you,' (was he staring at our row?) 'you're going to have to work hard too. We've got a full promotional programme lined up. The sooner everyone knows what they have to do and starts doing it the better.'

'Absolutely, yah! Freddy darling?' Fiona waved at Nervy-Corduroy-Guy. 'Would you be an *angel* and run off copies of the handout? *Now.*' Nervy-Freddy hadn't jumped to it quite fast enough. 'And, while we're *waiting*,' she looked at all of us, 'we want to hear your opinion, yah?'

'Er . . . it's 11.43 a.m. already,' said Eddie anxiously before remembering his place in the hierarchy and sitting back down.

'Brainstorming, yah?' Fiona waved her arms around enthusiastically. 'Let's think totally out of the box!'

'In my experience,' chipped in Amber, 'the healthiest way to get through what's ahead is to think of the marketing process itself as a spiritual journey of discovery.'

'That's *great*.' Jonathan smiled tightly. 'So long as what we *discover* at the end of it are record-breaking box office profits.' He was terrifying. 'Let's get back to the media plan please, Fiona – not many spiritual or truthful discoveries to detain us there.'

Within minutes, a pile of satisfyingly warm

photocopies was being passed along the line like a physics worksheet (if your physics teacher asked you to 'take one and pass it along to the A-lister on your right'). *Connecting with traditional press media/ reaching out to key influencers/leveraging social media* . . .

'Hopefully,' chirped Fiona, 'this will give you an idea of the 360° strategy, yah, that we, at PPRrrr have devised to *get this movieee noticed.*' I skimmed some more. Promo had a chill vibe, no? Maybe not. This was full-on. There were pages and pages, most of which didn't make sense to me (so *very* like a physics worksheet). *Teasers and trailers/tracking public reaction/broadcast media* . . . Fiona powered on. 'We're going to be playing to our strengths, the proven star power we can count on,' she smiled over at Sam and Amber. 'Sam can really talk up the action elements of the film without ignoring his own dark and compelling personal journey.'

'You mean you want me to talk about rehab?' Sam didn't sound surprised.

'Only where that's going to translate into public sympathy and ticket sales!' Fiona replied brightly. 'Anyone else with a tragic backstory? No?' Jonathan glared at her. Havelski glared at her. 'No.'

'What's "sexy feminism"?' Amber asked reading her handout. 'And why am I meant to be talking to *Cosmopolitan* about it?'

'Because you're the perfect person to *tap into*

the female market and highlight *Raw's* feminist, empowering overtones, yah? Without killing the vibe of the interview by getting on to any actual issues like equal pay, domestic violence or reproductive rrrrights. We'll rethink if we get you a slot with *The Guardian*? Yah? It's all about finding the perfect pitch, OK?' Amber breathed deeply, composed herself and unscrewed Sam's hipflask. Possibly it wasn't OK.

Fiona turned to Carlo and me. 'And we're relying on you guys to appeal to the youth vote. Everyone loves a star-is-born narrative.' No one more than me. Odd how every word uttered in this weird twitchy meeting was making me feel less confident about that particular dream. 'That's going to be your angle. Your USP.' Everyone was asking questions at once now but I just sat there in mild shock.

An obvious truth was belatedly dawning on me: the film wasn't the only thing they were putting out there.

'To really get the most out of these appearances,' Fiona was still talking, 'we need to ensure we're tying them in across all your social meediaaa platforms and deploying your social influence to the max.' My social influence? 'We need to know that each and every one of your fans is on board and spreading the word about *Raw*.' My fans? 'Bringing your ready-made audiences to the table?

Yah?' Umm ... Not so much. 'Don't look so worried, Elektra! We've looked at your figures – lots of work to do, hahaha! So we're planning some extra help for you. PPR are going to help build you a hot-young-thing personaliteee and it's going to be *fun*!'

Briefing Doc for Elektra Ophelia James (Straker/Second Junior Lead) prepared by Fiona Hull at PERSONALITY PR – campaign to support release of Raw (Panda Productions)

Primary media target for Elektra – aspirational up-and-coming-hip-young-actor and social influencer with a reach we can exploit to the max.

- Action EOJ: Set up fan-friendly social media accounts. Make it GLAMOROUS! Make it MEMORABLE! STAND OUT!

- Post photos with Raw co-stars and other high profile industry figures across all social media – as many with Carlo Winn as possible, GOSSIP = BUZZ = TICKET SALES! Suggested hashtags: #RawTalent, #RawLOVE, #RawSquad, #RawTeens, #SquadGoals, #TeamRaw

- Production stills, video clips and trailer and teaser content will be released to you with a schedule for posting and re-posting on your media. Suggested hashtags: #ReadytoRawrr #IntheRaw, And, for any clips that showcase the fantastic original score, #HearUsRawrr

- Project an image of a buzzy-yet-on-brand-hip-and-happening-breakthrough-talent-young-actor personal life that ties in with Straker as a character and remains on brand. THINK action hero! THINK strong feminist icon! THINK bug-eating survivor!!

- Tap into social media buzz around warrior exercise (yoga poses/cross-promote with Amber Leigh); raw eating etc. Suggested hashtags: #RawGreens #WarriorPoses #RawSpirituality #VegansLove RawMovies

- Post red-carpet events to highlight glamorous lifestyle – be sure to thank your #glamsquad and always tag the photographer, tag the designer, tag the make-up artists, tag the shoes, tag the stylist. Suggested hashtags: #Rawontheredcarpet #RawStyle #RawSquad Style #celebstyle

POST regularly – not less than four times per week on each platform.
ENGAGE with key users and influencers.
BUILD followers, fast.

CHAPTER 4

'From the moment I turned [social media] off to the day I turned it back on, I was free.'

Hailey Baldwin

'Let's talk about *Raw*.' Stella looked happy but maybe that was just because she was wearing bat ears in the agency office in the middle of the day. To be fair, it was Halloween.

'Please tell me they want me to reshoot something?' Going back for the meeting had made my Fairmount FOMO even worse than usual.

'You don't have any reshoots scheduled. I just wanted to know how the meeting went?'

Oh. 'It was ...' I tailed off. I couldn't explain the weird muddle of excited and scared it had made me feel. 'It was *intense*. I didn't think they'd want me to do much publicity because nobody knows who I am.'

46

'But the plan is to change that! To get everyone talking about you!' That was definitely Personality PR's *very* ambitious plan. 'And talking about *Raw* obviously.'

There was an awkward pause while we both thought about how many people were already talking about *Raw*. 'Everyone's saying it's going to be terrible,' I blurted.

'People love gossiping about films before they come out. Films they haven't seen. Stop listening. Especially stop reading stuff on-line. *It will all be good*.' Stella didn't look as confident as she sounded. How could she be? She knew all about the rewrites and the delays.

I didn't know if *Raw* was going to be any good – I didn't even know what the bits I was in were going to be like. And I definitely didn't know if I was going to be any good. And now I wasn't busy on-set any more (couldn't they just keep filming indefinitely?), I was starting to think about that. A lot. In fact, I'd thought about little else since I'd left the meeting. I kept opening my old scripts and trying to remember exactly how I'd said the lines and then wondering if I should have said them differently until they didn't look like real lines on the page any more. 'Stella? Can I ask you something?'

'You can ask me *anything*.' She adjusted her bat ears, she was listening.

I took a deep breath. 'If *Raw* bombs, will I ever work again?' This was my current fave 3 a.m. worry.

'Of course you will!' And then she spoiled it by adding truthfully. 'Except anyone that makes promises in this industry is *insane*.'

I needed to get cast in something else before it came out. 'I haven't had anything for ages,' I said. I wasn't moaning; I was worrying. I'd thought getting an agent was the hard part and then I'd thought getting a role was the hard part *and then* I'd thought getting a big role in a movie was the hard part *and then* I'd thought filming the role was the hard part (that was the best part) but now I couldn't decide whether it was braving the movie coming out or getting cast in anything ever again that was the hard part.

'Building your social media for *Raw* will actually help.' Stella rallied me. 'It's part of the casting equation now. For better or worse, Casting Directors use it to decide who's hot.' Like school, then. 'You're on it?' I nodded. Obviously I was on it. I'd struggle to live without it but I wouldn't describe my haphazard, random and occasionally rogue social media as 'on fire'. 'I saw the briefing document PPR sent over,' she went on. '*Exciting*.' I nodded again, but less certainly. How had they described my 'target'? *Aspirational hip up-and-coming young actor and social influencer?* Okaaaaay, I was going to have to up my game.

Charlie (Stella's assistant) came out of the tiny

kitchen with a plate of iced gingerbread ghosts and came to join us. I flinched (not at the carbs obviously, but because she had a large and lifelike spider glued to her forehead). 'Just post lots of pics of avocados and hot-young-actor selfies,' she said and then quickly added, 'but, like, PG rated. This will be one of the funnest, easiest challenges yet.' Yeah, I'd voiced a squirrel, I'd eaten bugs, I'd played quite a few dead people, I'd screen-kissed Carlo. And now I was being offered the perfect excuse to spend hours on Insta. This was *all good*. 'And raising your media profile will help make you attractive to the big boys.' Sorry? I woke up from a little Insta red carpet #glam fantasy and paid attention. 'To the big *agencies*,' Charlie clarified. 'When you leave us.'

'*Leave you?*' I crunched off the ghost's head in one single panicky bite.

'You can't stay in a kids' talent agency for ever, Elektra,' said Stella (but she glared at Charlie). 'You know that! We've talked about it.' I suppose we had, but I'd buried it in the file of things-that-are-too-scary-to-think-about (in between Physics GCSE and the orthodontist). 'Most of the queries we get here are for younger kids' roles.' She guiltily shifted a large pile of files out of my eyeline. It was busy enough that they both worked on Saturdays. 'If you want to make a career out of this, you'll need to leave the nest for your own good.'

I gulped. 'But ... not yet?'

'Not yet.' She handed me another edible ghost. 'Let's get you through *Raw* coming out.' She made it sound like I was getting my appendix out. 'And in the meantime, we *will* find you another part.' She looked hopefully at Charlie like she might be hiding one. 'What about the *Worried Witch* production?'

'They want someone younger now. Nobody's commissioning the Troubled-Teen-Witch-At-School trope any more.' I could have told them they were making a terrible mistake. 'What about that indie film with the snake-charmer's rebellious daughter?' I'd vowed never to work with snakes *but* ... Maybe it would be a cute snake? A small snake? A rubber snake? I sat up straighter and tried to look like the sort of actor who was cool with reptiles.

'It's already been cast,' said Stella. It was probably for the best. 'Has it gone quiet on *Double Death*?'

'As the grave. Could we try her on Sally Upton again?'

'What? For the *Fortuneswell* guest role? The party-loving cousin who pops up as a plot device?' Charlie nodded. 'Sally *might* see her again.' I fake-coughed to remind them I was there. 'Sorry. Do you remember *Fortuneswell*, Elektra?' Sadly, I did. 'Classy Regency drama focusing on the—' Stella made little air quotes, '"*loves and misadventures of a family of high-born and high-spirited sisters*"?'

'She won't see me.' I'd auditioned to play one of those sisters and messed it up so badly that it had left a little failure scar.

'Upton's *tricky*,' (that was one way of describing her) 'but it's worth me calling her. You can be wrong for one part and perfect for another. But the Clemency role is small – just a few days' filming – would you be OK with that after *Raw*?'

I'd be *fine* with that. They could stick me at the back of a crowd scene with no words as long as they let me back on a set.

'Where's your costume? Two hours later, Moss was at my door wearing a little red devil dress and carrying an enormous pumpkin. She'd gone all out and matched her lippy to her glittery horns. But then, she was going on to Jenny's Halloween party and I – because I was still under house arrest – wasn't going anywhere.

'I'm wearing black because I'm in mourning for my social life.'

'They still won't let you go?' I shook my head. 'Savage. Here.' She thrust the pumpkin at me and came inside. 'We've got loads of time to carve this before ...' She tailed off.

'Before you go to the party,' I finished for her, carting the pumpkin to the kitchen.

'I feel *bad*.'

'Don't. It'll be a good night. Everyone will be there.' Except me. I wasn't bitter.

'You should still dress up.' Moss would wear costume to school if she could. 'Halloween vibes.'

'I'll draw on some whiskers or something.' There was a limit to the amount of effort I was prepared to make for a bit of pumpkin carving and an evening alone with my social media. How was I going to build myself as an aspirational social influencer if I was never allowed to leave the house?

'Whiskers? Like a hipster?' Moss looked confused. I'd been thinking 'cat' but whatever. 'Why are you looking at *Twitter*?' She was nosying on my open laptop. 'Are you stalking teachers?'

'I need to set up an account. For work.' Moss snorted. 'Seriously, it's part of the casting equation.'

'You're not making any sense but let's do it now.' Moss sat down at the table and took control. 'What are you going to call yourself?'

'Er ... "Elektra James"?'

'No. Go for something *exciting*. New identity. New you.'

'I think you might be missing the point of this exercise. Brand Elektra. LOL.' I was getting a nagging feeling this promo stuff had serious cringe potential.

'Odd,' she said but typed in @ElektraJames. 'You need a profile pic so you don't look sinister.' The doorbell rang and I left her scrolling photos. 'OK,

I've found you three classy options,' she said when I got back (having cheered up a small crying bat with most of our supply of marshmallow ghosts).

Option one: photo of me aged thirteen, licking Jenny's Justin Bieber poster.

Option two: photo of me aged ten wearing a unicorn onesie.

Option three: a very fuzzy one of me at the end of my party – after Archie had arrived. The best that could be said was that it was quite hard to make me out.

'Really helpful, thanks.' My phone barked. Sadly it wasn't Archie (who was living the Halloween dream and night-filming in a haunted forest in Transylvania), it was Carlo. A shirtless Carlo. **What do you think of my costume, E?**

What are you meant to be? Other than a narcissist.

A vampire. Obviously.

I was an expert on the vampire aesthetic. I spent many happy hours scrolling pics of Archie in costume. **Why no cloak/fangs etc.?**

Send it to Moss

You literally just sent me a shirtless photo so I could send it to Moss?! That is TRAGIC. Also ... she is right here

Show her BUT DON'T TELL HER I ASKED YOU TO

'He's not even cool about you, Moss. You bewitched him.'

She looked, shrugged and went back to Twitter. 'You can't use the same photo for everything. You should show another side of yourself. What about this one of you saving an endangered species?' That would be the photo of me lifting a dripping Plog out of the bath. I wrestled back laptop control and uploaded my headshot.

'So. *Carlo*.' He'd made me promise before I left Fairmount that I'd put in a good word for him. 'Have you accepted his friend request?' Moss shook her head. 'Why not?'

'Why do you want me to? What happened to the whole "Carlo's a pathological flirt" line?'

'I'm not suggesting you *marry* him.'

'He flirts with you.'

'Not for *ages*. Because we're mates.' She looked at me suspiciously. 'And it was never proper flirting, it was just because I was there and he was bored. OK, so he sort-of-flirts with everyone and he gossips nearly as much as me, and he doesn't always give the best advice,' (I possibly wasn't doing the best job of selling Carlo), 'but he's *funny*, he's hot, he's my friend and it's a bit aggressive not even to friend-accept him on Facebook.' Especially when you've already wept all over him, I thought, but didn't say.

'It's not a good time,' she said, playing with her fringe.

'Not because of Torr?' He was precisely the

reason it *was* a good time. '*Please* tell me not because of Torr?'

'Torr?'

'Yep, Torr. You know? Your *ex*-long-term-almost-boyfriend.' The one that had been playing mind games with her for the last fortnight. She looked all shiny with make-up and excitement and I had a bad feeling. 'What's Torr doing for Halloween?'

'He said he might be going to Jenny's.'

'But—'

'Hello, Moss! I didn't hear you come in. You look gorgeous.' Mum had come into the kitchen – wrapped in a bath towel and carrying Plog (which was a precarious combination).

'That's because she's going to Jenny's party,' I said pointedly. 'You've still got time to change your mind.' I looked at Mum pleadingly. Moss might not want me as a chaperone but she definitely *needed* me. 'You used to be hopeless at grounding me.' I missed those days.

'You didn't use to throw parties. Which reminds me, Dad and I are out tonight.' Of course they were, because Halloween was a night when people had fun. Other people. 'Don't eat all the treat sweets and make sure Plog's OK – there might be fireworks.' She dumped him into my lap, secured the slipping towel in the nick of time and left. There were going to be fireworks at Jenny's party. I really wasn't bitter.

'We should get this pumpkin started.' Moss surreptitiously checked the time but then she had a party to go to. Not bitter at all.

'Or, we could not bother and you could tell me what's going on with Torr.' I opened a packet of party rings because that was as close as I was going to get.

'Nope.' When Moss didn't want to talk, she didn't talk. She was flitting round the kitchen finding knives and newspaper like a nurse setting up for an operation.

I gave up. 'What are we going to carve?'

'Well, the pumpkin,' replied Moss, laying out the knives in size order.

'No, I mean, what pattern? It's like an *art form* – we need to take it seriously.' And I wanted to Insta it. I googled for inspiration. 'There's a cute little owl? Shall we go for that?'

We sat for a bit, looking hopefully from the knives to the pumpkin and back again. 'Elektra?' asked Moss. 'Is there anything that says *how* to do it?'

I delegated door-answering-treat-duties to her and googled some more. 'It's pretty straightforward,' I said when she got back. 'We just need a keyhole saw, a fleshing tool, a sharp awl and a couple of templates. Easy.' We looked at each other. 'Or we could just wing it?'

Twenty sweaty minutes later (with several

interruptions to hand out Haribo Fangtastricks to various miniscule witches and a couple of actually scary skeletons), we had ... something. 'Does it look like an owl?'

'What it looks like is a pumpkin with holes in it.'

Mum came back in – at least this time she had clothes on. 'I'm off. Oh you've carved a skull!' Looked at from some angles, we possibly had. 'Have a lovely time at your party, Moss. Don't growl, Elektra darling. And put the laundry in the tumble dryer for me when it's done, will you?'

This was abuse. 'Shall I clean the house top-to-toe while you're out then retreat to my tiny room in the attic with my pet rat and singing beetle?'

'I have no idea what you're talking about but, yes, if you could unload the dishwasher when it's finished running too that would be great.' The doorbell rang *again*. 'You get it,' said Mum, presumably because once you've started ordering Cinderella around you might as well keep going.

'You should go too, right?' I asked Moss when I got back.

She shook her head. 'I hate turning up to parties early.' I'd never known her arrive early or even on time in her life. 'I'll wait until I know ... people are there.' She checked her phone – so until Torr was there. 'Let's do your first tweet, what's it going to be?'

'How does it work?' No one I knew was on Twitter.

'Ummmm ...' Moss 'researched' a bit. 'You could live-tweet your period or talk about Trump?' Okaaay, I wasn't sure that was *exactly* the vibe PPR was after.

The door rang again – aggressively. 'I'll get it. You concentrate on composing something that makes me look brilliant.'

The pumpkin was in pieces on the floor, spewing gory remnants all over the tiles. I'd only been away two minutes.

'It fell,' said Moss.

'No, it didn't.' A few seeds had splattered onto her devil dress. 'What happened?'

'I've messed up,' she said, her voice was wobbly. 'I was trying to sort it out but I've ruined it.' She wasn't talking about the pumpkin. 'Torr's not going to Jenny's.'

He was a serial flaker. I didn't even ask her what his excuse was this time. 'It'll still be a great party.' I started picking up the biggest bits of pumpkin.

'I'm not going. Obviously.' She took off her glittery horns and chucked them on the table.

'Don't cry, Mossy, he's not worth it.' There wasn't a sexy-lopsided-grin™ in the world that was worth all this. 'Go to Jenny's without him. Go on your own. Or don't go. Stay, and we'll make a pillow fort and watch a scary movie – or a not-scary movie. But please don't cry.'

'But it's all my fault,' she said after some miserable snuffling.

'You can't *still* be guilt stressing about that *tiny* get-with at my party?'

She shook her head. 'I've done something much worse.'

'I'm sure you haven't,' I said soothingly, offering her a mini Mars bar.

'I have. I don't think I can even tell you.'

'You can tell me anything. I won't judge you.' The doorbell rang. I ignored it.

'I might have ... *I am such an idiot*.' I handed her the whole bag of mini Mars and waited. 'We were FaceTiming last night ...' It was a worryingly long pause.

'You and Torr?' She nodded. 'What did you *do*, Mossy?'

'It's what I *said*.'

'It was about time you said something to him,' I said fiercely.

'But what I said to him was ...' Another *long* pause and then in a single word vomit, 'I-told-him-that-I–loved-him.'

I stared at her. 'Like, "Love you!" in a casual I'm-hanging-up-the-phone/leaving-now   way?' She shook her head. 'Like, I-love-you-when-you-don't-make-me-watch-boring-documentaries/talk-endlessly-about-yourself   sort   of   way?'

Apparently not. 'Like, "love you *babe*"?' I desperately handed her a tangerine because there was no more chocolate.

'No,' she said flatly. 'Just "I love you". There wasn't a casual vibe.'

'Oh, Mossy. What did he say?'

'Nothing,' she said. 'He said *nothing*.'

'That's good,' I said, breathing a sigh of relief. 'I bet he didn't even hear you.' I was clutching at straws. 'He probably wasn't listening to you.' That was more credible.

'No. He heard me.' This was *horrible*. 'I thought it was OK because he was still going to come to Jenny's. I thought it was maybe even … good, but, no.' She held out her phone. 'It's definitely not good. Read his texts. All of them.'

God, there were dozens. I scrolled through. **I've been thinking a lot about what you said last night/ It's nice to know how you feel/ About me/ I'm all about honesty and openness/ I'm just not sure I can handle the depth of what you're feeling/ For me/ I don't know if I can give you the emotional attention you need/ Obviously/ I rush into things before I've thought about whether I really like someone/ Someone like you/ I just don't want to see you getting hurt/ By me/ Look after yourself, Moss and I'm sure I'll see you around/ I thought it would be kinder not to come to Jenny's**

Such a kind guy.

TheBizz.com

1 November

Georgie Dunn has been causing fireworks on the *Fortuneswell* set again — and not just because of *that* Halloween costume. To be fair it must be hard to remember to turn up to set at 7 a.m. when at 5.30 a.m. you're still partying with three ghosts, one skeleton, two Donald Trumps, a bear and Vladimir Putin (the last four were together, cute!).

We asked *Fortuneswell* director Amrita Sharma, known for her easy charm and laid-back manner, what was going on but got the frostiest 'No Comment' we've ever had (which at *The Bizz* is saying something). A nameless source (who was also headless when we spoke to her at Jonathan Ross's Halloween Eve bash) says that Georgie (who's playing Mary, the prim and prissy sister, no type-casting there) is pushing all Sharma's buttons — and not in a good way.

Whatever's going on it isn't hurting the pre-release buzz for this series.

Move over *Poldark*.

Sit back down *Downton*.

Nobody cares Colin Firth, put your shirt back on . . .

From: Fiona Hull at Personality PR
Date: 1 November 10.01
To: Elektra James
Cc: Stella Haden at the Haden Agency

Subject: HELPFUL ADVICE!
Attachments: List of links to key influencer accounts

Dear Elektra,

Great to see you've made a *start* on your social media and set up the new Insta and Twitter accounts that you'll be using for promotional purposes!!!

But remember, this is your chance, not just to promote *Raw,* but also to put yourself out there to the world!!! At least ninety-five per cent of your posts should feature your FACE or the good bits of your BODY!!! And even if you were going to go the *arty/quirky* route, a smashed pumpkin is maybe a bit too RAW! Hahaha! You need to think glossier, think GLAMOROUS!!!

I'm attaching a list of links to the social media accounts of some of the best young actor and model *Insta-Influencers* (I've asterisked the PPR clients!) *So much* you can learn from them!!! Take the time to get it right!!!

Love & Hugs,

Fiona

P.S. *Please* delete your existing Insta or at the very least change your user name to something *unrecognizable* and set the privacy accounts to the highest level!!

* PPR * ON FIRE in Soho since 2010
Follow us on Twitter @Personality Facebook: PersonalityPR
Insta @PersonalityonFire

WAITING

- % of time spent alternately being excited about *Raw* being released/being terrified about *Raw* being released: 70%
- % of time spent worrying I'd never get a part again/never get signed by another agent and would be 'famous' only for 'star' turn as bug-eating weirdo in epic movie-flop: 67%
- % of time watching Regency rom-coms fantasizing I'd get an audition for *Fortuneswell*: 49%[*]
- % of time spent listening to Moss mourning Torr: 47% (% of time trying not to say 'I told you so': 47%)
- % of time spent fantasizing about having the kind of life that looks good on Instagram/sounds good on Twitter: 34%
- % of time spent at school having the kind of life that doesn't look good on Insta/sound good anywhere: no idea but felt like 113%
- % of time spent hanging out with Archie: 0% (% of time spent imagining hanging out with Archie, not disclosed)
- % of time spent loving Plog: 100%.
- % of time spent missing Digby: 100%

---

[*] All percentages are 'estimated' i.e. made up) and should not be assumed to add up to 100%

From: Charlotte at Haden Agency
Date: 12 November 16.01
To: Elektra James
Cc: Stella at the Haden Agency; Julia James

Subject: *Fortuneswell* Casting
Attachments: Casting Brief, Character Sides, Google maps

Dear Elektra,

Sally Upton's assistant has confirmed that they'll see you for the Clemency casting. They've squeezed you in at the end of their packed all-day session this Saturday 14th November (be there by 5.30 p.m.). The brief and script etc. are attached. <u>Know that script back to front this time!</u>

One *tiny* thing, I may have slightly overestimated your *skills*. Just nod if Sally asks if you're up to speed with Regency-era ballroom dances . . . I'd be really surprised if she asked you to demonstrate but maybe look it up on YouTube, just in case.

Charlie x

130

Days to Go . . .

CHAPTER 5

*'I wonder if, over years of doing auditions, I've
stopped allowing myself to believe the dream.'*
Eddie Redmayne

'Do you have any photos of me as a cute baby?'

'Hundreds,' said Mum. 'They're all in the albums.'

'I've looked in the albums but they're either out
of focus or I don't have any clothes on.'

'There's nothing cuter than a naked baby,' she
said, rumpling my hair.

'I don't think naked babies are on brand,' I said,
pulling away because, boundaries.

'On brand?'

'My brand,' I said. Eeeeurgh, I should probably
know what that was by now but I was struggling.
Like, Sam had his Heartthrob-on-the-edge vibe,
Amber had her Spiritual-Goddess-of-Screen vibe, I

was meant to be coming up with something better than a Year-Eleven-on-the-edge vibe. That wasn't going to tick all Fiona-aa's 'hip-and-hot' targets.

'Are you going to become an It Girl?' Inexplicably, mum found that very funny. 'Give up the acting and sell contouring kits.' Snort.

I had great respect for people who could sell contouring kits. Even more now I was getting an idea how long all this took. 'It's for the *Raw* promo, my work Insta needs to be more *Instagrammable*.' I'd gained twenty-three followers and lost fourteen this week. Obviously fewer people were excited by Oreo sculptures than I'd thought. Baffling. I needed to post now. According to Fiona-aa and my in-depth on-line research (*How to build a KILLER social media brand*, *FEEL GOOD ways to build an online platform*, *Super Easy ways to get LIKES* and *Terrifying Tricks to TAME TWITTER*), if I wasn't posting – sorry, and engaging – daily, I might as well give up and go back to the twentieth century. And I had a bit of catching up to do on account of losing my phone three times in two weeks (which is something that could have happened to anyone but mostly happens to me). Raising my social media game was proving harder than I'd thought it would be. Time to fall back on a classic. 'Have we got any avocados?'

'No. You hate avocados. I haven't bought one since the green projectile vomit occasion.'

'I'm not going to eat it. Obviously. I'm going to photograph it in an unironic way.'

'Why?'

'Because that's what people with aspirational Instagrams and films coming out do.'

'Aren't avocados a bit over? You know, as a trend?' If she'd heard about it, yes. 'Bertie?' Dad had come into the kitchen. 'Avocados are over, aren't they?' Sure, ask a middle-aged architect, they're bound to know.

'Probably,' he said, filling Plog's water bowl (a bowl I'd lovingly graffitied with 'Digby Top Dog' when I was seven). What was I meant to do? Switch to broccoli or goji berries? I opened the fridge. Where could I go creatively and aspirationally with a pint of milk, some cheese and a plate of something undefinable covered in cling-film? This was more challenging than my art coursework. It was a relief when the doorbell rang.

'Bonjour, cherie!' Eulalie was standing at the door with a baguette in one hand and a bottle of red wine in the other, like a walking stereotype. She kissed me multiple times, breaking the baguette in the process.

'You're back!' I said. She'd been in Paris with Havelski – officially to enjoy le culture but looking at what she was wearing I think that mostly meant le shopping.

'*Bien sûr*, I am being back.' Ah, yes, because otherwise she wouldn't be standing in my hall smelling of expensive perfume and bearing only slightly battered gifts. '*Ça va?*'

'I've hit a new low,' I admitted. 'My parents are advising me that my Insta-goals are tragically out of date.'

'I adore le Insta.' Of course she did; Eulalie had couture gowns and the Eiffel Tower to post photos of, not half a packet of cheddar and three tomatoes.

'How is Havelski?' I asked once we'd made it to the kitchen, she'd said hello to Mum and Dad, and the wine had been opened.

'Sergei is being sometimes deliriously happy,' said Eulalie, breaking off the crusty baguette tip and feeding it to Plog. He looked at her with utter devotion. She handed me some perfume of my very own and I looked at her in exactly the same way.

'Because he's with you.'

'Non. Well, *oui*, but also because he is nearly finished with that *cafouillage* of a film.' I didn't need to speak French to understand what she meant.

'Is he worried about it coming out?' I'd had an anxiety dream last night that they'd decided to screen the premiere at my school.

'*Un peu.*' If upbeat Eulalie said he was a little worried, Havelski was probably sitting in a darkened room rocking silently from side to side. She shrugged. 'His reputation will be surviving it.'

I wasn't at all sure that my reputation would be surviving it. The latest from Carlo (who was *still* filming – I was encouraging him to text me all the on-set gossip so I didn't feel excluded and sad) was that one of the writers had checked into a discreet clinic for rest, recuperation and rebooting, and Sam and Amber were delaying finishing the new love scenes because they were enjoying them so much. I shook it off. It was ages away. Sort of. Who knew what might happen by then?

'He is having many exciting new projects to consider. There is maybe going to be one about revolting soldiers.'

'Uggers or mutinous?'

Eulalie looked confused and refilled her glass. Never mind, whatever she meant, there probably wasn't a role in that for me. I'd have to find my own something exciting ... 'You need to keep everything crossed that I get cast as a Regency minx.'

'The audition is today?' I'd told her about it. '*Non?*'

'*Oui!*' I looked at the clock on the wall and gulped. 'In about two hours. You can read the casting brief if you want?' Eulalie nodded and I pulled it up on the laptop and angled the screen for her.

CASTING BRIEF

FORTUNESWELL: Series One Overview

This series (already filming on location in Dorset and in London) is an Autumn schedule lead production commissioned by ITV from Aphrodite Productions.

Set in 1813 in an England adjusting both to the excesses of the Prince Regent and the impact of the war against Napoleon, the series centres on the lives and loves of the wealthy and aristocratic St Clair family. Lord St Clair, Baron of Lowpuddle, has left England to fight under the command of General the Marquess of Wellington, leaving behind his worried wife and four daughters – three of whom (Sophia, Belle and Mary) are at that dangerous marriageable age. Without the firm rule of their father, the girls are soon entangled in any number of romantic misadventures. Sophia, the eldest, fast falls into the clutches of the caddish but ruggedly handsome and much older Captain Allerton, while bookish Mary and beautiful Belle both fall prey to the myriad charms of the irresistible young Viscount Luddington.

Episode 5, Coming Out Ball: Overview

In this episode (to be filmed in London's Mayfair) the three eldest St Clair girls are in London to attend the coming out ball of their vivacious, flame-haired, minx of a cousin Clemency Barton-Wood. Captain Allerton and Viscount Luddington are both to be present. The sisters gossip to Clemency of their crushes. She is shocked and excited in equal measure – not least because she's attracted to the Viscount herself . . .

Production Details

Shooting dates Ep. 5
One day rehearsal/dance instruction/costume fitting; two – three days ball-room and supper scene **19–23nd December (tbc)**

Company:	**Aphrodite Productions Ltd**
Director:	**Amrita Sharma**
Casting:	**Sally Upton CDG, Upfront Casting Ltd**
Location Ep. 5:	**Brook St, Mayfair, London W1**
Pay Category:	**Paid.**

'Red haired!' said Mum, reading it again over my shoulder and focusing in with laser-like precision on the only possible problem. 'I didn't notice that before. You don't have red hair.'

I drew her attention to the asterisk, 'But if,' (big if) 'I get the part I will have.'

'You have *lovely* hair.' I had the sort of average brown hair that only a mother could love. 'Why does this Clemency character need to have red hair? Why can't they just make her a brunette?'

'Because she's a flame-haired Regency party girl.' Duh.

'This is *formidable*,' said Eulalie. 'You are being perfect for this role!' Maybe not perfect but I was up for it.

'Except for the hair,' said Mum in an increasingly

73

desperate voice. 'Statistically, I'm sure brown-haired girls outnumbered all the others in Regency England.'

'I don't think TV works that way.'

'Are you sure about going up for something else this year? You've got such a lot going on.' Please don't say it. 'With exams.' She said it.

I was so sure it hurt. I embarked on my well-practised and one hundred per cent heartfelt wanting to act/needing to act/it's-a-tiny-part-in the holidays/I'll still get all my schoolwork done/I NEED to get something before *Raw* comes out, monologue and then (fortunately, because no one was really listening) I had a flash of inspiration. 'You do know that Lohan Winter is playing Captain Allerton?'

Mum's jaw dropped. 'Lohan Winter. *The* Lohan Winter?'

'Oh, yes.' The very same Lohan Winter she'd had a tragic crush on since he'd played a bare-chested nineteenth-century lawyer in *The Trial of Sir Montmorency*, also a bare-chested sixteenth-century officer in *The Retreat from Pirate's Leap*. And now he was going to be playing a (probably) bare-chested eighteenth-century army officer in *Fortuneswell*. 'Just think, Mum, you and Lohan hanging out in catering. Or, even better, you and Lohan hanging out in Costume. You handing him his cloak before he steps on set. You—'

'Lohan Winter—,' breathed Mum, only to be interrupted by a siren going off somewhere nearby. 'Make it stop!' It was *very* loud.

'Oh, God,' said Dad leaping from his chair. 'It's our car alarm.' He raced from the room as if pursued by the Warri tribe.

'*Corsets*,' said Eulalie happily, rolling the 'r' so it sounded even more extravagant. No corsets in *RAW the Movie*.

'The car!' Mum ran to the window.

'Ball gowns!' said Eulalie. Definitely no ball gowns in *Raw*.

'It's still there!' shouted Mum.

'Dangerous marriageable age!' said Eulalie with loud glee (plainly not ruling herself out of that category).

Dad came back inside. 'False alarm,' he boomed, not sounding as happy about that as he should.

'Then why is it still going off?' shouted Mum.

'Drop!' said Dad sternly to Plog.

Plog looked guilty.

'Can you worry about Plog's teething later and *do something about that racket*,' said Mum.

'Give. It. To. Me,' said Dad through clenched teeth. Plog looked *really* guilty – but also stubborn. 'Drop!' bellowed Dad and Plog finally disgorged the car keys onto the floor. We all looked at him. He looked back at us with big pleading eyes. Dad grimaced and picked up the slobbered-over key fob. The noise stopped abruptly.

'So what do you all think?' I asked when some sort of order had been restored and Plog had been sent for some serious time out in the garden. 'Dream role?'

'Corsets,' repeated Eulalie with a dreamy look on her face. 'And the men are being in britches and the britches are being very tight and—'

'And,' I'd lost track of the time. 'If I'm going to have any chance of getting over the minor hurdle of getting cast, I've got to get going.'

'Do you want to practise the lines one last time?' Everyone spoke together.

'There's no time.' I tore around throwing things into my bag – script, concealer, hairbrush, brain, nerve, talent.

'Come in, come in.' Two hours later (one of which was spent just waiting anxiously to be called) and it was my turn. Mrs Upton gestured impatiently and looked from her notes on the table to me and back again. 'Elektra James?' I nodded nervously and her assistant made a little tick against my name. We were in a boxy grey (originally white?) room with bars on the window in the same church hall where they'd held the last auditions – bad energy. There was a free chair but I didn't dare sit down. 'We saw you for the part of Mary St Clair. I remember. You weren't quite right.' I wasn't confident she meant just for the role; she wasn't smiling. 'But this is a *much* smaller role and I hear that you've been working with Sergei Havelski for the last couple of months.' I nodded. 'I expect that was quite an education?' I nodded again. Words were deserting me, which wasn't a good start. 'Let's get cracking, I've had a long day.' I started to thank her for seeing me. 'Never mind all that, are you off-book?'

I nodded. Lots of things might go wrong in this audition but not knowing my lines wasn't going to be one of them. Not this time. 'Where do you want me?'

'Where you are is good. And standing will work for this. So, it's the night of your coming out ball. You're *fizzing* with excitement. Just imagine, you're newly sixteen, you've led a sheltered life and this is your first real grown-up party. Your first time "out" in society. The room is packed with friends and strangers.' Yep, I could imagine that quite easily. 'Your cousins, the St Clair girls, and their mother have just been announced and you go over to greet them. You are about to drop the bombshell to Mrs St Clair that your mother is pregnant again. Tracey?' Her assistant, who was now behind the camera, nodded, she was ready. 'All right, Elektra, kick off any time.'

Me/CLEMENCY
You're here at last!(*embraces the sisters*).
Good evening, Aunt (*drops a curtsey*). I
hope your journey was without incident.

Mrs Upton/MRS ST CLAIR
The weather was so treacherous I feared
the carriage would overturn but the girls
would not hear of us turning back (*tinkling
laugh*). I swear we could have met a
highwayman and the girls would have ordered
him to stand aside and let us pass to get
to your ball. (*She looks around the crowded
ballroom.*) Where is your dear mama?

Me/CLEMENCY
Resting in the small drawing room, Aunt.

Mrs Upton/MRS ST CLAIR: (*looks concerned*)
Whisper to me child — is she unwell?
Distempered? I have not had a letter from
her for some long time.

Me/CLEMENCY (*leans in close*)
She is ... *increasing*.

Mrs Upton/MRS ST CLAIR
Clemency! Hush child! Have you forgotten

where we are? You shall be overheard
and then your mama will be the talk
of the town!

Me/CLEMENCY
I couldn't possibly be overheard in
all this hubbub. *(Says with joy)* It is
such a crush!

We ran a couple more lines and then she cut. 'Let's try it again but this time accentuate the RP.'

'You want Clemency to sound posher?' I vaguely remembered her complaining I'd sounded too posh when I'd auditioned for Mary.

'We're at her coming out ball in her home in Mayfair, I think we can risk it.'

Fair. We did it again.

'Let's try a scene between Clemency and Mary,' said Mrs Upton. She flicked through some scripts. 'I know you won't have seen this before so take your time, have a read through.'

I could feel her watching me while I read but it didn't feel as hostile as before. We weren't in biscuit territory but at least she'd stopped checking her watch. Tracey set up and we were ready to go again.

Mrs Upton/MARY *(anxious)*
Do you think he'll come?

It was the same monotone voice she'd used for Mrs
St Clair but then she wasn't trying to cast herself.

Me/CLEMENCY (*eyes twinkling* — that's a tough
direction to pull off but I did my best.)
  If you mean Viscount Luddington — and I
know you do — I *know* he will come. He is
even now in the card room!

Mrs Upton/MARY
Oh Clemency! Isn't he the handsomest man
you ever saw?

I struggled not to laugh as Mrs Upton utterly failed
to get in touch with her inner lovelorn teenager.

Me/CLEMENCY
He is very agreeable to look at.

'Do that line again Elektra, and really emphasize
the "very" – Clemency is as struck by the handsome
and gallant Viscount Luddington as every other
young woman in that ballroom. In fact, she has a
long-standing crush on him although Mary doesn't
know that.'

Me/ CLEMENCY
He is *very* agreeable to look at.

I could picture him now, tall, strong jawline, great hair … odd – he resembled Archie in my overheated imagination. I gave a little swoony sigh.

'How would you feel about dyeing your hair red?' Mrs Upton asked when the camera had been switched off and she was sitting back behind the desk.

'I'd feel very good about it,' I said. 'Very good indeed.'

She *almost* smiled at me. 'Well, Sergei Havelski has taught you something.'

I texted Moss on the way home. **Do you think I'd suit red hair?**

Yes!!! Do you want me to dye it for you?

Maybe … One hundred per cent no. Not even to cheer her up.

I texted Eulalie, **Should I dye my hair red?**

You should dye your hair whatever colour or colours you wish. It is being your hair. Surtout if it is for being pour la Regency Belle xx

Eulalie gave the best advice. I smiled and texted Archie **You around?**

Yep, just finished filming a riding scene. I'm chilling

with Angelina. Angelina was Archie's horse for filming and he was in love with her.

Archie Mortimer Would Like FaceTime.

I pressed 'Accept' and there he was.

'Hey, Angelina,' I said, waving at her. In real life, I'd probably have run away from her but I was safe at this distance.

'I told you she was beautiful,' said Archie, like a proud parent. He'd not only told me; he'd shown me about a thousand photos. 'She made me look really good today.' He *did* look really good today but that might have had more to do with the mud-spattered britches and the dishevelled locks. Viscount Luddington had nothing on Archie Mortimer. I watched him pat Angelina's nose and felt a little bit jealous (not because I wanted him to pat my nose). 'Good day today—,' he broke off to say 'hi' to two crew members walking past carrying a coffin – presumably a prop coffin because everyone was very upbeat. All this FaceTiming was great for our relationship but less good for my filming FOMO. 'But we had to start at the crack of dawn to give Count Plogojowitz,' (vampire and lead villain), 'time to stack up a decent body count of newly undead in his attic.'

'That sucks,' I said but only because I have a very juvenile sense of humour – I'd have happily got up at the crack of dawn to murder some innocents, or even rescue them, if that's what a director wanted. 'Do you think I'd suit red hair?'

'Sure.' Archie hesitated and peered at me. 'Oh, God, is that a trick question? I mean your hair is nice already. Red would be equally good—' This time he was interrupted by a passing (blonde) maiden-of-staggering-beauty who wanted to say 'hi' to him. 'I'm good with all the hair colours.'

'If I were to be cast as, for example, a flame-haired Regency minx?'

'You had the *Fortuneswell* casting?!'

'I did.'

'And? I'm sensing it went well.'

'I've literally just left so I don't know, I can never tell *but* . . . I don't know, there was just a *vibe*. And the casting director made me do an extra scene.'

'That's a good sign,' he said.

'Sometimes.' I'd made the mistake of trying to read the omens before and getting it wrong. 'She asked me whether I'd dye my hair. They're filming in the Christmas holidays.' Which would be good because less parental resistance but also bad because I wouldn't miss any school. 'So they'll have to cast quite soon.' And then there was an awkward couple of minutes while another random (blonde) maiden tried to get his attention. Just weeks ago, that would have triggered a scary bout of paranoia. It was still quite annoying. 'I've got lots of *hopes* and that'll make it worse when they're cruelly crushed,' I said when it was just the two of us again (and Angelina). 'I've been literally fantasizing about wearing a ball gown and flirting with viscounts.'

He laughed. 'Good to know.'

'When are you home next?'

'Not until we wrap – but it's only a week or two now. It's my last scene with Angelina tomorrow.'

'The one where you ride up too late to save a minor maiden from a horrible death and all the roses turn to ash and the screen fades from colour to black and white?' It's possible that I was following the shooting schedule of *The Curse* more closely than was strictly necessary. 'Are you OK about finishing?'

He nodded. 'Right now, I'm more than OK with it. I want to be back in London for a bit.'

'I want you to be back in London for a bit too,' I said and then went red because I was still the least smooth girlfriend in the world.

From: Fiona Hull at Personality PR
Date: 23 November 10.13
To: Elektra James
Cc: Stella Haden at the Haden Agency

Subject: *MORE* HELPFUL ADVICE!!!

Dear Elektra,

Quick reminder that you should be posting MUCH more regularly – and if we send you over some content then we do expect it to be reposted ASAP and for you to ENGAGE with any positive on-line chatter.

- We want you to PUT YOURSELF OUT THERE. Bare your soul. Talk about your craft. *But* there are a few things to bear in mind:

- AVOID POSTING ABOUT SCHOOL.

- It might be safer to AVOID ALL NON-INDUSTRY SOCIAL LIFE!! (Although photographs of your cute family pet might be productive if more artistically framed – and without the references to his house training). The key is to remember that real relationships and personal preferences have no place in promotional activities – unless we ask you to deploy them!!

- DON'T POST INAPPROPRIATE/OFF-BRAND images #RawandClean! I do appreciate that your pig-patterned mini

85

pyjamas (yesterday's Insta #OutfitOfTheDay post) are in fact less revealing than your Straker costumes but *we can never be too careful* (or, at least not without an excellent photographer).

Whatever you do, DON'T try to be FUNNY about any disappointment or concerns. DON'T share any negative news or rumours. *The Bizz*, sadly, can get their message across without your help. Avoid SARCASM. ***FEAR OF FAILURE IS UNHELPFUL AND CONTAGIOUS!!!***

And please don't forget make-up. This is your chance to LOOK GOOD – make sure you do – for you and for *Raw*.

Love & Hugs,

Fiona

P.S. We'll sort out some invites for you to industry events, get you mingling. That will help! #RawGlamour

* PPR * ON FIRE in Soho since 2010
Follow us on Twitter @Personality Facebook: PersonalityPR
Insta @PersonalityonFire

CHAPTER 6

'You go into a room, and there's ten other people who look just like you or better than you or more interesting than you in however many ways, and it's all set up to make you doubt yourself.'

Ryan Gosling

Unit B 675: Hostile world and Investigating the Shrinking World. Who names these exam papers? Dystopian script writers? Fatalistic cult leaders?' I moved the heap of practice papers off the kitchen table.

'Geography teachers,' said Moss sadly. She was practically living at mine (a bit because we were 'revising together' and a lot because her mum had a new boyfriend and she was finding the PDAs traumatizing). 'They're on the dark side. They lure us into signing up with the mellow pond habitat and pictograms stuff, and then – *bam* – two years later it's all deforestation, natural hazards and choropleth maps. Is it too late to switch to media studies? You could be my case study. *"Unknown wannabe-actor Miss X exploits social platforms like a pro and joins the A list"*. How's it going?'

'Not great.' I sighed so deeply Plog fell off my lap. 'There was another piece on-line last night predicting *Raw* would hit new cinematic lows and I still haven't heard anything on *Fortuneswell*. I don't think it's going to happen.' It was time I stopped tragically refreshing my emails every five minutes and 'rehearsing' made-up scenes in the shower. It was time to let hope go.

'That's *bad*, but I didn't mean your whole "career".' The sympathy would have come over better without her air quotes around 'career'. 'I just meant the publicity stuff.'

Ah, that. 'It *will* be good.' It had to be good. 'I just need to find my media *thing*.'

'What? Like inflatable flamingos?'

'Possibly not. But I need something. I haven't got enough followers.' Maybe that was why *Fortuneswell* weren't calling me back. 'And I hardly get any likes.' I was endlessly checking my popularity rating as if I were back in Year Eight (and it hadn't done much for me then). 'I'm spending *ages* on it and I'm still not building brand.' Moss looked at me like I'd morphed into Flissy (Berkeley Academy's very own

Regina George and, it pains me to admit it, a queen at social media). 'Seriously, Moss, I thought this was something I'd be OK at.' I'd 'practised' at it enough, if you counted hours on Insta and Buzzfeed. 'But ... it's weirdly *hard*.' I showed her the most recent 'helpful advice' Fiona-aa had sent over. 'I'm not doing it right.' I felt like I was handing in my posts as homework and getting them all back marked 'could try harder'. And I was sixteen and Fiona-aa was a forty-year-old woman who liked stripy knitwear – it was a bit ... demoralizing. 'How am I meant to "put myself out there" while simultaneously avoiding anything that resembles my actual life?'

'LOL, no photos of me then.' Moss read on a bit. 'She wants you to avoid sarcasm? Challenging. It doesn't leave you with much.'

I nodded sadly. 'And I don't have time to conjure up a whole new sparkly personality.' Definitely not if I was going to finish my geography. '*Unless*,' (I stopped fretting and pointed to the 'P.S.' – the good bit), 'unless Fiona really does get me into VIP events.'

'Like?'

'Film premieres? Maybe ... after-parties? I don't know, handbag launches? You can be my plus-one.'

Moss snorted. 'The day your mum lets you go to the after-party of a handbag launch is the day I get a hundred per cent in chemistry.'

'I won't tell her.'

'Good luck with that.'

Moss was in a weird mood – possibly the geography but probably Torr who hadn't even bothered to breadcrumb her since The Great Love Declaration. I opened up my laptop. 'Carlo's media is making me feel inadequate. Look at his Insta.' It wasn't the subtlest tactic.

'It's just him doing vaguely sporty things without his shirt on.'

'Not just that.' Mostly that. 'He's even got *Twitter* banter.' I never knew what to say and if I did say anything, I panicked in case it was the wrong thing and deleted it and then I panicked in case anyone noticed (PPR noticed). It was exhausting.

'You're in that photo.' She pointed to a group shot of me, Carlo and half the crew paddling (i.e. mucking about) in the "stream". '*The Bizz* will start calling it a *thing*.' She was full-on stalking his Insta now.

'So ... you're messaging?'

'I suppose you already know we are?' I nodded. He'd mentioned it. 'It's not flirty,' she said defensively.

'But it could be? Which would be funny.'

'I'm not going to embark on a virtual rebound thing with Carlo just to amuse you, Elektra. Anyway, he's not into it in that way. And I'm not. Obviously, because he's an *actor*.' I glared at her. 'I still think he's ... Anyway, *I'm* not into it. I'm not. I'm really not. Just, no.'

'But—'

'No, Elektra. It's not happening. I've friend-zoned all males,' she said primly. 'Possibly for ever.'

'I'm off now.' Mum came into the kitchen. 'I'll drop you off at the Heath, Elektra, you can walk Plog and then pick up some shopping for me on the way home because I won't be back till late. Moss? You look like you could do with a nice brisk walk too. You're both turning blue from that screen light.' We really weren't.

Moss politely declined. What a surprise.

An hour later, I was freezing, I was bored and I was walking at a rate of what felt like ten steps an hour. I turned and looked back at my small but very wilful black and white dog. I tugged at his lead, he sat down more firmly. I pulled him along a few steps ignoring the you-are-a-dog-abuser looks from the competent dog walkers around me. This was ridiculous. He was a dog. Dogs liked walks.

'Come on, Plog, get with the programme.'

No movement. None. I sat down on a bench and plopped him on my lap for warmth. He practically smiled at me and set to chewing the end of his lead. I checked my phone – two messages from my mum asking me to pick up random vegetables, one from Eulalie with a photo of her laughing with Havelski against a backdrop of golden pineapples (nope, no idea) and one from Archie. Two words, **It's over**

Never a great text to get from your long-distance boyfriend but I was pretty sure I knew what he was talking about. **You just shot your last scene???**

Yes. All over. ALL OVER. OVER. 😞😦😦😦😦/🔪🔪 🔪🔪🔪/💜💜💜💜💜/👻👻👻👻👻

Did everyone cry? Everyone had cried at my last scene, but then it had been a harrowing death scene. My death.

NOBODY cried. It was a green screen scene. There was only me, the third AD whose name I still don't know, a bunch of techies and two hundred invisible bats

No audience of sobbing maidens? He'd live. **It's only over if they don't pick up another series . . .**

I can't even think about that right now. I've got three months of unwashed clothes to pack up, about a hundred people to say goodbye to and a flight to catch in about two hours

And in about five hours my boyfriend would be living one bus ride away again rather than stuck in a forest in Romania with a squad of hot co-stars. **Will you get me an obscene amount of chocolate in duty free?**

I've got precisely four euros left so probably not. But I will come over tomorrow and help you train Plog or something. Any joy on Fortuneswell?

Nope. I'm giving up on the corset dream

He texted back immediately, **I'm never giving up on the corset dream. Got to go, see you tomorrow xx**

And then I saw I'd somehow missed a call from Stella. *News?* Was hope still alive? I pressed callback. 'Stella? Hey ... it's Elektra ... *Get down!*'

'Sorry?'

'Not you – Plog. He's my new puppy,' I added, in case Stella jumped to the unlikely conclusion that I was being molested by a short person with a weird name.

'Hello, Plog!' Stella chirped, and then, when he didn't answer. 'What are you up to?'

'Me? What? Now?'

'Yes. Right now.'

'Nothing. No! We're not going to play now!'

'*Sorry?*'

'Plog again.' Obviously. 'Is there any news on *Fortuneswell?*' I tried not to sound desperate.

'Just a loud silence from Upton. But we're hearing on the grapevine that it's cast.' Probably someone with a million Insta followers. 'I'd chalk that one down to experience.' Hope bludgeoned to death. Again.

I took a deep breath and tried to sound like I cared a lot less than I did. 'At least I won't have to learn the quadrille.'

Stella laughed. 'One day, Elektra, one day. But now

I need you to get yourself over to Shoreditch by four p.m. latest. Is that do-able?'

'For an *audition*?' For an audition anything was do-able. Was hope scratching at the lid of the coffin?

'Yes.' *Yes?* Hope was now tap dancing on its premature grave – this conversation was the emotional equivalent of being on a seesaw with a chronically indecisive giant. 'It's a pilot for a family comedy,' I tried to calm down and focus on what Stella was telling me, ' . . . two overworked parents, a teenage kid who might or might not be a member of The Undead and a new baby.' Yes! It wasn't a corset role but I could work with the whole undead thing. Or dead thing. Either was good. 'For reasons known only to the producers, the working title is *Strawberry Jam*. No script but I'll mail you a map.' And she was gone.

Ah.

Leaving me with just one tiny problem.

The sort of tiny problem with four paws and a weak bladder.

I couldn't just abandon Plog on Hampstead Heath. I couldn't drop him home first because both my parents were miles away and wouldn't be home before six and I'd *misplaced* my door key. Aaaaaaagh. I tried Moss and then Daisy. Their phones went straight to answer.

This wasn't good. I called Stella back. 'You've

reached the answering machine of Stella Haden. I'm away from my desk right now, leave your name and number.' I called Charlie. *'I'm away from my desk right now ...'* I tried Stella on her mobile. *'You've reached ...'* I didn't have any other number for Charlie. Panic and adrenalin were making me sweaty. I paced around for five minutes and called every number I had again. *'You have reached ...'* I looked at my watch, nearly 3p.m. I was low on options.

I got there five minutes before the deadline. Of course I got there. There was a sign on the door that looked like it had been typed on a vintage typewriter.

> If you're looking for Kat Casting go through
> the café to the back room and up the stairs
> to the first floor. May you find fame and
> fortune - if that's what you really want.
> If in doubt, stay downstairs and try the
> Sriracha Lobster Kimchi Mac & Cheese ...

It was the kind of coffee shop where they ground their own beans in the basement and shared the premises with a bicycle repair shop, the most frivolous cake was carrot and everyone had moustaches. On the upside, this was Insta heaven, on the downside, there was literally *nowhere* I could stow a small dotty dog. I took a deep breath, channelled my inner Amber Leigh and dropped Plog into my bag. He looked a bit surprised but settled happily enough between the empty crisps packets and my sports socks.

'Hey, Elektra James, right?' Katya (presumably) had the door open before I'd rung the bell – possibly because of the noise I'd made when I'd knocked over her bike. She was wearing a beanie and had only the teensiest of moustaches. 'I recognize you from your headshot ...' She had a strong American accent. 'Oh. My. Gaaawd. *Gorgeous.*'

I wasn't used to this reaction from casting agents. It was nice.

'What is he?'

Ah. Plog had stuck a paw out of the bag and was basically offering to shake hands.

'He's a ... dog. I'm SO sorry,' I began. 'I got stuck with him and I didn't know what to do and I couldn't reach Stella and—'

'*Your* dog?'

I resisted the strong temptation to make up something about how he'd been foisted on me by a foolhardy stranger and nodded shamefully.

'A Dalmatian, right?' He was getting dottier by the day. 'I LOVE Dalmatians.'

'Should I leave him out here?' I looked around desperately for something I could attach him to.

'Oh, don't worry,' Katya said breezily. 'Bring him in. We have an office pug.' There was a big difference between an office pug and Plog.

'He's house-trained,' I burbled hopefully but not entirely professionally.

'No worries. Polly's so ancient she needs diapers.' Katya pointed out a wheezing dog curled up on a leather sofa in the corner. Part-pug/part-cushion. Polly farted loudly in welcome. 'Sorry about the Saturday/short-notice/no brief thing. The clients messed up but you didn't hear me saying that. OK, it's a demo they're shooting for a sitcom. Think *Outnumbered* but with issues. Well, that's what they told me.'

'What sort of issues?' I pulled Plog away from a tempting camera lead.

'Parental neglect. Kids falling behind at school. Bullying. Zombies. Maybe bullying zombies? That sort of thing.'

'But funny?' I was trying to get some idea of what they were after before she put me on tape.

'I suppose it's a dark comedy. *British humour.*' Katya sounded a bit doubtful. 'Possibly with overtones of social realism, or maybe it's magical realism? I'm never quite sure what that is but there are definitely some dream sequences.' She absentmindedly dived into the cookie jar. Excellent. She handed a biscuit to Plog. He was enthusiastic. I was waiting. Nothing.

'Anyhoo,' she went on, letting Plog lick the crumbs off her fingers, 'the scene we're going to film now couldn't be simpler.' She handed me a page of script. 'You're reading for Meg. She's in the kitchen with her mom. It's a standard teen-parent-squabble scene – but with an *undead* element. Easy as apple pie.'

I had a quick skim. Not many clues to my character. Maybe Katya would give me helpful direction but she was ignoring me and cooing over Plog again. I needed to be the perfect Meg. I focused and read the pages *really* carefully, over and over again until, at last, she got up from tickling Plog's tummy and moved behind the camera.

'I'll read the mom's lines from here,' she said. 'Ready?' The little red light on the camera was already blinking. Katya morphed from chilled-out puppy pamperer to stressed out Hockey-mom.

Katya/MUM
'Hurry up, Meg. You're going to be late for school *again*.'

Me/MEG
I'm not going.

Oops, I'd inadvertently given Meg a strong American accent too. Between us we'd just moved this bit of British humour to Texas.

Katya/MUM
You'll get into trouble if you don't go.

I was pretty sure Katya was one of the large percentage of casting agents who'd started out as actors. She was really getting into it.

Me/MEG
You don't want to start imagining the sort of trouble I'll get into if I *do* go.

Plog, high on sugar, was leaping up and down beside me. Nooooo. 'I'm so sorry,' I said breaking off. 'I think he got into shot. Can we go again.' Five minutes for her to cuddle Plog and we started off again.

Katya/MUM
What are you talking about?

Me/MEG
I've been suspended.

Katya/MUM
What? *(shocked)* why?

Me/MEG
It was a miscarriage of justice. Obviously.

```
One tiny little death in the classroom and
I get accused of it. Classic.
```

Plog jumped up and barked. He wanted to play;
I wanted to die. I tried to fend him off without
sending him flying across the room. I read the
line again. **It was a mis . . .** There was an
anguished yelp.

'I'm so sorry.' I missed Digby – he'd never have let
me down like this.

'No. Wow, that was amazing!'

It was?

'Seriously, Ploggy is so smart.'

Ploggy.

'Like, he totally got that you were upset in that
scene. Wow. He's like, so empathetic.'

He was? Maybe he was; now he was looking at me
with big guilty eyes.

'Oh my God, he *so* deserves a treat for that.' He
so did not but Katya stepped away from the camera
and went over to the cookie jar. She took out two
this time. Sadly, they were both for Plog.

I got two more goes at it; ten per cent screen
time for me, ninety per cent Plog interrupting and
claiming biscuits.

Hope was back in intensive care.

WEEKEND RECORD
Celebrity news . . . Film & TV

The pastoral peace of Affpuddle in Dorset was shattered today as filming on *Fortuneswell* moved outdoors. Residents of this bucolic corner of England have become used to fleeting glimpses of stars of the small screen and hordes of crew buying up all the light bulbs and batteries in the village. But now they're filming a village fair scene and that means fans can get close to the action.

Most of the people fighting for a good view today were hoping to get close to Lohan Winter, resplendent in scarlet uniform, who plays Captain Allerton, catching the eye and winning the heart of the beautiful Sophia St Clair (played by Ally Sheer). 'If I was thirty years younger I'd be fighting her for him,' said Dawn (aged fifty-four) proprietor of the village convenience store. Malia had come all the way from Winnipeg just to catch a glimpse of Mr Winter in the flesh. 'I did think he looked fine in uniform,' she said

ecstatically. 'Although I'd been hoping to catch a glimpse of his famous abs.' But Mr Winter wasn't the only heartthrob with a crowd of fans panting after him. Handsome young James Moore (last seen in *Floreat Eton* and winner of last year's *Gives Good Posh* Prize at the Oxford University Alternative BAFTAs) is playing Viscount Luddington and is no doubt enjoying being fought over by the St Clair sisters (Belle, played by Lucy Morton and Mary, played by Georgie Dunn). 'He took a selfie with me!' squealed fifteen-year-old Sofia ecstatically. 'Best day ever!'

'I haven't seen pigs paraded through the village like that since I was a lad in shorts,' added Willy Ellis, at ninety-eight years old, the oldest resident in the village.

Readers in London will be pleased to hear that there will be some location filming in the capital in December.

★ CHAPTER 7

'I feel relatively immune to bitchy criticism now.'
Sienna Miller

'It's an offer. We need to talk about it, I suppose,' said Dad. 'And they're obviously keen. They took a decision fast; they must really want to get the ball rolling on this.'

'I suppose it is time sensitive,' said my mum. 'Playing age is going to be a factor. And it is such a big decision.'

'It might interrupt progress in what is a very important year.' Dad passed me the milk. We were all having breakfast late because, for once (for some undisclosed so possibly scandalous, teacher reason), I didn't have to be in school till eleven.

'And we really need to think about the impact

of long days on set,' added Mum. 'All that waiting around.'

'And only on-set catering.' What was Dad talking about? There was absolutely nothing wrong with on-set catering. Anyone would love it.

'What worries me is where it will all *end*. I just don't know how healthy it is.' Mum sighed.

'Look at Lindsay Lohan,' I added. 'All those young actors that go off the rails.'

'That's usually my line, Elektra,' said Mum catching Dad's eye and laughing.

Brutal.

It wasn't that funny.

I read Stella's email for the third time.

From: Stella at Haden Agency
Date: 24 November 08.51
To: Elektra James
Cc: Julia James, Charlie at Haden Agency

Subject: Kat Casting Pilot X/ Strawberry Jam (and update on *Raw*)

Dear Elektra,

Kat Casting emailed me after hours yesterday with some *interesting* feedback. Katya really enjoyed meeting you (I'm pretty confident she won't forget you!) but sadly, they're going in another direction with this one. But there was more feedback and this is where it gets *weird*!

Elektra James, what were you thinking?! I've never had a client turn up to a casting with their dog! The wrong script, yes, banned substances, yes – a pet? *Never.* As a general rule, it's probably not a great idea.

That said, there is *client interest* ... Plog, as you probably know, managed to get in shot quite a bit, and when Katya sent the tapes over to the client they were very impressed with him. They've asked whether you would consider Plog playing the part of the family dog in the pilot? The client is confident that he'd bring exactly the energy and vibrancy to the scene that they're after. They'd pay proper rates – taking into account chaperone fees, he'd be getting an hourly rate a little *higher* than we could have charged for you.

Although we'd *love* to have Plog's headshot on our wall we don't really have the expertise to represent him so I'm going to pass your contact details to Katya and you can deal with her direct. If Plog wants to take it further, he should think about getting his own agent (here's a list of some reputable animal casting agencies)!

Tell him well done from us. He's plainly a dog of unusual talents 😄.

And on *Raw*: while I remember, I know that Fiona from PPR is working on lining up some industry event invites for you to build your public profile.

Julia – I'm just flagging this up to you because I'm aware that it's an important school year for Elektra and no doubt you'll want to make a family call on the extent to which you'll be happy with her doing this sort of work (important though it is) around the acting ... Don't feel under any pressure. I'll back you up with whatever decision you take.

Stella x

This wasn't the audition feedback I'd been hoping for. I looked over at Plog who was conked out in Digby's big basket. He was snoring, soft little puppy snores. But then he could sleep deeply. He wasn't the one who was failing to get cast in anything. He looked cute. Maybe I should post a pic – plug with Plog, now he was going to be a star. My phone barked again; my ring tone was mocking me. Another email for me – and yet, once more, not really for me.

From: Kat at Katya Casting
To: Elektra James
Date: 24 November 09.09
Subject: Plog in Strawberry Jam!!

Hi Elektra,

Did Stella tell you that we're DESPERATE to make Plog a star?! He is PERFECT. Can you send me some pics and details? All the usual: height, age, eye colour etc.

SO exciting!

Katya

P.S. So sorry we didn't cast you Elektra! You definitely came over as a stressed-out-dead-but-real teenager to me but perhaps I misread what the client was after. It was a tricky one. Maybe next time!

'Aaaaaw,' said Mum reading over my shoulder. 'They think he's perfect!' She abandoned me to cover my four-legged baby bro with love and affection. '*You are perfect, aren't you, my little pooch.*' He wasn't 'her' little pooch. He certainly hadn't been 'her' little pooch when he'd vommed up half a (stolen) sausage on the carpet. 'Is it difficult being overlooked in favour of Plog?'

'It's not like they wanted him for the same part,' I said pettily. 'My ego will survive.' But possibly not my career. 'I don't know about his.'

'I don't think dogs have egos,' said Dad. 'I'm not even sure that humans have egos.' He muttered something incomprehensible about Freud and unproven concepts. But then Dad didn't hang out with girls in my class. Or actors.

'I've been reading up on the inner life of puppies and they are highly intelligent social animals,' said Mum. Poor Plog, any minute now she'd be drawing him up a list of improving reading and feeding him brain food. On second thoughts, if he was going to steal my parts he might as well sit my GCSEs.

'He's got a lot to be proud of,' said Dad.

We all looked at Plog, who'd woken up and was licking his bum. 'He'll be getting invites to VIP events soon,' I said – the silver lining in the email.

'Don't think for one minute that you're going to be gallivanting off to any "VIP events" whatever they may be,' said Mum immediately.

'Come on! It's work.'

'Not happening,' she said firmly. 'Not a chance.'

I looked at Dad. 'I agree,' he said. 'There's a world of difference between resigning ourselves to the fact that you're pursuing this acting stuff and letting you wander off in the evenings to get your photo taken at random events. Huge difference.'

'But I'm *sixteen*.'

'Precisely,' he said.

Ugh, they were hopeless. My phone barked again.

Angelina's coming home

'Is it Archie?' asked Mum. I nodded. 'Send him our love.' No, I was not going to do that.

She's on a German motorway right now. Finally on her way back to her luxury Ascot stables. I'm going to go and see her at the weekend. He was missing that horse more than any of the Maidens of Outstanding Beauty; Angelina was growing on me.

Come with me?

I can't. I've got to go to a one-day 'Negotiating the rocky landscape of Social Media' course at the Actors' Centre

Sounds grim

Just slightly less grim than the one-day actual rocky landscape revision course being put on by our geography department. I heard on the Zombie casting. They literally just got in touch

And?

They didn't want me.

Crap. Forget it. Zombies are over

Zombies are never over. That's kind of the point . . .
They made an offer

???

To Plog

Hahahahahaha

Apparently he's a natural in front of the camera

Hahahahaha. Sure

I'm not joking. They want him. I told you your dog shamelessly scene-stole

My dog? Our dog Elektra. We should be proud. We need to support him in making his dreams come true

Not funny Because I was wallowing in my massive sense of humour failure.

A little bit funny. Does he want to do it?

I have no idea what the answer to that question is

*

'I don't really mind if this assembly runs over into lunch hour,' said Mrs Green (the least pastoral 'head of pastoral care' in the history of the school) a few painful hours later. 'But I'm not releasing you until we've gone through everything on this agenda.' She held up something that looked like the Dead Sea Scrolls. 'Mocks,' she said. 'You'll no doubt be thrilled to know that we've finalized the timetable.' We were a tricky audience. Thrilled wasn't the vibe in the room. 'Depending on your subject selections, exams will fall between the 19th and 25th of January.'

'It's ages away,' said an optimist from the back row.

'You'll find it sneaks up on you very quickly,' said Mrs Green (who'd never been optimistic about anything).

'We might not have finished everything by then,' said Molly into the miserable silence. Molly was the only girl in our year who probably would have finished everything. Some of us might not have started very much.

The questions will mostly be on what you've covered in class.' Mostly? And the rest was just an invitation for optimistic guesswork? 'Deadlines will give you all the push you need to start taking this year seriously.'

'Because until now Year Eleven has just been fun, fun, fun,' muttered Flissy. Sometimes I didn't mind Flissy.

Mrs Green ploughed on. 'Here's what you need to know. You must avoid stress, panic and low grades.' At the mention of low grades we all started stressing and panicking. 'Use the remaining class time well because there isn't very much of it. If you don't understand something, *ask*. It will be too late when you're sitting in an exam room.' Somebody let out a low moan. 'You need to start looking after yourselves. No late nights.' She stared down Flissy who was rolling her eyes. 'No pointless distractions – you've got time to sort out your romantic life after your exams – or, if you've got any sense, after you leave school.' This was grim. 'And you need a revision timetable. I've got *planners* for you all here.' She pointed to a big heap on her desk. Oh, God, they were A3. 'Filling them in will boost your motivation to revise, revise, revise. Go through the past papers on the school portal and practise, practise, practise. It goes without saying that you must switch off or block all social media when you're revising.' Fiona-aa would have something to say about that. 'And forget everything you've read about revising with a friend.' She looked at Moss and me. 'It's a hopeless waste of time. *Obviously* from the school's perspective it's your *well-being* and the development of your *moral* character that matters most. *But* just bear in mind that while feelings are temporary, exam results last for ever.'

*

'Well, that was depressing,' said Moss when we were finally released and were walking towards the lunch hall.

I nodded. 'And we're so late for lunch there'll be nothing left but salad and fruit. I swear we could have revised an entire module in the time she took to lecture us.' We could have, but we wouldn't have. I sighed. I needed to start soon, though. I didn't want to fail.

'Does anyone want this planner?' asked Molly. 'I've already got one. It works better if you start at the beginning of the academic year. By this stage you're already in catch-up.' She had no idea.

'I'll take it.' Jenny grabbed for it desperately.

'You don't need two planners,' I said. I should probably have taken it. One for my countdown to exams and one for my countdown to *Raw* coming out.

'I already cried on mine and the dates have smudged.' Jenny was one of my best friends and I loved her but nobody could describe her as resilient. I gave her my last Haribo.

'Are you even going to have to do the exams, Elektra?' asked Flissy, who as 'luck' would have it was now behind us in the queue for lunch. 'Or are you going to pull the "I'm filming" excuse?' She gave it the full air quotations treatment. 'Except, you haven't had anything for ages, have you?'

'A few months isn't "ages". It's not even a long time.' I lied. It felt like a very long time.

'I bet you thought when you got cast in that weird dystopian film you'd never be back here. That's *tough*.'

'I didn't think that.' The long and painful year before I'd got cast in anything at all had taught me something. Pessimism. And I was getting a nice little refresher course now.

'Be fair, Flissy,' said Talia (her loyal side kick). 'Elektra's definitely a professional actor. We all know that now.'

'Maybe not "all",' said Flissy. 'We're still a very small and select group. How many likes does your new Facebook *fan page* have, Elektra?'

'I think it's about seven, isn't it?' said Talia.

'It's probably more by now,' said Flissy. 'I tagged at least a dozen people last night. It's good to spread the word.'

'You need a bit more content, though,' said Talia. She had a point. So far all I'd had time to post was my headshot and a link to some official site.

'Maybe add some funny stuff?' suggested Jenny who was failing to pick up on the vibes.

'Oh, it *is* quite funny,' said Flissy. 'But it's a bit disappointing that you're not engaging with your *fans*, Elektra. When people go to all the effort to comment and they don't even get a reply.'

Her comments being, if I remembered properly (and sadly I did), *'What even is this?'* *'Wait, wait, are you famous? LOL!'* and, *'This what I was talking about 😒'* followed by about twenty tagged names sadly and predictably including @ArchieMortimer. Just slightly less painful than the post that read, *'I can't wait to see you on the big screen, darling! Xx'* That one might not have been ironic, but the forty-seven likes definitely were. I needed to go into settings and block my mum before she *engaged* with me again.

'But *Raw* is going to be *epic*,' said Flissy loudly. 'That's what it said in *The Bizz* yesterday.' I was torn between greed and the urge to run. I'd looked ahead and counted and if I stayed in line there was a very high chance I'd get the last slice of pizza. Greed won. I held my ground. '"*An epic disaster in every sense*" is, I think, how they put it.' Flissy was playing to the whole line now.

Of course I'd read it. And if I'd missed that one, a quick Google would have turned up any number of apocalyptic predictions. 'Good to know you're following it so closely.' That's where I should have stopped but, no, I added, 'and thank you for your critical input and soothsaying.' Hunger had apparently made me brave, reckless *and weird*. Where had that even come from?

'*Soothsaying*. LOL. You're hilarious Elektra.'

I really didn't need pizza. Sometimes retreat is the best option.

I should have retreated from the rest of the day.

14.03 Late slip for being 'shockingly late' to Maths. Third in a row so the only event I was going to be going to this week was detention #RawBehindBars

14.50 Called up in front of class to demonstrate my 'original' French pronunciation. Held up as an example of 'what not to do'. Public humiliation and a classic example of the way Berkeley Academy tramples over my human rights on a daily basis #RawExposure

15.35 Made to sit in the front row at PSHE because I was talking to Moss instead of concentrating. Because our PSHE teacher thinks we're still in Year Six. To be fair, I should have concentrated; it was the 'Stress and Anxiety' module #RawFear.

'I've been thinking about it,' I said when I got home. I'd had a lot of time to think about it because the bus had broken down. 'Why shouldn't Plog have his moment in front of the cameras?' I scooped him up for a cuddle.

'I thought we'd all agreed it was a mad idea,' said

Mum. She and Dad had agreed it was a mad idea. I'd just sulked and not said anything. 'What made you change your mind?'

The honest answer was that Moss had pointed out to me that I'd get hard cash and it wasn't like I was going to get hired if he turned down the job, but I went with, 'It's funny, it'll give him something to tell his grand-puppies about.'

'You don't have time to look after your own career, far less Plog's.'

'It's not like I'm filming anything right now. It's in the holidays and I'll take revision with me. I always work really well when I'm hanging around sets.' That was a lie. 'Please. He is *my* dog. I won't even ask you to drive us to the set. You won't know it's happening.'

'It sounds like a recipe for disaster to me,' said Mum, 'But I suppose so long as it is the holidays and you get all your revision done it's up to you how you spend your time. Better than hanging around in a park drinking lager.' What was she talking about? I'd never done that in my life.

WAITING

- % of time spent being excited about *Raw* alternately dreading *Raw* being released/being a massive fail: 81%
- % of time spent fantasizing about having the sort of life that would look #Rawontheredcarpet 54%; % of time spent being #Rawontheredcarpet 0%
- % of time spent concentrating/panicking at school because EXAMS: 13%
- % of time spent listening to Moss mourning Torr: 21% (% of time trying not to say 'I told you so': 21%)
- % of time spent failing to train Plog for a life of stardom: 11%; % of time spent loving Plog: 100%.
- % of time spent missing Digby: slightly less than 100%. Always loved, never forgotten.

106

Days to Go . . .

From: Charlotte at the Haden Agency
Date: 11 December 15.23
To: Elektra James
Cc: Stella at Haden Agency; Julia James
Subject: *Fortuneswell*. Glandular fever: Good News
Attachments: Location details, Google map (confidential)

Dear Elektra,

I've just got off the phone from a call with Tracey, Sally Upton's assistant. Their first choice to play Clemency Barton-Woods in *Fortuneswell* has been hospitalized with severe glandular fever. You're their second (obviously better) choice – so you have the part. It's very late notice (it's still shooting **19–23 December**) but you're a pro, I know you'll be off-book in time.

We hope you've been keeping up that dance practice? Seriously, DON'T PANIC, there'll be a run-through with the dancing master on the first day and Tracey says there won't be much more than curtseying and the occasional turn and twirl for Clemency. It's amazing how good they can make even the most average of dancers look.

You'll be fitted for costume on-set so you need to fill in the measurements form attached. Even though it's a big costume department and there'll be a seamstress on hand, try to be *really precise with your measurements* – it will speed everything up.

And you'll need to get your hair dyed at least a couple of days before filming (in case it goes *horribly wrong* . . .), so call me and we can sort out a time. Can't wait to see you as a red-head!

I'll be in touch later today about the contracts and performance licences etc. etc.

Charlie x

CHAPTER 8

'Remember not to joke.'
Ruth Negga

I was revising with Moss and Jenny. We'd made ourselves a little study pod in one of the school corridor alcoves. It smelled strongly of cheese and onion crisps and we had to sit on the floor but there wasn't anywhere else to go.

'Elektra gets made love to at a ball,' said Moss giving up on irregular verbs. 'By a lord.'

'He's only a minor squire,' I clarified happily. Jenny still looked puzzled. 'I got *Fortuneswell*!' I did a little sitting dance of glee. It might just be a couple of days' filming but I was back in business.

'Love-making at a ball? It sounds a bit dodgy.'

'It's eighteen-thirteen dodgy. He clasps my gloved

hand and he may or may not whisper sweet nothings to me over the ices.' No awkward love scenes, no on-screen get-withs. No blood. No explosions, no gore, no bugs, no hessian sack. The only action, twirling in the arms of a squire. The more I thought about it, the more I liked costume dramas. I was finding it quite hard to feel sorry for their invalided first choice.

'A hot minor squire?' asked Jenny.

'All of Elektra's drama boys are hot,' said Moss.

'Is Archie OK with that?'

'Annoyingly so – but then he spends months surrounded by hot co-stars himself.' Just one of the reasons I was so happy he was back in London.

'Weird,' said Jenny, drawing little cows all over her copy of Silas Marner.

'I haven't seen "Minor Squire" yet, he might be ugly.'

'He won't be,' said Moss morosely. 'He'll have posh boy hair and a jaw that could shatter glass.'

'I need to take up an interest where I'm going to meet a long line of eligible minor squires,' said Jenny.

'Farming?' I suggested.

'Seriously, my life has dwindled to a dark, lonely, text-book-filled place where the social highlight is ... no, there's no social highlight.' Jenny added crying faces to her cow drawings.

'We can live vicariously through Elektra,' said Moss, handing me half her last Oreo. 'Our smug married friend with the film and TV career.'

'So just smug then,' I beamed. I'd been in a nauseatingly good mood since I got Charlie's email.

'Will you get to wear a dreamy ballgown?' Now Jenny was trying and failing to make her cows look like they were dancing.

'I *really* hope so.' Although with my luck on costumes I'd probably end up in something that looked like a nightie worn by a slightly pregnant woman. My phone barked. **Pyrotechnics** 🔥 🔥 🔥 🔥 🔥 🔥 **AWESOME** Carlo had added some photos for extra jealousy.

Where does fire come into plot?

Warri tribe camp gets destroyed in flaming apocalypse

I thought it was a watery apocalypse? I swear it wasn't normal to be this confused about a film you're actually in.

Why have a watery apocalypse when you can have a watery AND a fiery apocalypse. There is a MASSIVE flame-thrower. MASSIVE. They wouldn't let me operate it 😩 😩 😩 😩 😩. On the one hand his enthusiasm was getting a bit psychotic, on the other hand, *why was I missing all this?* I showed the texts to Moss.

'Does he text you *all the time?*' she asked with a hint of judgement.

'He keeps me posted on all things *Raw*,' I said. 'So I don't feel left out.'

'I swear he texts you more than Archie does.' And again with the judgey voice.

'That's because it's end-days chaos on the set and Carlo has his phone with him all the time now because nobody's bothering about the rules.'

Also I was hit by a falling branch. Fake, but still heavy enough to do me a bit of damage

I bet it was your own fault

I miss you, E

Moss looked at my screen. 'Seriously?'

'Not in that way.'

'Is it not enough that Archie has to worry about the minor squire?' said Moss. 'Do *you* miss *him*? Carlo?' There was definite edge.

'I miss *it* – the set, everyone, being someone else in front of the camera, *working* . . .' Too hard to explain – so I gave up.

'How can they *still* be filming?' Jenny was baffled.

'They're nearly finished. It's just a few reshoots and there's already lots of post-production stuff going on.' I think I was pulling off the 'expert' thing quite well. **The beaten-up look suits you** I texted.

Yeah, it's hot. Do you think Moss would go for it?

'*That's* why Carlo's being so nice to me,' I showed them the text. '*Come on, Moss.*'

'Put him away,' she said sternly.

'If you don't want him, I'll have him,' offered Jenny, who'd been selflessly googling images of Carlo for the last couple of minutes. 'Just let me know. I'm going to follow him on everything.' She started to collect her stuff together. 'I can't concentrate now. I need to find a cool corner and fill in my revision planner. It makes me feel in control of my life and my destiny.'

'But does it make you feel in control of the Periodic Table?' asked Moss.

'What do you think? See you in Biology.'

'Why don't you just meet up with Carlo?' I said when it was just the two of us. 'He's wanted to since my party and you must be into him or you wouldn't be messaging – I know you are.'

'Because he tells you everything?' Ouch. 'I'm surprised he didn't tell you that we did meet up then.'

I was so surprised I swallowed the gum I'd literally just put in my mouth. '*You* didn't tell me!' That was not OK.

'I don't tell you *everything*.'

'But *I* tell *you* everything.'

'Only because you've got the wrong sort of face for keeping secrets.' Sadly, that was true. She started gathering her things. 'It was an impulse thing. And I would have called you if you hadn't lost your phone. *Obviously*.' Ah. Fair.

'Misplaced,' I corrected her. 'Misplaced for all of half a day.' Half a day and I'd missed *this*. (It had turned up in Plog's basket so I probably wasn't even to blame). The bell rang and she attempted a getaway but this was worth a late slip. '*And????*' I tugged her back.

'It was a humiliating disaster and I never want to talk about it.'

'I. Will. Literally. Kill. Him!'

'It wasn't his fault.'

'What. Did. He. Do?'

'*It wasn't him.* It was me.'

'What is your problem? You never blame the guy.' But then I blamed the guy even when it wasn't his fault. 'When? *And what happened?*'

'Yesterday, and nothing happened.' She stopped dead in the corridor (possibly because I wasn't letting her pass). 'I turned up at Starbucks and he was already there and he got me coffee and I spilled it because he made me feel nervous and then I didn't know what to say and he was sort of sitting there *smouldering* hopefully and I got even more nervous so I said I'd "suddenly remembered" that my mum was sick – or, maybe I said she was in hospital, possibly on the brink of death, or maybe it was my dad, or both? Whatever, it was *bad*.' She drew breath. 'And then I walked away.' Walked? 'So, yeah, there wasn't much to report to you.'

Not much to report? 'We should one hundred

per cent analyze this,' I said when I'd recovered the power of speech.

'We are never analyzing it. We are never talking about it again. And I'm glad he didn't tell you.' I was glad too. Carlo had to get marks for that. 'I'm incapable of seeing this guy without making a complete fool of myself so I'm never going to see him again.' I'd never seen her move to class faster.

'*Frogs*,' said Mr Williams, waving us to our seats. 'These frogs are going to be our teachers today.' He tapped the lid of an innocent-looking Tupperware box.

'Do we have to do this?' asked Molly. 'I mean, we're not going to get *examined* on our dissection skills.' She was talking very quickly – she'd been doing that a lot recently, like she could learn more if she speeded everything up. 'I want a *nine*,' she added. 'I need a *nine*.' The rest of us died a little.

'Education is about more than exams.' Mr Williams snapped on a pair of latex gloves. He looked like he might burst into tears. 'And I have quite a few frogs in this box and we need to do something with them.'

'We could let them go, sir?' suggested Jenny.

'Brilliant idea,' he said, opening the lid. 'Anyone with long hair tie it back, lab coats on and grab some gloves. I'm going to put you into groups.' He looked around the room. 'Elektra, Moss and Talia, take the back-left bench.'

'So this new part,' said Moss while Mr Williams was sorting out all the groups and Talia was off in a corner styling herself into scientist Barbie and sulking about being grouped with us, 'there's going to be an actual ball?'

'But Carlo—'

'We're not talking about that.' I'd leave it – for now. 'The ball – I'm amazed you're so calm about it.'

'I'm super excited!'

'But not freaking out.' Moss left a pause for me to freak out. 'I mean you *can* dance. I've seen you dance. At parties. Also, not at parties. In your bedroom. In my bedroom. But ...'

'There's a half-day with a "Dancing-Master".' I was clinging on to that.

'Nothing to worry about then. Dick did wonders for your running.' Dick Murphy trainer-extraordinaire-to the-stars and to me on *Raw* had taken weeks and weeks just to teach me to stop running like an electrocuted chicken. But if dancing was what I needed to do to be allowed to *be* Clemency Barton-Wood, I was up for it. And it was only dancing – not linear algebra, or thermionic effect. And it was *acting-dancing*. 'All I have to do is stand in a line opposite my partner, curtsey, smile sweetly and spin around a bit. Plog could probably do it.' Although I hoped he wasn't going to edge me out this time. (Which reminded me, I still had to persuade my mum to chaperone him because our shooting dates clashed – acting dynasty problems). 'I've watched *a lot* of costume dramas.'

'So have I, but they didn't teach me ballroom dancing.'

'Then you haven't been paying close enough attention. I've been pausing at all the dance-y bits. I've watched like, every version of *Pride and Prejudice*.' Everyone's Regency gateway drug. 'And there's stuff on YouTube.'

'Oh, well, you'll be *fine* if you've learned it off YouTube.' Before I could work out if that was sarcasm, Mr Williams was dropping frogs onto the benches like some biblical plague and calling us all to attention.

'Right, girls, observation first – make sure your frog is the right way up.'

'Which way up is that?' I asked.

'So you can see the face,' he said, as if it were obvious. 'First off, determine if your frog is male or female.'

'How do we do that?' I asked poking around a bit.

'Check the innermost digit on the forelimb . . . yes, that's right, you're looking at the fingertips. If it's a male you'll find an enlarged darker patched pad – that's what the male uses to grab on to the female during mating.' Mr Williams clicked his magic pen-thingy and a noisy video of a couple of frogs mating filled the whiteboard.

We checked our frog.

'Philomena's a good name for a frog,' said Moss, peering intently over my shoulder. 'Oooooh, look at her cute little face.' She was getting into it. She was also delusional.

'Elektra, did you get a chance to talk to Carlo about me?' Talia asked. Why would I have done that? 'Carlo?' she prompted me. 'Is it just that you don't *want* to put us in touch?' I could sense Moss sending out little spikey vibes of dislike in Talia's direction. 'Have you got a thing for him? I mean, I get it if you do. But if he hasn't tried to get with you yet, it's probably not going to happen, is it?' She was impressively uninterested in Philomena. 'Oh, and I guess you've got Archie,' she added snidely. (Talia and Archie had history, not much and very historical history but, still).

'a) I'm not into Carlo; b) Carlo's not into me; and c) I'm going out with Archie – except you can reverse the order. Oh yuck, I've got to pull her tongue out. Will someone else do that bit?' Apparently not. I did a little sick in my mouth but got the job done.

'Right,' said Mr Williams. 'I need you to turn your frogs ventral-side-up.' Half of us raised our hands. He clarified, ' … lay it on its *back*. And then I need you to *pin its four limbs down*.' This was the most intense biology class I'd ever been in and human reproduction in Year Six hadn't been a breeze. 'I'll do one for you and you can all watch.' He elbowed Moss out of the way, flipped Philomena-the-Frog like a burger and started pinning her out (Philomena, not Moss, obviously).

'Then you can set me and Carlo up,' said Talia, ignoring the masterclass in crucifixion going on inches away from her. Was she mad? There was as much chance of that happening as of Philomena leaping about on lily pads again.

'If your frog is very stiff, you might have to break the legs.' What? I was seeing a new dark side to Mr Williams. 'Why don't you stop worrying about your love life for ten minutes, Talia, and make the first cut.' Philomena was 'ready'. Mr Williams held out the scalpel.

'Sorry, I can't,' she said, flicking her ponytail. 'I'm a vegan.'

'I'll do it,' I said because we couldn't just all stand here looking at Philomena until whatever was preserving her stopped working.

'Just one sharp incision . . .' Mr Williams directed me and moved on to the next bench.

'Carlo's really into someone else,' I said when he was safely out of earshot.

'Who?' Talia was paying attention to what I was saying if not to what I was doing. 'Amber Leigh?'

'Scissors, please.' If the acting didn't turn out, maybe I could be a surgeon. 'Amber's about twenty years older than Carlo,' I said, snipping away. 'So, no.'

'Who then? I bet it's someone famous,' said Talia.

'Not really,' I said and offered Moss a turn with the scalpel.

From: Fiona Hull at Personality PR
Date: 11 December 16.22
To: Elektra James
Subject: Corpse!!!

Dear Elektra,

Just a quick note to suggest you delete the Insta posts featuring the strange little grey dead reptilian thing, haha!! It doesn't play *visually* and you don't want to get into hot water with the anti-dissection lobby. At least it wasn't vivisection or hunting!!!

Love & Hugs,
Fiona x

* PPR * ON FIRE in Soho since 2010
Follow us on Twitter @Personality Facebook: PersonalityPR
Insta @PersonalityonFire

***

From: Fiona Hull at Personality PR
Date: 11 December 17.12
To: Elektra James
Subject: WELL DONE!!! #COUPLE GOALS

Dear Elektra,

You didn't tell us you were dating Archie Mortimer! *This is
great news!* I know that he's currently relatively unknown but
with *The Curse* expected to be one of the lead shows in the
autumn schedules, this is really something you should start
LEVERAGING in your social media (so much better than toads!!!).
It will help to build BUZZ if you're seen as one half of a hot young
acting couple (#couplegoals). *Good job!*

Love & Hugs,
Fiona

P.S. and no reason not to have lots of photos of
you with Carlo Winn out there too ☺. Remember
GOSSIP=BUZZ=TICKET SALES!!!

* PPR * ON FIRE in Soho since 2010
**Follow us on Twitter @Personality Facebook: PersonalityPR
Insta @PersonalityonFire**

***

From: Fiona Hull at Personality PR
Date: 14 December 10.12
To: Elektra James
CC: Stella Haden at Haden Agency

Subject: URGENT

Dear Elektra,

We've been trying to call you all day as there's a bit of an EMERGENCY on your Insta!!

For some reason you've posted a photo of yourself eating what appear to be noodles but this time the carbs aren't the only problem . . . you MUST DELETE ASAP the description *'Warri-ors eat bugs. . . .'* and the hashtags #NoodlesAreBetterThanBugs and #Rawllyrank. The struggle over resources and the near starvation diet forced on the warring tribes by the eco-disaster that sets up the narrative is an *important part of the PLOT*. We don't want to be giving that away before people have bought their tickets! *Obviously*. You've posted a *massive* SPOILER!!

We shouldn't PANIC *too* much because your follower numbers are still on the *disappointingly* LOW side, but we wouldn't want this to be your first post to go VIRAL, would we??!!

Love etc.
Fiona x

P.S. Take a look at how Amber Leigh has been promoting-with-diet. She posted a mini-video of herself mixing green smoothies filmed to the Raw soundtrack!! #RawStrength.

* PPR * ON FIRE in Soho since 2010
Follow us on Twitter @Personality Facebook: PersonalityPR
Insta @PersonalityonFire

From: Fiona Hull at Personality PR
Date: 14 December 15.43
To: Elektra James
CC: Stella Haden at Haden Agency
Subject: **EXTREMELY URGENT**

Dear Elektra,

We've been trying to reach you all day. The longer that SPOILER
stays up, the BIGGER the PROBLEM. Please DELETE
that post NOW.

Can you also ping over all your social media log-in details so if
there's another **DISASTER** and we can't get hold of you, we can
DEAL WITH IT FOR YOU!!!

Fiona

* PPR * ON FIRE in Soho since 2010
Follow us on Twitter @Personality Facebook: PersonalityPR
Insta @PersonalityonFire

***

From: Charlie at the Haden Agency
Date: 14 December 17.34
To: Elektra James
Subject: URGENT! GET IN TOUCH WITH PPR! ASAP

Hi Elektra,

You're not answering texts or picking up your phone – have you lost it again?! Fiona is going nuts about something you've posted on Insta. CHECK YOUR EMAILS!

Charlie x

⭐ CHAPTER 9

'I feel like fear is a really boring waste of time.'
Idris Elba

It was 4.45 a.m., hours till it got light but I was on a mission. I'd read the articles (*5 a.m. Superwoman!, Get Up And Get Ahead!, Winners Wake First!*), I'd made a plan. From the ashes of disorganization and disaster would rise a new shiny me. There was a deluded bird chirping outside the kitchen window. Why did it sound so happy? Why? And why was it so loud? I fumbled for my phone.

Eulalie? Are you awake?

Oui! I have been dancing

With Sergei?

Oui, but now he is being asleep and I am still dancing. You are not dancing, I am thinking

137

Non. No dancing. Will you help me with Twitter? The new shiny me was going to be a social media legend for the right reasons. **You are my ONLY follower.** Not much of an exaggeration. I was now up to one hundred and thirty-three. Ten less than my neglected private Insta (*I missed it*) and not even enough for one very small cinema. **How did you get all yours?**

They just came. It's like going to a party. You are being friendly and you are making all the new friends. Très amusant. Give it time

I don't have any TIME because SCHOOL. And I haven't got anything to post about because SCHOOL/ Except I posted a SPOILER by accident and everybody hates me – or they would if they followed me. (I was picking up Fiona-aa's ALL-CAPS habit.) **The publicity woman definitely hates me** 😞 😞 😞 😞 😞**/ The only thing I've done that makes them happy is date Archie.**

Well, that is making us all happy! A minute later she texted again. **Are you wanting that I tell Sergei to make it stop?**

No! Don't tell him! I was pretty sure that even if he was madly in love with my step-grandmother, Sergei Havelski would neither know nor care what I was doing on social media.

Plog can be doing le Twitter. I am already following two dogs and a horse. Stop worrying and go to sleep, cherie xxx

But I couldn't go back to sleep, too much to do. And I couldn't concentrate. I put my head down on the table and closed my eyes. Oddly comfortable. I'd just stay like this for a minute. For five minutes . . .

'What are you doing?!'

I jerked awake. Mum was standing there in her dressing gown.

'You should be asleep!'

'I was.' How much time had I *wasted*?

'In. bed. Not. At-the-kitchen-table-with-the-laptop-open.' I slammed down the lid. 'What. Are. You. Doing?'

'Just . . . work.'

'Even I don't think five-thirty in the morning is a sensible time to be studying. It's not a sensible time to be doing anything other than sleeping.'

'You're not sleeping.'

'I'm old and I don't have school. And I heard you and I thought it was Plog so I came down to check on him.' Priorities. 'I thought he might be worrying about his filming coming up.' Because Plog was totally on top of the calendar. '*Five-thirty*.' It didn't sound better the more often she said it.

'It's Magic Hour.' The bird started up again. I hated that bird and his whole happy carefree vibe.

'It's the middle of the night.'

'If I do all the things I have to do now then everything will be fine. I'll be *sorted*.' I looked anxiously at the clock. My golden hour was nearly gone and I hadn't updated even half the media stuff and I hadn't started my homework; I didn't have time for this conversation.

'Are you feeling all right?'

'No' was the honest answer to that. 'I'm going to dominate my day before breakfast,' I said. It had seemed like the obvious solution when I'd pressed 'next episode' on Netflix eight hours earlier.

'What have you been working on?' Mum opened up the laptop before I could stop her. 'Elektra! Please don't tell me you're up in the middle of the night just to muck about on Facebook.'

'Don't look at my computer,' I said, desperately trying to reach the high ground.

'You shouldn't be wasting time like this right now.' She was not happy. I slipped back down to the low ground.

'I'm not wasting time. I'm working.'

'Don't be ridiculous.' She looked; of course she looked.

God, this was embarrassing.

'Elektra!'

Nobody wants their mother to see this stuff. The Magic Morning/new Me stuff was *nearly* OK but there were a lot of tabs open. *Is the Kardashians' next move into acting? 10 Actors who posted HUGE spoilers on Social Media. Red hair FAILS. Is Sam Gross losing it? Is*

Sam Gross losing his hair? Should Cara stick to modelling? Is it time for Havelski to go back to making small budget art movies?

'What. On. Earth . . . ?'

'Work, Mum.' So much hard work. 'And research.' So much depressing research. *Fifty Reasons why so many Child Stars don't make it as Adult Actors. Twenty movies that killed careers. Ten Spoilers that ruined movies. Two hundred career-killing movies and the stars they ruined for ever.*

'This isn't work, this is madness.'

'You don't understand.'

'No, I don't think I do.'

'I'm building a *platform*. Which is very difficult to do without a life to talk about. I can't believe you wouldn't even let me go to that TV award/ party thing.'

'Why are you taking this stuff so seriously?' She peered at me. 'And why are you wearing make-up? Please tell me it's not for photos.' Obviously. 'But Elektra, you're not a social media star.' I was aware. 'You're *shy*.' Something I was doing my very best to hide (so much harder without a costume and character for disguise). I glared at her. 'Look, whether or not you post something at five in the morning on wherever it is you post things – with or without blusher – isn't going to make the blindest bit of difference to how well *Raw* goes or anything else.'

'But it's cumulative. If I persist . . .'

'If you persist, there are two things that will happen.' She was less angry now and more serious. It wasn't an improvement. 'The first of these is that you will mess up everything at school and you're too smart for that – and probably out of school. The second – which is very closely connected – is that we will have to revisit what seemed like a very sane decision to let you pursue the acting with our support. And I don't like this media nonsense.' She didn't even know what media was. 'You don't need to put yourself out there like a tin of beans.'

'But I *do*. Maybe not a tin of beans but . . . an avocado. Everybody says so, even Stella says it matters. I need to be a *better avocado*.'

'You're not making sense. Go to bed.'

'It's not worth it now. It's practically getting up time. Listen, the birds are cheeping.'

'It's pitch dark, the birds aren't cheeping. You're hallucinating with tiredness.' Was that a thing? Was she even here?

'I'm not going to get back to sleep. If I promise to put away everything else, can I just sit here and get back to my homework?' The last homework of term and the straw that was breaking this camel's back.

'Well, I'm going to have a cup of coffee.' Mum boiled the kettle.

'Can I have a cup?'

'You don't drink coffee. Just sit there and cuddle Plog, he'll relax you. Are you seeing Archie soon?' Was that a non-sequitur or just weird?

'He's coming over on Friday. He's going to test me on stuff again.' Maybe. 'Please can I have a coffee?'

She tutted but poured me half a cup. 'It's not good to get reliant.' She didn't specify whether she was talking about Archie or the coffee.

Neither did I. 'It's got to be worth a try.'

Dad came into the kitchen. 'Morning, Plog,' he opened the door to the garden for him.' What are you doing up so early, Elektra?'

'It's not that early.' Not now my Magic Hour had been so brutally wiped out. 'God, this coffee stuff is *amazing*.'

'And now you can't unknow that,' he said sadly, like all my innocence was lost. 'This is the earliest I've ever seen you voluntarily out of bed unless it was to get to a film set.' I wished I were going to a film set. Then I'd only have one thing to worry about. 'Today's the day though, right? Last few hours as a brunette. Is that why you couldn't sleep?'

'I've still got reservations about the hair.' Looking at Mum's face, they were quite big reservations.

'Too late now,' I said because the *Fortuneswell* people had booked me in to one of London's finest (by which I think they meant most expensive) salons. By the end of the day I was either going to have the flame-coloured tresses of my dreams or look like an orange Pomeranian. But first, I needed more coffee.

'*Someone's* got quite poor quality hair.' Leanne the colourist came over and prodded my head judgementally.

'Er . . . sorry?'

She pursed her lips 'Do you take hair vitamins.' She fastened the gown tighter around my neck. She basically garrotted me.

'Yes.' No. What even were hair vitamins? Leanne raised her eyebrows. 'Yes . . . I take them . . . every day.' Speech was tricky.

Leanne gave me an intense look. She was definitely on to me. 'Right, let's look at these swatches.' The *Fortuneswell* people had sent over some little sample bits of hair pinned to a board like I was some weird interior design project.

'They all look quite similar to me,' I said.

'No! There's a world of difference between *Light Extra Red Iridescent* and, for example, the *Dark Extra Red Copper Blonde.*' There was? 'We need to work out what's going to work best with your skin colouring.' She turned my face from side to side and stared at me until I felt deeply uncomfortable. 'Yes, definitely the 6.64. OK, I'm going to go mix the dyes. You don't have any allergies, do you?'

'I don't think so,' I said, immediately worrying that I did.

If you don't want to do this it's not too late to back out It was Mum.

I think it is

Leanne was back with a little trolley of chemicals and foils. 'I'm going to cut off most of the hair to start.'

WHAT?!

'Hahhahaha! Only joking. Gets people every time.' Hilarious. She pinned back some of my hair and got out her little paint-brush. 'Aaaaaw, look at your little face! You look like a frightened bush-baby.' God, I was sophisticated. 'It's going to be great. Trust me.'

I did not trust her.

Leanne folded the last bit of tinfoil into my hair. 'The dye will take about an hour to *take*. Do you have something to read? Want a magazine?'

'I've got some maths revision stuff.'

'Perfect.' Was it perfect? Was it really? I eyed the pile of trashy magazines in the corner of the room with longing and pulled *GCSE Maths Made Simple* out of my bag.

I swear my head was heating up but maybe that was just arithmetical effort or a side effect of getting up at 4 a.m. I tugged the gown a bit looser and picked up my phone. My scalp was definitely getting warmer. And itchy? That couldn't be good. Clemency didn't go through this for her flame tresses. I tried to focus. *There are 5 lemon sweets and 4 orange sweets in a bag* ... No question, my head was hot and it was itchy. And the more I thought about those two things the hotter and itchier it got. Which meant that if I stopped thinking about it, it would go away. Probably. I scratched a bit through the foils. *Kiran takes one of the sweets at random* ...

My phone barked. It was Archie. **How's it going? Are you a ginger yet?**

Past the point of no return. Also on the verge of a panic attack. Do you think dye is meant to make your head hot? Also ITCH??

Oddly enough I don't know the answer to that question. Ask a hairdresser

I'm too embarrassed

It'll be more embarrassing if all your hair falls out. Two seconds later. **Or you die**

Good point. 'Er ... Leanne ...' I waved out to her as she was walking past. 'My head's sort of warm.' Hot. Really hot. 'Is that OK?'

She poked at a couple of foils in a casual way. 'It's fine. You're just cooking.'

How reassuring. First they'd covered my head in chemicals, then they'd wrapped bits of it in tin foil and now they were boiling it. **Apparently it was all in my head** On my head. **It's taking FOR EVER. And I'm**

STRESSED. What if it's awful. What if I literally look like a tomato? Or a pumpkin? Or an orange? Or, if it doesn't work, a BLORANGE?

Stop customising red food groups, it will be great

Or a carrot – that would be bad

Carrots have green hair, stop stressing. Also I'm guessing it's too late now??? Snap when you're done

If you haven't heard from me by tonight, send help and a balaclava

'Good wow or bad wow?' asked Leanne who was smiling at me staring at myself in the mirror.

'You know the answer to that question,' I said and jumped out of the chair to give her a big hug.

'I told you it would be worth it,' she said. 'And start using conditioner.' I would do whatever she told me. Even take vitamins.

The woman was a genius.

CHAPTER 10

'I still go into panic mode about seventy-five per cent of the time.'

Robert Pattinson

'Do you genuinely actually like it?'

'That's the seventh time you've asked me,' said Archie. 'And I still genuinely, actually, love it.'

'Are you sure I don't look like a red-haired troll doll?'

'Well ...' he hesitated. What? No! This was not OK. He looked at my face. 'I'm *joking*, Elektra.'

'Or the love child of Ed Sheeran and Queen Elizabeth the First?'

'Probably not.'

'Daphne from Scooby Doo?'

'No.'

'You were meant to say yes to that one.'

He laughed. 'Stop fishing for compliments. Fill me in on *Fortuneswell*. I want to see what scenes you've got with Minor Squire. Or that James Moore guy.' He didn't look that threatened but then he was sprawled all over my sofa and I was making him a sandwich (more because I was very hungry than to reinforce the patriarchy).

'Sorry, I know my hair still smells weird.' I edged Plog out of the way and snuggled into him. 'I'm glad you're back. Really glad.'

'Are you OK?' He shifted so he could look at me. 'You sound a bit ... *flat* for someone with excellent hair.'

'Yeah ... no, sort of. Just tired. It's been a really long day.'

'And?'

'I'm just stressed because I've been messing up *Raw* stuff. My latest Insta disaster was to post a spoiler.' It made me sweaty thinking about it. 'I accidentally – OK, stupidly – revealed to the world that Straker eats bugs.'

Archie looked at me blankly. 'And that's a problem because ... ?'

'It's a plot point. Who knew.'

'It's not like you posted the ending.'

'I'm not sure I know the ending,' I said and he laughed.

'You can't worry about this media stuff.' He

sounded so *rational*. All they seem to care about on *The Curse* is us not posting stuff from set. Forget it.'

'I'm not allowed to. I've got to be on it.' And I wasn't good at it. They hated everything I did. Well, nearly. 'You're the only thing I've done they approve of.' He looked confused. 'The publicity woman has found out that we're dating and she finds that *very exciting*.'

'Fair. So do I.'

'The email header was "*Well Done #CoupleGoals*".' He found that funnier than I did. 'But it gets worse. She'd like . . . I'm not quite sure how to put this.' Use you? Exploit you? Eeeeeurgh, this wasn't good.

'What did she say? *Show me.*' I cringed but pulled up the mail on my phone. 'Seriously, what does this even mean? How are you meant to "leverage us in your social media"? God, this industry's messed up.'

'We both want to stay in it, though.'

'I don't think it's much of a plan for future screen domination but post what you want. I've posted pictures of you.' Mostly untagged and with Plog in front of my face. I knew Fiona-aa well enough by now to know she'd want something a bit more 'curated' than that. 'Maybe I was subconsciously rolling out a PR plan all along.' He stopped joking and added, 'They're going to spin you and Carlo too?'

'Fiona didn't say that.'

'She pretty much did. How badly do they want to sell tickets?' Very badly. Was he annoyed? But he put down my phone and pulled me back into him. '*Stop worrying about it*. Think about nice stuff. Like your hair. And *Fortuneswell*. And Christmas. And me.'

'Archie? Can I ask you something?' He looked a bit nervous, but I wasn't after any 'leveraging'. 'Will you teach me to waltz?'

'I'd love to think this was some rogue form of flirtation but I'm guessing you've moved on to panicking about the ballroom scene?' I nodded and he shrugged. 'I'll try. We need something with a three-four beat.' He started scrolling.

'I've no idea what you're talking about but I won't feel it unless I've got proper waltz-y music.'

'Oddly enough, I don't have *Greatest Waltz Tunes* on my phone.' He looked at me. 'You're going to make me download some, aren't you?'

'I'm not going to *make* you.' But I was quite pleased when he did.

'OK, let's do this.' He wolfed down the last of *my* sandwich and got to his feet. 'Come on, don't leave me and Strauss hanging.'

'I don't think you're doing it right,' I said, not moving from the sofa.

'I haven't started,' he protested.

'You have to ask me to dance. I'm not passing up my only chance to have you bow to me.'

'You are a very demanding girlfriend.' There was the tiniest attempt at a bow, and then he swung me off the sofa. He turned *The Blue Danube* up to top volume, Plog skittered under the sofa for safety and I was in Archie's arms. This was the point at which I should have magically found my dancing groove and *twirled*.

But, no. 'Sorry, sorry, sorrreee …'

'It's *fine*,' he said stoically. 'I'm not sure how you managed to step on both my feet at once though. That takes some skill. Let's try again.'

'Will you bow to me again?'

'Under the circumstances I think you should be bowing to me. Stand on my feet for now till you get a feel for it.'

I made quite fast progress despite all the distractions. We were literally (almost) *twirling*.

This was #CoupleGoals but oddly enough, it could stay private.

My phone started barking aggressively from down the back of the sofa. It was killing the vibe. I went to turn it off and checked the screen.

ELEKTRA

It was Carlo.

CHECK

YOUR

EMAILS

RIGHT

NOW

I went into Mail very nervously. Two new, just arrived emails. The one from Jonathan the producer guy was short. 'Trailer out. **Link** attached. Best, J.M.' *Oh God.* I hovered over the link – nope, too scary. There was another email, this one from Fiona-aa. This one was longer – but then she had to fit in lots of exclamation marks. *'Archie!'* It came out as a weird squeak. He and Plog were beside me in seconds. I put my phone down on the table and we all peered at the screen.

From: Fiona Hull at Personality PR
Date: 15 December 17.23
To: Straker Cast and Crew
CC: Jonathan Martin at Panda Productions

Subject: TRAILER!!

HI ALL!!

Thrilled to be able to reveal that the TRAILER FOR *RAW* HAS FINALLY DROPPED!!! Here's the link for you all to watch AND REWATCH!!
While I'm sure you're all *Raw*ring (!!!) to share this with everyone you know, please be aware it's **embargoed** until **18.30 hours** BST TODAY so – until then, show NO ONE.

At **18.31** TODAY I expect you all to be sharing, sharing, SHARING. On all your social media platforms. We'll all be using the caption: **If you're looking for #RawNerve, #RawAdrenalin and #RawEmotion ... it's time to #GetRaw.** If you want to add your own stamp of personality – which we strongly advise against (!!!), please do that LATER when *re-sharing*.

We think the trailer is FANTASTIC!!! And we hope you love it too! It's so COOL! It's so EPIC! Let's make this teaser launch go with a BANG to counteract ALL the negative press we've been getting recently.

Love & Hugs,
Fiona x

* PPR * ON FIRE in Soho since 2010
Follow us on Twitter @Personality! Facebook: PersonalityPR Insta @PersonalityonFire

'Aaaaagh, I can't open it.'

'You have to!' Archie and Plog were practically biting their nails.

'I *can't*.' Was this what it felt like when you had to open exam results? 'Anyway it's TOP SECRET to you for,' I checked the time, 'thirty-five more minutes.'

'Yeah, right – stealth-watching classified-embargoed-trailers very slightly early, let's live on the edge.' Archie handed me the laptop (my dad's) that was lying on the table. 'We need a proper screen.'

I steeled myself, hacked in (password 'Digby007'),

opened Fiona's email again, gulped and clicked on the link . . .

Blackness and some sort of strange incantation.

An explosion.

The word **RAW** in stark white lettering flashed up on a black screen. A tracking shot panned over trees. The chanting gave way to discordant 'music'.

NERVE

The trees exploded.

For no apparent reason.

RAW

Some jolty shots of people's feet running through dirt. I saw a flash of hessian, one of those feet could *definitely* be mine.

ADRENALIN

Oh look, another explosion. Might be in the cave, but then again, maybe not. Then a close-up of Amber's face, with artfully defined dirt streaks. The music took a turn for the romantic and *swelled*. Amber opened her eyes, wide – zoom in.

RAW

More running, some of the creepy wolf-like creatures, a shot of a man (not sure who) falling from the Cliff of Dreams into the lake. A few more explosions sprinkled on for seasoning and another new and exciting feature which (probably) had no relevance to the plot – a *tsunami* ripping through the forest . . .

EMOTION

Now we were back with the creepy chanting, this time over a shot of Amber and Sam staring deeply (and possibly meaningfully) into each other's eyes against the flattering but otherwise gratuitous background of an out-of-control forest fire.

RAW

Limbs. A pile-up of limbs. Quite random but mostly legs and mostly severed. Blood. *Everywhere.*

EXCITEMENT

So many exciting severed bloody limbs.

RAW THE MOVIE
PANDA PRODUCTIONS
FROM THE DIRECTOR OF TERROR ISLAND. COMING SOON. GET READY TO BE PUSHED OVER THE EDGE ...

And a final shot of a bloodied Sam and Carlo leaping from the edge of the Cliff of Dreams.

'Brilliant,' said Archie before it had even faded from the screen. *Was it?*

I pressed play again. 'What do you really think?' Because I had no idea what I thought.

'Awesome. Classic of its genre.'

'What is its genre?'

There was a long pause while we both watched it over. 'Action,' said Archie confidently. 'Definitely action. Also blood. Is that a genre?'

'Would you go and see it?'

'Obviously.'

'If I wasn't in it.'

'Yes. Perfect date-night movie.' We watched it again. We watched it a lot of times and every single time it seemed to get louder and more bloody and make less sense. 'You've got to post it now,' said Archie, checking his watch.

I hesitated. 'It's going to look ... *boasty*.'

'So what. You earned this. Just do it,' he said. I gulped and went into my 'work' Facebook. 'Don't forget the hashtags.' Oh God, those hashtags. My hands hovered over the keyboard. '*Come on* ... It's time to #*GetRaw*. You have ten seconds and then I'm posting it for you.' I typed a few letters, deleted them, started over. Deleted ... Archie grabbed the laptop. 'If you're looking for #RawNerve ...' he started typing. 'Should I add in some extra hashtags just for you?' He was finding this way too funny. '#StrakerIsRawllyHot ...'

Nooooooo! I wrestled for the laptop. He pulled it just out of reach, I lunged at him and we fell in a giggling heap onto the sofa. Plog barked and joined in. There was a crash behind us.

'Your dad's computer!' We all (dog included) looked at it like it could be an unexploded landmine. Archie took a step forward and tentatively lifted the lid. It turned on and we breathed again.

'That was awful. Like watching a child nearly drown.' Definitely the ~~most~~, ~~second~~, third most stressful thing that had happened today.

'But it's all good, so come back here.' Archie pulled me back onto the sofa. 'You can stay on the floor, Plog.'

About ten minutes later my phone rang.

'Ignore it,' whispered Archie, pushing a strand of hair off my face.

It rang again. And again. Finally I picked up. 'What?' I asked aggressively. Archie stifled a laugh.

'Elektra James? This is Fiona Hull. Look, I don't want to disturb you – you're obviously *busy* – but everyone here at PPRrrr, and probably at Panda too is quite *worried*, yah.'

'Worried? About the trailer?' Surely it was a bit late now.

'Your *post*,' Fiona took a deep breath, 'is now eight minutes lateeee. We thought somethinggg must have happened to youuuuu?'

'Yes um … no I'm, I'm on it.' I fumbled for the computer. Archie had totally lost it.

'Do you remember the captionnnn?' she asked.

Yes. Unfortunately. Yes. I did.

'Don't even look at the comments,' Archie advised. 'It literally doesn't matter.'

Was it worse to get loads of really awful ones or

none? Of course I was looking. OK, there definitely weren't none – I had one hundred and twenty-eight notifications.

Random stranger 1: 'Love this'
Random stranger 2: 'So cool! Sam Gross 🖤 🖤 🖤 🖤 🖤'
Random stranger 3: 'Can't wait for this to be out.'

This wasn't so bad. And I was gaining a lot of new followers. Fiona-aa was going to be pleased.

Random stranger 4: 'Wow. It's loud.'
Random stranger 5: 'This looks crap'
Random stranger 6: 'What??'

And yet, I couldn't stop reading.

Sensationnel! Étonnant! Merveilleux!

No prizes for guessing.

Carlo: THIS IS COOL
Carlo: I AM NOT BIASED
Moss: You are a goddess
Moss: SLAY QUEEN

She'd also sent me a message saying that it would have been better if I'd been in it more and that the bit at the end looked like Carlo and Sam had swapped dystopia for a sick holiday and were jumping off a yacht. That was actually true.

Jenny: This is awesome

Random Stranger: I heard this was really bad

Talia: Are you even in this tho

>Reply: Flissy: Yeh thought you were a 'starring' role?!?!??

>>Talia: Maybe she's one of the feet?

>>>Flissy: Then she SERIOUSLY needs a pedicure

>>>Talia: No, it's just the #RAWLOOK!!!!

Random Stranger: I swear #GETRAW means something else

>Reply: Another Random Stranger: I don't get it

Twenty-seven Random Strangers posting links to movie gossip sites reporting that it was going to be crap.

Fifty-three random strangers and twenty-seven people I knew: *What's it about?!*

This felt like a point of no return.

Raw was coming soon.

It was coming soon even though they hadn't finished filming it.

It was coming soon even though nobody knew what it was about.

It was coming soon whether or not I was ready.

I wasn't ready.

Winter was coming.

★ CHAPTER 11

*'I don't wanna half-ass this – if I'm gonna tap
dance, I wanna tap dance. I don't want to cheat it.'*
Emma Stone

ROAD CLOSED. FILMING

It wasn't just the signs that gave it away. There were
rows of trucks and trailers double-parked in front of
the sort of houses that could easily be concealing a
ballroom or two. It was nothing like the Fairmount
studios but there was something about the buzz
that was the same. Crew in the usual 'uniform'
of black everything, workmen's boots and walkie-
talkies, were rushing around and actors, some in
normal clothes and some rocking a weird Regency
ballgown/puffa jacket fashion vibe, were standing in
little gossiping groups. It was frosty cold. Two huge

guys wearing light-up reindeer antlers and pushing racks of shrouded costumes apologized their way past me. To be back in this sort of madness was heaven. Scary, but heaven.

I went up to a big guy with **SECURITY** written across the back of his jacket and gave him my name.

'I'm meant to be checking in with the assistant director,' I checked my phone, 'John Price, and then going to hair and make-up.'

'John?' He called over to a middle-aged man who was walking past. 'New victim for you.'

'Elektra James? I recognize you from your tapes. Red hair suits you.' He stopped to tell a couple of crew members carrying armfuls of silver candlesticks where to go (in a non-offensive way). 'Great timing. You're in exercise kit, right?' I nodded. 'So, the dance run-through will take most of the day.' I stifled a little nervy squeak at the mention of dance. Oddly, I was losing faith by the hour in my in-depth small-screen research into Regency ballroom scenes. 'But you'll get let out for lunch.' He pointed at a big trailer as we walked past. 'Catering.' Two guys in white aprons were serving people coffee and chocolate muffins and bacon rolls from a hatch. 'You grab whatever you fancy, find yourself somewhere warm to eat it,' he gestured at what looked like a couple of converted buses kitted out with benches and tables, 'and then follow everyone back to the ballroom.'

'Do I get fitted for my costume today?' I was looking forward to that more than the dance-y stuff.

He shook his head. 'No need. I've spoken to wardrobe, you're a pretty standard size and they've got lots of options. We've set your call time tomorrow for 7 a.m. and you're not needed on-set till the afternoon, so heaps of time to get you fitted out. Right, shall we make our way to the ballroom? Follow me.'

I did. Embarrassingly quickly. I'd have followed anyone who said we were going to a ballroom. We went into a huge panelled hallway that would have been gracious if it hadn't been full of cables and ladders and up one side of a double staircase.

Oh. My. God.

This was Disney-level stuff. Huge double doors opened out onto the biggest room I'd ever seen outside the Fairmount lot. Camera gear pushed up against the panelled walls, reflecting in the pockmarked windows. French windows opened onto what looked like a narrow terrace. I looked up – crystal chandeliers – *and up*, there was a huge painting on the ceiling of some near-naked goddess flanked by dodgy demonic cherubs. There were gold curly bits *everywhere. Lots of curly bits and lots of gold.* I'm more of a *Frozen* kind of girl but I can appreciate some *Beauty and the Beast* vibes when I see them.

'Keep moving, Elektra,' said John who'd bumped

into me when I'd stopped dead in the doorway to gape. 'The guy over there in the pink t-shirt.' He pointed out a middle-aged man in black leggings and a delusional t-shirt with the slogan '*Hotter than Darcy.*' 'That's Danny the dancing master. Just do what he tells you and you'll be fine. Follow the crowd at the end of the session and you'll find yourself back at Catering.' And he was gone.

Eeeeeek. Everyone else seemed to know everyone. Huddles of people in chattering groups. I recognized Ally Sheer who was playing Sophia leaning onto Lohan Winter for balance while she stretched out one impossibly long leg. Lucy Morton who played Belle was sitting on the parquet floor surrounded by guys. One of my friends, Daisy, had acted with her in something, apparently she was nice as well as perfect. I knew I was staring. I would never get over the weirdness of seeing stars in the flesh.

'Everyone!' Danny-the-dancing-master was clapping his hands and yelling in a strong Scottish accent; there was no escape. 'Let's get you into your couples. It's all on the big list.' He gestured at what was indeed an enormous list stuck to one of the big gilded mirrors.

I smiled nervously at the strangers round me and checked the list: **CLEMENCY/ELEKTRA: MINOR SQUIRE/MIKE**. OK, I wasn't getting paired up with

Lohan Winter but finally I was getting to meet *Hot Minor Squire*.

'The plan is to start NOW! Not wait till global warming hits Glasgow,' bellowed Danny and everyone started to sort themselves out with a bit more purpose. I searched in vain for someone who screamed Squire. 'And Penny,' he gestured at one of the crew,' you're a decent dancer. Stand in for Georgie Dunn, will you? She's decided against gracing us with her presence again today.' He didn't sound happy.

A tall, painfully skinny, chinless guy came over and stood next to me. What? No. Where was *Hot* Minor Squire? They'd got it wrong. 'Minor Squire?' I asked. 'Sorry, I mean Mike?' He nodded. I searched in vain for another lurking Squire. 'Clemency's partner?' He nodded again. Well, this was disappointing. I smiled nervously, he didn't smile back. I tried some small talk but it wasn't his strength. We stood side by side not talking.

'*La Pastorale*,' announced Danny as if we were all in for a huge treat – maybe we were?

'I'm not good with anything that starts with French,' I said. Mike looked at his feet. 'Have you done this before?' Nothing. Did he only talk when someone gave him lines?

'It's a cotillion,' bellowed Danny, 'but you probably already know that.' Well, no. 'Everyone happy with the cotillion?'

165

There was a murmur that I realized with horror was assent. What about the waltz? And what were these people doing with their lives that they'd just casually picked up the steps to the cotillion?

'Then you've obviously been practicing. Brrrilliant! Remind me, anyone new in the room?' I put my hand up (there had to be a cooler way to get people's attention). 'Ah, yes, it's our Clemency ... they warned me you'd be in for the run-through. Welcome, Allegra.'

There was a muddle of hellos. 'It's Elektra,' I said, adding to the pile-up of embarrassing names.

'Elektra? Odd name. You're ticked off as having all the dance skills to competent level. So, you're au fait with the cotillion?'

A sentence I'd never expected to hear, especially not said by someone who sounded like he chilled with the Loch Ness Monster. 'Not exactly ... au fait but I've watched lots of ...' I tailed off.

'Och, well, don't panic.' Too late. 'Has it been a while since you've done that one?' That was one way of putting it. I was an imposter and I was about to be found out. 'I'll tell you what to do and just follow everyone else's lead. It'll all come back to you.' It definitely wouldn't all come back to me. 'Your partner knows what to do.' He nodded to Mike-Minor-Squire who just looked back blankly. Perhaps he had hidden rhythmic depths.

'Form two circles.' That sounded simple enough, I followed Mike out onto the dance floor. 'Bit tighter.' We all squished in a bit. I had Mike on one side of me; and Lohan Winter, dashing and distracting on the other. He smiled at me and I wiped my sweaty hand on my leggings. 'Better. And . . . music.' Danny said this with such a flourish that I half expected an orchestra or at least a string quartet to materialize, but instead he just pressed a button on a sound machine that was almost as old as the cotillion. 'Dum de dum, diddy dum . . .' He was making more noise than the backing track. 'Let's all just remind ourselves of the cotillion beat. 'All together now, dum de dum, diddy dum . . .' You can say this for actors, they don't hold back – within a minute the room was resounding with rousing dum-de-dums. Even Mike got stuck in (but quietly). 'OK, now, eight bar intro.' I had a blank. What was a bar again? No time to consider, he was directing us over the music. 'First lady,' he gestured to Lucy Morton, 'and gentleman opposite,' he nodded to Lohan Winter, '*contretemps* towards the right couple, *rigadon* around each other and cross into opposite place.'

What was he even saying? People were moving. They were *dancing*.

Unfortunately, I was still standing where I'd started.

Danny gave me a little jab in the back and now I was moving too. 'Hop-step-step, hop, step, step, hop, *simple!*' No, no, it really wasn't simple. 'And step-step and now the *rigadon* hop-step-step. More effort! This is like watching haggis run round a mountain.' Lohan Winter laughed but then he looked nothing like a haggis. 'This dance is meant to be a dance of courtship, not death! Hop-step-step and ... *plié* ... jump.' I was a dead haggis. 'Let's start again because that was a bit *ragged* in places. Allegra, just try to do what everyone else is doing.' That might have been good advice if everyone in this ridiculous dance had been meant to be moving in the same direction at the same time. '*Rigadon* and cross.' Now Danny was literally manhandling me around. That was better ... but also worse. This was harder than our physics practice paper. I couldn't breathe. 'We'd better take a break. Allegra ... Elektra, breathe, *breathe.*'

I slumped down against a wall, sweat pouring down my back.

'Well-earned rest, Clemency.' Lohan Winter walked past and grinned. I'd probably embellish that exchange a bit when I told my mum.

Lucy Morton came over. 'Hi, Cousin!' she said. She didn't know my name either. 'Are you surviving?' The answer to that, no matter how hard I tried, was sadly obvious to everyone. 'I brought you some water.' She crouched down and handed it to me like a relief worker tending to the wounded at a disaster zone. 'Don't look so worried. They'll cut away if you're messing up a step.'

'I've got some lines while we're dancing, though.'

'Then they'll be more focused on your face than on your feet.' Lucy gave me a little pat on the shoulder, unfurled her ridiculously long limbs and went off to talk to the real members of the cast.

By the time I limped out (following the crowd) to the Catering trailer, they'd chalked up a menu on a blackboard outside. I stood and stared. I'd expected to grab a sandwich; *somehow* from inside what was basically a caravan, they'd rustled up a feast – no, a choice of feasts.

Menu

Pappardelle with lamb ragù
Turkey, cranberry & grilled brie toastie
Vegetarian fajitas
Salt & pepper squid & rocket

***

Christmas Pudding Ice Cream with hot brandy sauce
Salted caramel popcorn pot
Toffee apples

The queue was moving fast, everyone stamping their feet to keep warm, and gossiping. Obviously I couldn't stamp my feet because I'd basically seized up and I couldn't gossip because they all knew each other and I knew no one. Everyone was smiley to me but I was guest 'talent' and I didn't know what they were talking about (although I heard 'Georgie' more than once). But the good thing about it being a non-filming day was that – so long as we followed all their strict no-posting rules – we were allowed to keep our phones. I had an email from Fiona-aa. More media 'encouragement'? More 'helpful advice'?

From: Fiona at Personality PR
Date: 19 December
To: Elektra James

Subject: *Raw: Revised strategy for Elektra/Straker*

Dear Elektra,

We've been keeping a close eye on how the media platform building has been working out for you and we think that this might be a good moment to try a new STRATEGY!!! We haven't got long now until RELEASE (yay!!! Exciting!!!) and your media audience numbers still aren't building as fast as we'd hoped. And this last week you've barely engaged on media at all! We understand too, from discussions with your agent, that there are still *disappointing* restrictions on your availability for evening industry events etc.

We've had your log-ins since the *unfortunate* SPOILER incident and you might have noticed we've started dropping some lovely PROMO CONTENT in for you – just to save you time!! We think it's time to ramp things up and we'd like to get stuck into posting loads of STARRY and HIP content. We really want to get you noticed!

There are some print and online media opportunities coming up too. With the smaller non-traditional PR slots (Fun Facts, Twitter chats etc.) it would make sense for us to go ahead and build that content on your behalf and *get it out there*. We promise we'll give you a really fun, upbeat PERSONALITY!

Of course you must let us know if you're not happy with any of this! It's absolutely your shout, we're just offering to HELP.

RELAX and let us carry the burden of the virtual build. Your image is in safe hands with Personality PR!!!

Fiona xx

Well, this was humiliating.

Maybe PPR would do my twirling and GCSEs for me too.

CHAPTER 12

'I hope we can get to a point where a woman can wear a low-cut gown and still have some relevance.'

Amy Adams

Another day, another oversized caravan – this one with blacked-out windows.

'Don't just stand there! Come in, before we all die of frostbite.' I jumped to it – literally, the trailer was quite high off the ground. And then I regretted it because ALL MOVEMENT WAS PAIN.

'They've done a good job on the colour.' Mel-the-make-up-woman was lifting strands of my hair and inspecting them closely. 'That's the perfect shade for you. Grab yourself a tea or coffee.' She pointed to a counter groaning under thermos jugs and mugs and half-opened packs of digestives. It was like a miniature, portable, version of the Hair and Make-Up department at Fairmount, sinks and hairdressers' chairs and make-up mirrors (sadly, not the ones framed with lightbulbs). And it smelled the same – eighty per cent hairspray, twenty per cent chocolate. Bliss. 'Choose a chair and we'll get started on you in five minutes. You're last on our rota. We just need to get the others out the door.'

'Hey, Clemency, hope you've recovered from yesterday.' Lucy waved at me vaguely from one of the chairs. I smiled back nervously – maybe not *recovered* exactly; I was just glad that I hadn't had an email firing me before I ever got on the set for real. Half her head was decorated with tall, curling white feathers. She looked amazing but it made me nervous. I wasn't sure I could pull off feathers. Georgie Dunn was sitting next to her. Finally, I was meeting her in the flesh. Well, sort of meeting her. She didn't acknowledge me so I sat one chair along so I didn't mess with their starry-main-cast space. My phone barked. **We're here! Nice and early!** It was Mum (who had caved and was at the *Strawberry Jam* set chaperoning Plog in my place). 'Are we allowed phones in here?' I turned down the volume.

Lucy nodded. 'So long as you don't take any photos. I couldn't survive hair and make-up without my phone. I've been here since six a.m.'

'That's because you've got *feathers*,' said Georgie.

'I'm lucky if I get a single ribbon. "Simple and charming" that's what I get. I mean, do I look like a *simple* and *charming* sort of person?' Georgie made it sound like an accusation right up there with kidnapping and genocide. 'No.' She pointed to her furry Gucci sliders. I could have mastered social media if I'd had those shoes. 'I do not. I want tackily extravagant hair.'

A muffled woof. **Two hours early.** Classic Mum. **I'll find someplace to have a nice cup of tea.**

'Big hair takes so long, though,' said Lucy. 'Over an hour and I've still got loads of feathers *and tendrils* to go.'

I picked up a magazine, pretended to read an article on celebrity tattoo fails and settled into eavesdropping.

'An hour is my absolute shortest time to get ready anyway,' Georgie said. 'I mean, if I'm *filming*.' She made it sound like penal servitude – which, even if her alternative wasn't GCSEs, was just *mad*. 'If I'm free, it's more like a whole day. I could literally just groom myself all day every day. I'm like a cat.'

'Or a monkey,' suggested Lucy, drinking tea through a straw because her make-up was already done.

'No, Lucy,' said Georgia coldly. 'Not like a monkey. Monkeys are not cute.' Monkeys were so cute! (If I hadn't been suffering from New-Girl-On-Set

174

syndrome, I'd have one hundred per cent got stuck into this conversation.)

'Did Amrita give you a hard time about yesterday?'

Georgia shrugged. 'She emailed me. So aggressive, it's like literally every little thing I do that she doesn't like I get an email. Like, if I'm even a *tiny bit* late, she freaks out. And she copies my agent. She's a nightmare.'

'She's really not,' said Lucy quietly. 'And to be fair, you weren't late this time.'

'No, I wasn't.'

'You didn't come at all.'

'Come on! There was no way that I was wasting a day on one of Danny's boring, boring rehearsals. Anyway, Mary never dances. She's way too uptight.'

'But on the callsheet it said—'

'Doesn't matter what it said on the callsheet. Mary is *no longer* dancing the cotillion and I took a personal day to have a life.' *Wow.* Havelski would have fired her.

My phone barked quietly; Mum again. **There's nowhere to have a nice cup of tea. I need tea. Chamomile tea. I think Plog's nervous.** I had a suspicion he wasn't alone. **Yes, Plog's definitely nervous. He's weeing a lot.**

Did you give him some of the chamomile tea?

Possibly

175

'When I say day, I mean night. Obviously. Guess who I met in the VIP room at Circus?'

'No idea.' Lucy sounded a bit bored. I was *riveted*.

'Kylie ...'

'Jenner? No way!' I'd forgotten I was both silent and invisible. I blushed and buried myself back in *Closer*.

OK ... we're in ... Mum made it sound like she'd broken into Alcatraz rather than been allowed onto the set. Two minutes later. **Everyone is LOVELY. They're making such a fuss of Plog.** Of course, he was a superstar thespian hound. Mum was positively lucky I'd had to delegate the chaperoning to her.

What's the girl playing 'my' role like?

Pale and very intense. I think she might actually BE a zombie. But everyone else is LOVELY. They're giving Plog biscuits. I ate another digestive. I'd never been on a biscuit-free set.

'Another day of watching James being out-acted by his floppy hair,' said Georgie. 'It should have its own agent. He's such a boring actor.' Was he? I'd always been too riveted by his chiselled features to judge.

'I don't agree.' Lucy was blushing.

'No?' Georgie fake-laughed. 'Well, I suppose you wouldn't.'

They stopped talking, it was a painful sort of silence. I checked my phone. **Oh dear, Plog's been sick. He found the Director's sandwiches. Tuna.** And then, **This is quite stressful.** And another one. **This is VERY STRESSFUL.** I was starting to feel guilty.

What's he done now? No reply.

Nearly two hours later, two-thirds of a packet of digestives and I was the last person in there.

'Eurgh, are they giving you proper hair?' Georgie reappeared, now in full costume, a lit cigarette in her hand.

My hair was real, actual human hair (if you didn't count all the chemicals) but I felt that wasn't what she meant. 'Like the full on . . .' she gestured wildly around her head.

I had no idea what sort of hair they were giving me but Georgie made me nervous so I just nodded.

'I'm literally the only person on this production with crap hair. And a crap costume. I look like a spinster aunt. They won't give me cleavage. It's ridiculous. One mention of bookish in the script and I'm consigned to wardrobe hell.' That did sound a bit discriminatory. 'Do you think I look pregnant?'

It took me a second. According to the Weekend Record's sidebar of shame there was a good chance she actually was pregnant. 'You look incredibly slim,' I said. She smiled; I'd made the right call.

'They should have gone with full-on waisted dresses. I wanted one of those corsets that make everyone complain in the press about the objectification of women. Nobody's going to objectify me in this, that's for sure. Have you seen my phone?' She picked up mine from the counter.

'That's my ...' I began but she was already scrolling the photos.

'Is that your boy?' She sounded impressed.

The 'boy' was Carlo in full Warri tribe get-up dangling from a polystyrene cliff face. 'No,' I said.

'Shame. Good upper body strength.' She scrolled some more. 'This one?'

'This one' was Archie in a billowing white shirt astride Angelina. 'Yes,' I said, desperately wrestling my phone away from her in as 'chill' a way as was possible.

'Also hot,' she said, sounding surprised. 'Have you got a thing about guys in costume?' Possibly. 'God. You're getting some stressy texts. Who's *Plog*?'

I grabbed back the phone.

I have never been so embarrassed/Not even by you
Either Mum had lost her memory or this was bad.

WHAT???

He savaged it

Savaged what???

The THING that looks like a small sheep on the end of the sound THING. He SAVAGED IT

Mel was back before I could think of a consoling reply – maybe there wasn't a consoling reply, 'Let's do this, Elektra.' She turned to Georgie. 'You shouldn't be in here with a cigarette. And you definitely shouldn't be in costume with a cigarette. Your phone's over there, if that's what you're looking for.' Within seconds Mel had shooed out Georgie and her hands were hovering ominously over my head. It looked worryingly like she was trying to curse me. 'Let's take out these curlers.'

She yanked at my head for what seemed like minutes and one tiny curler and about sixty thousand brain cells came away in her hand. This was not a good year to be losing brain cells. She was in a groove now, there was a heap of curlers in front of us. 'Okaaaay.' She pulled out the last one.

I had a literal and actual full-on perm. I looked like an electrified ginger poodle. I hated mirrors.

'I'm going to have to add a hair piece,' Mel tutted. 'You just don't have *sufficient* hair of your own to support this style.' She ignored my apologies, pulled out a little drawer and started colour matching what looked like dead fox tails to my head. Satisfied that my hair was now *sufficient* she disappeared into an enormous cupboard. She returned ...

'OH MY GOD, IT'S A TIARA!'

'I need you to be sensible, Elektra.' I wasn't being sensible; I was fan-girling over an inanimate object. 'This is a very serious piece of costume jewellery.' I was definitely telling everyone it was real diamonds. It was still the most glamorous, glittery thing anyone had ever let me within touching distance of. Mel twisted some of my curls up and started pinning. I lost another hundred thousand brain cells but I didn't care. 'We just need to create an even surface here for the base. You have a very uneven head.'

Finally, Mel lifted the tiara from its velvet box. Sprays of 'diamond' stars and 'pearl' corn sheaves quivered on tiny 'gold' filaments. She twisted some loose curls around the band so the hair and the stones looked almost interwoven. I gave a little disbelieving sigh of pure happiness and timidly put my hand up ...

'No touching! And no aggressive head movements. And don't muck it up when you're getting into costume.'

Minutes later, I was being handed a pair of white stockings and – my worst fears – what looked like a nightgown by a woman called Geila. What was it about me that screamed 'put this girl in a sack' (in a costume-y and not kidnap-y sense)?

'Ready, darling? Corset time.'

The corset looked like a cross between an intense (more intense?) Victoria's Secret push up thing-y and a full medieval girdle. It was made of white linen and some kind of boning – they couldn't really use *whales*, could they? There were ties up the front and tied on straps to go over the shoulders and cups for each boob that were worryingly far apart. This was quite intimidating. I stuck one arm in. So far, so good. Where was the other arm hole? Geila watched calmly as I flailed wildly. OK, I'd found it. Why was it so far away? I twisted my arm back as far as it would go. 'It's not very stretchy, is it?' I panted.

'That's the point of a corset,' Geila pointed out helpfully. 'That it *doesn't* stretch to accommodate the *bulk* of the body.' Seeing as Regency corsets only seemed to cover the boobs, bulk wasn't going to be an issue for me. Half my arm was in the corset; the other trapped behind me at a deeply uncomfortable angle. 'Do you need help?' I was trapped in a corset before it had even been done up. I clearly needed help. Help to get out of my immediate predicament. Quite possibly help more generally. I tried to pull the strap up my arm. It didn't move; it had embedded itself in my skin. This hadn't been how I'd envisaged becoming one with my character.

'Careful! You'll mess your hair! Can you just shift your arm a bit further backwards?' Not really, *no*. My arm wasn't going to move anywhere. Geila grabbed my arm and yanked. 'Right.' She spoke very slowly like she was handling a toddler. 'This time we're going to do it *together*—' she broke off. 'Oh my God.' She started to laugh. 'I *completely* forgot! The straps *untie*.' Hilarious. '*What was I thinking?*'

Two minutes later she was lacing me up. 'Tell me

if it starts to hurt,' she said reassuringly. 'Actually, just tell me if you can't breathe.' Less reassuring.

But the corset was oddly comfortable. I felt sort of supported, like being hugged by a needy whale – but good. And my boobs were definitely in the picture. Or, more accurately my boob.

My right boob was kind of stealing the scene while left boob . . . left boob was more of an extra.

Geila stepped back and looked at me with concern. She called over a woman who was brushing down tailcoats at the far end of the caravan. 'Is it just me, Janey, or do her boobs look *really* uneven?'

They peered at me like I was a mutated caterpillar, newly discovered in the Amazon. 'Oh my God! They are *so* uneven. I mean,' Janey turned to me, 'not uneven in a bad way, just from a purely neutral standpoint . . . they *are* . . .'

'Uneven?' I suggested.

'Yes,' she confirmed apologetically. 'You didn't say that when you sent over the measurements.' Well, no. There hadn't been a separate box for left and right. I'd been optimistic and evened upwards. 'Don't worry, darling, there's so much we can do!' They nodded sympathetically as if they'd just delivered the news that modern medicine had advanced to the point where uneven boobs were no longer *necessarily* terminal.

'I have a whole box of chicken fillets!' announced

Geila brightly. I was happy she was getting her intake of lean protein but I wasn't quite sure where this was going. 'Somewhere ...' and she went off to scan boxes and rummage like Ollivander looking for the perfect wand. 'We'll just slip one,' she held up the silicone enhancer – now I knew where this was going, 'in the left breast cup ... et voilà! This should be the *perfect* size.'

And it was.

Et voilà indeed.

My boobs were now perfectly equal. Perfect communist boobs. I had actual *cleavage*! The dream.

Geila started to unzip the single garment bag hanging on the rail in front of me.

The suspense.

And. There. It. Was.

My dress, Clemency's dress, was layers of white muslin, tiny seed pearls shivering in amongst the threads of gold around the neckline and clustering on the satin ribbon clinching the empire waist. Oh, and it had a *train*.

'It's *perfect*,' I breathed and reached out my hand and stroked it gently just to check it was real and not something I'd dreamed up.

This was a costume. Wearing this I could flirt with squires minor or major. I could flirt with Viscounts and Earls.

I could probably even dance.

From: Kat at Katya Casting
Date: 19 December 17.56
To: Julia James, Elektra James
Subject: Plog/ *Strawberry Jam*

Hi Julia and Elektra,

Aaaaaaaagh, I hate writing these emails and it's so much worse when it's a dog!

You one hundred per cent shouldn't feel bad about this, *but* the clients feel, upon reflection, that they probably don't need more from Plog than just the tiny cameo they managed to get today. They're standing him down for tomorrow – no need to turn up!

They asked me to stress that this decision has absolutely nothing to do with the fact that he destroyed the sound boom, ate the director's hat and peed on the shooting script. These things happen! They wish Plog all the best in his career going forward! We all do!

Katya x

P.S. Please don't show this email to Plog, I'd hate for him to be discouraged!

★
CHAPTER 13

'Darcy has never been a burden.'
Colin Firth

They'd just finished another scene so the room was filled with people standing very still at awkward angles so as not to mess up their hair or their dresses. So many beautiful dresses, (fake) jewels glinting in the light from literally hundreds of (fake?) candles. Also, lots of crew looking scruffy and busy and huge cameras and heaps of techy kit, but somehow that didn't detract.

'Sorry, can I squeeze past?' Ally Sheer was behind me in the doorway. Her dress was pink and *almost* as beautiful as mine. 'Clemency?' I nodded. 'That dress! Follow me, I'll take you over to Amrita.'

I took a deep breath. Well, as deep a breath as

my corset would allow. Ally was kind of gliding but there were a lot of people in that room and I didn't really know any of them and I definitely didn't want to mess up any of their costumes or trip over any lighting cables so I opted instead for a sort of sideways crab shuffle. 'Sorry, sorry, sorry, SORRY, sorry, sorry, sorry, SORRY, sorrryyyyy, sorry, sorry, sorry, sorry excus—, sorry, sorry. Ohmigod, I'm so sorry, sorry SORRYYYYYY, sorry, sorry, sorry.'

By the time I reached our director I was literally panting from the strain of being such an inherently awkward person. 'Hello ... I'm ... Elektra,' I managed. The corset must be addling my brain. I was starting to feel like all I was capable of doing was lying on a chaise longue reading bad poetry and producing spawn at regular intervals.

'Hi, Elektra, great to finally meet you.' Amrita was short and *she* definitely was pregnant. 'They gave you one of my favourite dresses!' She was very smiley. 'Do you like it?'

'I *love* it,' I said. 'I want to wear it all the time.'

She laughed. 'What do you think of your party?' It took me a moment to realise what she meant.

'It's unbelievable.'

'Clemency Barton-Wood's Coming Out Ball is going to be the talk of London.'

Danny-the-dancing-master came over and there

was nowhere to hide. 'Allegra! That is a better look than the leggings.' His t-shirt, black this time with the legend, *"In love with Miss Elizabeth Bennet"* printed across the front was also an improvement. 'I had a little chat with Amrita about the *challenges* you were facing with the cotillion.'

'I'm so, *so* sorry,' I said, praying that the fact that I was standing there in a corset meant that they weren't going to boot me off set.

'Don't worry,' said Amrita, giving me a little reassuring pat on my arm. 'Happens all the time. It's not that big a deal for the Clemency part or we'd have had you training earlier. We'll get enough shots of you looking like you know what you're doing.' Danny coughed. 'OK, we'll cheat with angles and close-ups. We can fill in the spinning around bits with dance pros – nothing is ever quite as it seems. And we're starting with the supper scene. There's no dancing in that.' I'd known this was a dance-free day but I still breathed out when she said it – well, I would have done if it hadn't been for the corset.

'While they're getting everything set up next door,' said Amrita (I could just see through mirrored doors at the end of the ballroom another room stretching out) 'let's chat through Clemency's motivations in this scene.' Obviously, you're the better-off, sophisticated cousin. You're far more used to these surroundings than the other girls – this is your home and balls are your natural habitat.' My whole sparkling social life had been method acting for this role. 'You've been taken in to supper by Squire Ellington,' (she motioned over to Mike). 'This is a blow. The man you want to be feeding you sweetmeats is Viscount Luddington but he's been asking you questions about your beautiful cousin Belle St Clair and treating you like a schoolgirl. The whole time you're forking up some delicious delicacy you're troubled by the fact that the man you have a romantic interest in has a romantic interest in *another*.' I could relate to that. 'And you've been hoping he will declare his love and ask you to marry him.' OK, that was *slightly* less relatable. 'You're trying incredibly hard not to show how much his interest in Belle is hurting you and all the while you've got to negotiate supper with the Squire-who-loves-you. Got all that?'. I nodded happily. It was like a nineteenth-century episode of *Made in Chelsea*.

'EVERYONE WHO'S NOT NEEDED FOR SCENE TWENTY-THREE CAN LEAVE NOW,' bellowed John. 'Be really quiet when you're on your way out because we'll be rolling again ASAP.' Some of the 'guests' started to drift from the ballroom.

'Have you had a chance to get to know Luddington – I mean James?' asked Amrita.

'I haven't spoken to him yet,' I said nervously, looking over to where he was standing, resplendent in tail coat and breeches. He was whispering something in Lucy's ear and she was blushing. I wasn't sure he wanted to be disturbed.

'Come with me. He doesn't bite. James, this is Elektra – she's playing Clemency.'

'Ah.' James smiled. 'Viscount Luddington's number one fan.' Everyone laughed. I laughed too – for just a tiny bit too long. It was uncomfortably close to the truth. Close up, he was *dazzling*.

'We're all set,' called John from the other room and I was shepherded through with everyone else who was in the scene. This room was about half the size of the ballroom (still huge but it looked smaller because of all the crew and cameras and kit). It was just as beautiful. A long table was covered in a snowy-white cloth, nearly every inch crammed with silver and china and food that barely looked like food, it was so beautiful. There were candelabra up and down its length, real candles this time, the smell of wax mingling with the smell of roast chicken and sugar and spices.

'Listen up—' began John. One of the production assistants raised his hand. 'Sorry, Amrita, sorry, John, before we start this scene, I have a quick message from the costume department.' He frowned at his phone screen. 'Right.' He coughed nervously. '"*If anyone gets food on their costume I will personally shoot them, wring their necks and stuff them like the game birds weighing down their entitled bourgeois table.*"' We all stared at the large platter of artfully arranged roast birds in the centre of the table. '"*Love, Your Friends in Costume P.S. obviously don't phrase it quite like this when you read it out*".'

Amrita laughed, but John was out of patience. 'For anyone who wasn't here when we were filming supper scenes last week – edible food is on the gold plates; fake stuff is on the white plates. You'll regret it if you forget it. Couldn't be simpler. Don't muck it up.'

I peered at the food on the gold plates and then at the food on the white plates. It all looked pretty much identical to me. I surreptitiously sniffed at a plate of roast venison on a white plate.

'Mostly brown bread and jelly glaze,' whispered one of the props guys. 'You could eat it at a push, but I wouldn't.'

'Elektra, stop poking over the savouries,' said John, 'we need to crack on with your scene.'

'Look at those little gingerbread cakes!' said Amrita. 'I think I've just got my first craving! Everybody make sure you leave one for me at the end of the day. Right. Elektra and Mike.' She gestured him to come over. 'So, Clemency, who'd dreamed of being taken into supper on the arm of

Viscount Luddington, is stuck with Minor Squire.' She smiled apologetically at Mike. 'Elektra, when Clemency says, "Are you acquainted with Viscount Luddington?" I'd like you to hold out your glass for Mike to fill with punch from the silver pitcher to his left. Clemency is *obsessed* with the Viscount so no matter what she is saying to Minor Squire and despite his increasingly desperate efforts to engage her attention, her eyes never leave the Viscount. Luddington in the meantime will be deep in conversation with Captain Allerton.' Lohan Winter moved to take up his place next to James. 'Got it?' I nodded. Mike nodded.

'Then Minor Squire will make the first of his stumbling *Love Declarations* while forking up some of the chicken on that platter. Everyone else around you will be feasting away. Elektra, you'll largely ignore Minor Squire and then on your line, when you try to swerve him by palming him onto Cousin Mary, I want you to take a scoop of the ice cream next to you.'

'Parmesan flavoured,' said the props guy. 'Authentic Regency recipe.'

'Actual *cheese* Parmesan?'

'Is there any other sort?' asked Mike (reasonably) and then we were hushed and everyone got serious about what they were doing.

'ACTION!'

CLEMENCY
```
And are you acquainted with Viscount
Luddington, sir?
```

I got through my first line and held out my glass in Mike's direction without taking my eyes off Viscount Luddington. It was no hardship – James was wearing exactly what Mike was wearing but he looked very different in it. James winked at me and I blushed.

They cut to sort out some problem with the sound levels.

'You're blushing! Great characterisation! Well done!' said Amrita. That would be because I was such a good actor. James winked again, torture. 'Action!'

'Er ...' Mike tried to get my attention. 'I finished filling up your glass ages ago.'

'Cut,' yelled John again and started lecturing Mike on not breaking out of character when the cameras were rolling.

'Sorry, Mike,' I said, while they were setting up again. 'That was my fault. It's just a bit tricky because I'm not meant to be taking my eyes off James. I mean Luddington.'

'I could cough? A little nervous cough. That's a very Minor Squire thing to do, I think. That can be a signal that you can safely move the glass.'

'Good plan.' I smiled at him. He was sweating through his powder.

'OK, guys, let's go again, start over from the top. Action.' John snapped the clapper board.

CLEMENCY
And are you acquainted with Viscount
Luddington, sir?

Eye contact with the Viscount, ✓; wait for the cough ... cough ✓

MINOR SQUIRE
I have not had that pleasure

I took a sip of the punch. Oooh, it was yummy. I took another. Quite distracting, what was my next line?

You must allow me to introduce you.

MINOR SQUIRE
But not yet. There are things ... that I
want ... no, that I need to tell you ...

CLEMENCY
(not paying attention) How do you find the
roast fowl, sir?

193

MINOR SQUIRE

I want ... I need ... I yearn to tell you ...

CLEMENCY

I trust it is not overdone?

MINOR SQUIRE

No, no, quite tender ... but not as tender as ... I cannot stay silent, I have *feelings*

CLEMENCY

Are you acquainted with my cousin Mary? (Such a brutal swerve, poor Minor Squire.) I am sure you would like her.

I peeled my eyes away from Viscount Luddington (that was what the directions said but honestly, it was hard) and reached past Mike/Minor Squire (who was simultaneously gazing on me with adoration and forking up chicken) to help myself to the cheese ice cream.

There was a worrying slither and plopping sound.

My left boob felt worryingly light.

I looked down at Mike's plate. There appeared to be *two* chicken breasts. One a lot more silicone-y than the other.

There was deathly silence.

Everyone was staring at me. Or more specifically my left boob. Or sudden lack thereof.

This was definitely the first time this many people had noticed my boobs and contrary to my expectations I was *not* enjoying it.

My chicken fillet ex-boob-enhancer slithered down slightly into Mike's gravy.

'OH MY GOD, IT'S A BOOBIE!' he screamed.

What? Seriously! Nooooo. Surely even Minor Squire must know that human breasts weren't see-through? Or shaped like weird kidney beans. And they didn't tend to fall, in one piece, onto people's plates at supper parties.

Also. '*Boobie*'?

'*Cut*,' yelled Amrita and John at the same time. I'd almost forgotten that cameras were rolling. Mike was hyperventilating; it was starting to feel kind of personal.

'That's not helpful, Mike,' said Amrita, rolling her eyes. Everyone else was silent – frozen, morsels of food halfway to their lips.

'I'm *so* sorry.' I clutched what was left of my supposedly 'heaving bosom'.

'It's not your fault, Elektra,' said Amrita. 'Right, does anyone ha—' She broke off to stare at Mike – everyone else was. He'd pulled the boobie/chicken fillet from its watery grave and was inspecting it in unsettling detail. I felt violated. 'For God's sake, Mike, put it down!'

He jumped about a foot in the air. Did he think he'd been being subtle? He'd practically got a magnifying glass out.

He dropped my silicon colleague.

It fell in what seemed like slow motion towards a particularly elegant silver bowl of cranberry sauce.

Lohan Winter made a heroic grab for it.

Too late.

There was cranberry sauce on my boob. The silicon one. And the actual one.

There was cranberry sauce on Mike's necktie.

There was cranberry sauce in Lohan Winter's hair. His beautiful, beautiful hair.

'It ... it was slippery,' stuttered Mike.

Someone fished the silicon boob from the bowl. It was dripping with layers of gravy and cranberry sauce – a worryingly innovative chicken dish.

	Clemency's Coming Out Ball	Elektra James's 16th
The Preparation	*16 years of dancing, posture, elocution and conversation instruction. Very effective.*	Wikihow article: 'How to stop your teen party trashing your family home.' Very ineffective.
Outfit	*Oh, just a silk muslin empire line gown with gold embroidery, embellished with seed pearls and a diamond and pearl tiara.*	Oh, just jeans and a nice top.
The Boys	*Amazing bone structure combined with either gentlemanly or rakish charm (except for a spattering of chinless minor squires)*	Tragic. Except the ones that brought dogs.
The Dancing	*The cotillion*	Definitely not the cotillion. Beyond that I'm not entirely sure.
The Food	*All manner of savouries including roast chicken breast. Also, flummeries. All deemed excellent (although the Parmesan ice divided opinion)*	None. Strangely no one ate the carrot sticks and hummus my mother had left in the fridge. What a shocker.

The Gossip	*Unspeakable.*	Unspeakable.
The Aftermath	*Four silk gloves, two fans and an engagement.*	Three shoes, a puppy and a bucket hat.
Parental Reaction	*'Darling, I do believe that the young Viscount would be a truly advantageous marriage prospect, forsooth why ever did you not charm him with your many accomplishments?'*	*unintelligible screeches of anger*

CHAPTER 14

'There are times I put something up and I'm like "Please don't think this is me. This is work."'

Hailey Baldwin

'It wasn't funny.' Moss and Eulalie wouldn't stop laughing but then I probably shouldn't have made a clean breast of it. I'd meant to take it as a secret to my grave (the sort of secret shared only with thirty cast and crew including two cameramen) but baking this Cranberry Orange Layer Cake was triggering traumatic memories. 'OK, it was funny. But *before* it was funny it was embarrassing. Like, literally one of the most embarrassing things that have ever happened to me.' And I wasn't a stranger to embarrassment.

'Did they get you a new fake boob?' asked Moss, tying Christmas ribbon in a bow around Plog's neck when she should have been cutting up perfect circles of parchment paper to line the cake tins.

'No. They literally just wiped that one down and I had to stuff it back in. It was *sticky*.'

'Did your real boob fall out too?'

'Not so far as I noticed, but honestly that would have been less embarrassing.' Eulalie nodded. Nothing embarrassing about a real boob. She wasn't even pretending to help with the baking. 'The director was lovely about it. She called a break and fed me pastries until I'd calmed down.' Nobody had fired me – or even killed me off early.

'How did the dancing go in the end?' Moss picked up Plog's paws and made him do a little jig. Weirdly, he didn't seem to mind. He'd been super chill about the premature end to his acting career too. I needed to be more dog. 'You didn't report back.'

'There wasn't much to report. They used a stand-in for all the fast bits.' Shaming, but definitely for the best or we'd either all still be there or I'd be dead. 'I had to do a lot of curtseying, which is harder than it looks.' I demonstrated. Challenging – but after Boobiegate I had a strong sense of perspective. 'I had so much *fun*,' I said wistfully. It was over so fast.

'Something else will come along.' Eulalie patted my arm consolingly just as I was sieving the flour.

'But will it?' I brushed myself down. 'What if I don't get another part? Ever. And then I won't get another agent. Ever. And then I *definitely* won't get another part. No more acting. It could all just stop. *Disappear,*' I wailed.

'Elektra James,' said Moss sternly, 'in a couple of months we're going to the cinema to watch a film starring several A-list actors and you. That is the opposite of disappearing.' I'd have explained (not for the first time) that the whole being-on-a-cinema-screen thing was not just terrifying but, if the trolls were right, would make it even harder for me to get another part but she was still talking. 'I love you but you are being quite *annoying.*' Oh God, was that fair? I had a bad feeling it might be. It was time to start keeping the fear to myself. 'Stop moaning and tell us whether you had to kiss Minor Squire?'

OK, OK. 'No. No kissing for Clemency Barton-Wood. Do you think that's "light and fluffy?"' I held out the bowl and they both shrugged. I was beginning to feel the burden of leadership on this bake. 'Clemency is a model of breeding, virtue and sensibility.'

'But she was a flame-haired minx, non?' Eulalie had found a glossy magazine and was circling all the outfits she wanted.

'That too. She's a complex character.' I missed Clemency and not only because I wanted to have red hair for ever.

My copy of the *Fortuneswell* shooting script was lying on the table. I'd been reading it like a book (it would be months before it aired). Moss picked it up and flicked through the pages. 'It was easier in period-drama days. All the rules, everyone knew what they were meant to be doing.'

'Nobody in history has ever known what they were meant to be doing,' Eulalie said, and she had many decades of experience to draw on. 'This designer, he is not knowing what he is doing any more.' She pointed to a dress that appeared to have no armholes and made my Straker costume look flattering. 'It is better now, non? No hangings, highwaymen, horrible teeth ...' She raised her voice over the sound of the mixer.

I switched it off and added, '... no mobiles, no Netflix, *no tampons.*' We all took a moment to ponder the horrors. 'No YouTube, no Buzzfeed.' Unthinkable. 'No Twitter.' Maybe not all bad.

'But the romantic stuff must have been quite relaxing.' Moss wasn't giving up on her theory. 'So much less pressure. Less competition.'

'Non,' said Eulalie firmly. 'There is always being the same competition.'

'But not competition about getting with people.' Moss persisted. 'Or followers, or favourites or likes. Just about whether you had the nicest dress or the hottest viscount or whatever.' It seemed mean to point out that we wouldn't have been hanging out with viscounts.

And yet. 'I remember a very charming marquis in the Eighties.' Eulalie gave herself a little shake and went back to being distracted by a Grecian-inspired Chanel gown in Vogue (if the Greeks had worn feathers and accessorized with diamanté).

Moss tipped the cranberries into a bowl and started snorting again. '*Boobie*. That is just the cutest.'

'What's wrong with you? A guy in a tailcoat shouting "boobie" at any sort of chicken fillet is *not* cute.'

'It sort of is.'

'Be careful or I'll set you up with him and "boobie" is one of the few words he speaks. Trust me, Carlo is a better option.'

'Ah! Le Beau Carlo.' Eulalie was a fan. 'You are ...?' She hesitated. What were they?

'He's probably messaging about five girls,' was all that Moss said.

I shook my head. 'I don't think so.'

'Yeah, I forgot. He tells you everything.' There was that edge again.

'He tells me a lot. We're good friends. *As I keep telling you.*'

Eulalie picked up on the vibe. 'Mais bien sûr they are talking all the time! They are still going through so much together. Stressful non?'

'Oui!' And then I remembered I wasn't meant to

be worrying about the *fast* approaching release of my Major Motion Picture, so I just went back to beating ingredients aggressively and therapeutically. 'Look, I get the whole virtual relationship thing, but you should meet up with him again.'

'No. I'm not over the trauma of the last time. I need a break from guys with egos. And guys without egos.' A much smaller category. 'I'm scarred.'

'Carlo is nothing like Torr.'

'You used to say he was a player.'

'Le reformed player can be being fun.' Was Eulalie talking about herself?

'He just talked a player game,' I said hopefully, 'testing' some of the cake mix. 'Look, it's *always a risk*, isn't it? And Carlo's funny and he's not mean and I know you like him because otherwise you wouldn't still be messaging him.' Or being all weird about him talking to me. 'And he is so into you.'

'Yeah, but maybe it's best if it's just into virtual me.'

'He'll like "real you" more. Well, if you stay long enough next time for him to get to know you.'

'Which is reminding me,' Eulalie dropped the magazine into her enormous tote bag, 'that Sergei will be waiting for me. We are going to be watching a film by a director he is hating and then we are going to eat cake and drink champagne and have a very nice time saying how terrible it was.' That was tempting fate. 'Ah! I was nearly forgetting.' She delved back into the bag and brought out a little penguin-shaped hand-warmer. Brilliant, just what I'd always wanted (or would have done if I'd known they existed.) 'Pour le très romantique ice skating.'

'Archie's taking you ice skating?' Moss snorted. 'He gave you a puppy, now he's taking you ice-skating. What's next? Rose petals showering your every step?' I tried to grimace as though I wouldn't actually *love* that. 'Changing his Facebook status to "in a relationship"?'

'Obviously not the last one.' My phone barked. **Agent's just emailed. It's happening** And again. **Confirmed. Talk properly later xx**

Moss looked at me. 'Who was that? What's the matter?'

'Archie. Nothing. It's good news.' I gulped.

'Seriously?' She looked doubtful.

I nodded. 'They've just confirmed the second series of *The Curse*. Way before the first has even aired. It's *amazing*.'

'You don't look like it's amazing.' Odd, I was sure I was smiling. 'Are you OK? It's OK if you're not OK.'

I took a moment. More virtual relationship time for me. We were much better at it but well, it wasn't *real* time. Was I OK? 'I'm happy for Archie.' Eulalie and Moss were either side of me. Real time was *much* better. I took a deep breath. 'I'll live.'

'Of course you will live. We are all strong and independent women, non?' Moss and I nodded uncertainly. 'It's better to be with an interesting man who is far away than a man who is dull and is living next door, non?'

'What's going on with the new @ElektraJames by the way?' asked Moss when it was just the two of us and when she knew that I *really* didn't want to talk about *The Curse*.

'You've noticed?' Fiona-aa had been dropping in posts for me in the last couple of days like I was a Kardashian.

'It's like you suddenly have an actual glamorous life.' Moss paused and added uncertainly. 'Not that you didn't already have an actual glamorous life . . . sort of.' Sort of. Like, I'd have thought I did if someone else described bits of it to me but mostly, I didn't. Because I spent ninety per cent of my life in school? Or just because glamour wasn't my vibe? I consoled myself with some more cake mix. 'But not glamorous like new @ElektraJames.' Moss was pulling up 'my' Insta. I was quite excited to find out what 'I'd' been doing. 'You've already got lots of new followers.'

'I think they bought them,' I admitted.

Moss shrugged. 'Would they pay me to follow you?' She scrolled a bit. 'I never knew you always started the week with a 5k run!' I should totally do that. 'Good to see your support for Actors Against Poverty.' I'd hardly be against it. 'And aaaaw, look, life advice: "Your vibe attracts your tribe".' Because it can never be said too often. Real me would rather have posted pretty much anything Eulalie said. 'You look really hot in these photos though.' Moss pointed at one where I was in work-out clothes on the *Raw* set. 'Is that even you?'

Sort of. 'They've filtered and face-tuned me,' I said. The caption underneath read, *Keeping up with my #RawWorkout #RawEnergy #RawAction*. I cringed at a post that strongly implied I'd spent last night having a brilliant time at an art collective opening (#RawArt) in Hoxton. 'I feel a bit weird about some of these.' Not least, because last night I'd been eating pizza in front of *Next Top Model*.

'So, don't let them post them.' Moss sniggered. 'I was a big fan of your early Insta work.'

'*Exactly.*' My (Real Me's) last post had featured a large block of cheese and a bag of Maltesers. 'PPR know what they're doing. And I know I'm lucky they're doing it for me. It'll help me get parts and stuff.' Stuff like getting a new agent. I'd scared myself last night by stalking glossy company websites.

'Do they do Carlo's for him?' She was scrolling his feed now.

'No. I'm the only one in remedial measures.' But then, Carlo hadn't posted a spoiler, he wasn't spending nearly all his daylight hours at Berkeley Academy and he wasn't locked up at home every evening by Victorian parents.

'Was it awkward kissing him?' she asked out of the blue – ah, not quite out of the blue, she was gazing at a ridiculously hot photo of Carlo halfway up the Cliff of Dreams. 'I mean, did you like it?'

'No! And, yes, it was horribly, horribly awkward.'

'Was he awkward about it too?'

'Yes, he was. I told you that at the time.' She obviously needed to be reminded.

'But if you like someone it must be quite nice.' She looked at me like she wanted to say more.

What else was awkward was this conversation.

'Look, maybe if you're having a thing with someone or you want to, screen kissing is ... OK. Sam and Amber don't seem to have a problem with it. But it's not like real-life kissing. There's so many people watching and judging you.'

'That sounds like your basic Year Eleven party.'

'No, trust me, it's really not.' How much detail did she want? 'Everyone is telling you what to do and touching up your make-up and making you do it all over again.' She didn't look reassured. 'No tongues.' This was painful. 'Also no ... connection. You're hyper aware of everything going on around you, people checking light levels and sound.' How clear could I be? 'Screen-kissing Carlo was not a romantic experience *at all* and I'm very glad that we'll never have to do it again.'

WAITING
(FOR SANTA)

- % of time spent trying and failing to persuade Dad to let me decorate the house in the style of the *Fortuneswell* ballroom: 32%
- % of time spent trying to recreate the *Fortuneswell* supper table for Christmas (OK, making mince pies with shop-bought pastry but it was a sound effort): 21%
- % of time spent searching the house for hidden Christmas presents: 11% (found seven for Plog)
- 0% of time spent styling the perfect Ice Skating Outfit: 12%
- % of time spent trying to resist singing cheesy Christmas songs: 45%
- % of time spent actually singing cheesy Christmas songs: 156%
- % of time spent wearing Christmas jumper and/or reindeer antlers: 100%
- % of time spent alternately dreading *Raw* never being released/being released/being a massive turkey: 1000%

★
CHAPTER 15

'Yes, of course [celebrities have celebrity crushes]!
Ryan Gosling's a given!'

Billie Piper

I met him outside South Ken Tube station.

'Elektra!' Archie pulled me into a big crushing hug only to pull away and look at me with concern. 'Are you OK?'

'I'm *fine*. Why?'

'It's just you're ... sweating.'

Ah, the perfect opening line to a romantic date. 'It was just a bit hot.' I waved in the general direction of the Tube tunnel. Of course I was sweating. It had been warmer than August down there, the bobble hat I was wearing was intensely 'cosy', and my pompom scarf was so long that I'd had to wrap it around my neck so many times

I looked like I was wearing a fluffy snake with attachment issues. But I'd worked long and hard on this look and you've got to stand up for what you believe in.

Archie was trying very hard not to laugh at me. 'We've got like an hour before our session so even if it takes ages to hire the boots I was thinking we could get hot chocolate,' he said. 'But that's maybe a bad choice? Iced tea?'

'Will there be marshmallows?' If I was going to go on a clichéd winter festive date I was going to do it properly. 'Oh my God, there's a massive Christmas tree!' I practically screamed. 'In the middle of the ice!'

'Yes? It is ... Christmas?' It was actually the day before New Year's Eve.

'But this is like *American-Movie Christmas!*' I wasn't going to specify that the American Christmas movies I was talking about were the ones where the baker/designer/cute-shop-keeper from Chicago/Boston/San Francisco meets the undercover European prince and at first she hates him but then she doesn't but his family hate her but they kiss in the snow and ... etc. etc. I looked up at the sky.

'What are you doing?' Archie looked up too.

'It should be snowing.'

He shook his head. 'It's not going to. Maybe the

end of next week.' By the end of next week I'd be back at school and about to sit Mocks. I wasn't going to think about the end of next week.

'Wait, I just need to send Moss a snap.' I ushered Archie into an obvious selfie-position. I was pretty sure 'I'd' already been here, Fake-Elektra, that is. These were nearly good enough that I could post them myself. I took another twenty or so and sent Moss the best ones.

Are you literally in a Christmas card? She snapped me back straight away. She looked disgusted.

I'm feeling so smug I ignored Archie who was getting bored and judge-y and took some more.

I can tell

What are you doing?

Nothing/I'm so bored/ I'm dying/ Send help/ Gonna watch University Challenge Christmas Special I got a stalker pic of Moss's mum looking almost relaxed on the sofa. And then a troublingly zoomed-in pic. **She will know all the answers**. Even more zoomed in. **She'll be assessing them for son-in-law potential/ What's wrong with your face though?**

Wait, what? I tried to examine my face in the snap camera.

It's really red. She'd helpfully coloured in the pic of her own face bright red. The extra time I'd spent before I came out, painting on a natural winter rosy glow, had been wasted. So, maybe I wouldn't post any of these anywhere.

The café had a toasty vibe. Unfortunately, it was also actually toasty. Two minutes in and Archie was unwinding my scarf. 'I get that I'm messing with your carefully constructed Winter Wonderland fashion moment.' He did? That was a tiny bit embarrassing. 'But seriously, you will die if you don't take that off.'

'I'm keeping the hat on,' I said stubbornly. 'I always wear a bobble hat indoors.' I was already about to look like a total idiot on the ice. I didn't need to look like an idiot with sweaty hat hair – even flame-coloured hat hair.

We looked out of the big windows. The massive, cathedral-like museum was all lit up, a backdrop to the rink. 'The ice looks cold,' I said. 'I mean, to fall onto.'

Archie laughed. 'It'll be fine. We can hang on to each other.'

'Can you skate?'

'Nope. But we can waltz so we can do it.' For some odd reason – possibly experience – that wasn't filling me with confidence. 'It looks easy. Look at that little kid, if she can pull it off we probably can.'

'She's a lot closer to the ground.' She was about three years old. 'Her centre of gravity is more centred. Look at exhibit B.' I pointed to a twenty-year-old-guy who had spent at least five minutes on his bum providing entertainment to all his friends. He was laughing along but he also looked like he was dying inside. And possibly outside. Bum-frostbite couldn't be a nice way to go.

'No one can stay upright if they're as drunk as he is,' said Archie. 'The ice is not his biggest problem. Have a mince pie.'

I sent Moss another photo. 'I'm torturing her with the romantic vibe,' I explained and munched. 'Hopefully, it'll encourage her to get back out there with Carlo.'

'Has she met up with him again?'

I shook my head. 'No, but I think she will and I hope she does. She's been worrying about ... something but I think that's OK now.'

'The you and Carlo thing,' he said casually.

'*Excuse me?* What thing?'

'Not an actual thing.' He was cringing. 'But Moss *thinking* there might be a thing.' He tried to distract me with the last mince pie.

'Er ... how do you know she was worried about that?' I waved away his offering.

'I ... guessed?'

I looked at him avoiding looking at me. 'No. You didn't guess.'

'OK, Moss asked me about it.' Archie shrugged like

that was going to be the end of the conversation. It wasn't.

'*Moss* asked *you* if I was into *Carlo?*' I spluttered a bit.

'No! No, she didn't ask that ...' But then he hesitated.

'She asked if *Carlo* was into *me?*' Only marginally less traumatic. Archie shrugged awkwardly. 'And *you* didn't tell *me.*'

'I didn't want to get involved.' Classic. But not good enough. I glared at him. 'Look, she obviously spoke to you about it eventually, so there's no problem, is there?' He wished.

'There is a problem. You guys have been talking about me behind my back.'

'We weren't really talking about you. We were talking about Carlo.'

'And yet I was part of that conversation. What exactly did you say?'

'Do I ask you for a debrief on every conversation you have with Moss that I'm mentioned in?' Thankfully not. 'She just wanted to know if I'd picked up any vibe with all the texting and stuff between you and Carlo.'

'And? Had you?'

'Obviously not. Chill. She wasn't implying you were flirting with him, just that *he* was maybe into you.' I was not chill. 'Stop looking at me like that. Moss just wanted a bit of reassurance about Carlo. Come on, don't sulk.'

'Don't tell me not to sulk. It's really annoying. And I'm not sulking. I . . . have a legitimate grievance.'

'A *legitimate grievance*, right. Don't spoil the day.' And I could tell that what he meant was don't spoil the day because he was going away again soon. Don't sulk, don't fight, because we don't have enough time in the same place together for that? So now I felt bad, and I still felt angry. Great.

Another text from Moss. **These photos are killing me. #SmugMarried** Whatever the vibe was now, it was a long way from #SmugMarried but I didn't reply because I was still angry with her too.

'They're calling our session,' said Archie. We both sat there stubbornly for another couple of minutes. They announced again. 'If we don't go now, they won't let us on.' And we both knew how much the tickets had cost.

We still weren't talking when we got to the gate (which took some time because how were we even meant to walk in solid plastic blocks?). The portal to cute wintry romantic hell. I took a deep breath and spoke into the frosty atmosphere. 'I don't think I can do this.' I hadn't really thought through the whole endangering my life, limbs and dignity on the ice.

'Come on, Elektra. You wore that Straker costume – you can do anything.' Well, at least we were speaking. 'It's gonna be *fun*! I'll hold you up.'

OK, I was still annoyed but somebody was going to have to hold me up. I let him pull me onto the rink.

I was moving! I was moving upright across the ice! Granted, I was clutching onto the wall and taking tiny penguin waddle steps but it one hundred per cent counted. I inched my hand off the rail ... I remained upright. I took a slightly larger penguin waddle step and then a bigger one and then I was ... kind of ... actually sliding along the ice. I was legitimately skating. That, or I'd already fallen over, got concussion and this was my crazed coma dream. Either way, it was an achievement.

'Elektra!' squeaked someone behind me. I swivelled – elegantly, obviously – to see Archie clutching on to the side by the gate with a traffic jam of angry children behind him. I *skated* over.

'Come on, Archie.' I smiled 'sweetly'. 'It's *fun*. I'll hold you up!' Karma.

He scowled at me. 'I can't move.'

'Of course you can. Just put one foot in front of the other and pull yourself along the rail.'

'But. They. Slip. Around.'

'That's kind of the point.'

'Not helpful, Elektra.'

'Just moooovvveeee,' shouted one of the traffic jam children.

Archie moved a skate and it sort of *kept moving* until it was in the air, and he was on the ground.

The icy, icy ground. It's really hard to stay angry with someone who's on their bum on the ice.

'Oh my God,' huffed another child, 'can you stop just sitting there?' Wow, seven-year-olds had got sassy.

'It's not like I'm just *hanging out* over here,' snapped Archie.

Great. My boyfriend was fighting a seven-year-old and the seven-year-old had the upper hand. One of the skating ... umpires? Bosses? Smug-sporty-people? stopped next to us with an offensive little flourish. 'All good over here?'

'Yuup.' Archie nodded sarcastically. 'Everything's *great*.'

'Fab!' The skatey-man gave us a thumbs-up.

'*Wait*,' Archie shrieked after him. He turned around. 'Um ... I'm ... I'm stuck.'

'Oooooo, he's stuckkkkk,' mimicked the children.

Skatey-guy laughed 'Let's get you up, mate.'

'That will only take another, like, ten thousand years,' moaned a small boy with a challenging spiked hair and fringe combo.

Skatey-guy yanked at Archie's arm and he was up ... Oh. No. No, he wasn't. He definitely wasn't up. He was very much *down*.

'Can't you just let us pass?'

Skatey-guy looked slightly terrified. It was good to know that the seven- year-olds were objectively scary and it wasn't just me. 'Um, maybe it is better if we move you out of the way,' he suggested to Archie.

'Yes, but the major issue of this whole situation is that I can't move.' I had a teeny suspicion that Archie was losing his sense of humour. Also perspective. Possibly will to live. It would definitely make everything worse if I laughed.

'If all else fails just sort of . . . shuffle.' Skatey-guy shouted a last tip as he abandoned us to go and rescue a toddler.

Archie shuffled. I tried really hard not to laugh. I failed.

'Tragggiicccccc,' crowed another one of the kids as they sped past.

'Oh my God.' Archie was finally back up again, just. 'Feel how cold I am'. He put one hand on my cheek. He was right, it was cold. He linked an arm around my waist and pulled me towards him. This was getting less cold. The frosty atmosphere had melted. Our faces were so close. 'See right now,' he whispered, 'it may *look* like I want to kiss you.'

'It may *look* that way?' I smiled.

'But *really* I just need to lean on you to stay upright.'

'Really?'

'No. Well, let's say I have mixed motives.'

'Get a roooooooooom.' Our fave seven-year-old sped past.

'Elektra.' Archie grabbed my hand. 'That's what I need.'

'What? What?' There was obviously some urgency. He'd lost all interest in kissing me.

'THE PENGUIN.' Archie pointed at a group of *very small* kids clutching sliding plastic penguins to keep them upright and then he clung onto me again – definitely for support this time. He was right that *was* what he needed. 'I think they're all gone. I'm going to have to steal one.'

'How?'

'Mug a child?' The dream date activity. 'You distract one, I'll swoop in. We'll be like Bonnie and Clyde.' That famous plastic-penguin-stealing-duo.

'Er ... Archie? Are you sure you can swoop anywhere?'

'Stop laughing at me, Elektra James.'

'Wait, Archie,' I shouted (I was getting way too´ into this whole immoral plan). 'That one, that kid – over there, getting dragged off the ice by his mum, he's abandoning his penguin!'

Archie gave me what in the *Fortuneswell* script would have been called 'a devilish grin'. 'Let's go.'

We both paused. 'How about I go?' I suggested.

'Yep, that's probably for the best. Can you just ... lean me up over there?'

Two minutes later I was back with a penguin. His gift of a puppy was starting to look pretty mundane.

'This is amazing. *This*, you should snap me with.' Archie did a small very slow twirl. OK, more of a ragged circle. 'Tree in the background?' And then his phone started buzzing – and kept buzzing and buzzing. That sort of urgency either meant a real-life emergency or an angry parent. 'You should look,' I said, dragging him and Pingu over to the side.

Sorry, Archie, but can you get off the ice, please. No skating, please.

Get off the ice, Mr Mortimer. That one definitely couldn't be his mum.

'Oh God,' he said. 'It's Production on *The Curse*. They want me to get off the ice.'

'How did they know?!' Was there a clutch of shady-looking producers lurking in a gothic arch?

'I guess they're stalking me online.'

'Flattering,' I said but then I wasn't in a position to judge.

'Creepy,' he said.

His phone buzzed again. **Off the ice NOW, Mr Mortimer.** They *really* wanted him to get off the ice. He read some more messages. 'Turns out I'm not insured for ice-skating.'

'To be fair, there is quite a high chance that you might injure yourself beyond repair,' I said.

'You could nurse me back to health.' He leaned in to kiss me. Which was actually quite difficult given that there was a substantial penguin in the way. 'It's mad.'

'I don't think they care about your health,' I said. 'But a vampire hunter would be at a disadvantage on crutches, right?' It probably wasn't OK to wish an injury on him to keep him in London.

'If I was on crutches, Count Peter Plogojowitz would probably win.'

I found it quite hard to think of Plogojowitz as a dastardly vampire now that his namesake was peeing on my carpet.

Something magical happened in London's Mayfair last night when the cast and crew of Fortuneswell spilled outdoors and danced as the snow fell. For just twenty blissful minutes the years were rolled back, men in tailcoats bowed to women in gowns and they waltzed up and down the street, pulling in passers-by and crew for an impromptu Winter Ball such as hasn't been seen since the nineteenth century.

'I dreamed all my life of waltzing with a handsome man,' said Marjorie (aged eighty-one) 'and finally, last night it happened. I will never forget it till the day I die.'

'It was better than Strictly,' said Mahira (aged fifteen).

And what of the stars? Did they have a night to remember? Well, James Moore and Lucy Morton were waltzing in each other's arms long after the music had stopped.

But not all the residents were happy. 'It is shocking that filming is permitted in this part of town at all,' said Mrs Cranford. 'We should not have to put up with this inconvenience. My Harrods deliveries have been held up three times this week.'

73

Days to Go . . .

7

days till exams . . .

☆ CHAPTER 16

'Fear can be incredibly motivating. It makes you work harder.'

Daniel Radcliffe

Now it was snowing. Big fat show-offy snow-globe flakes and all it meant was that the inside of the Lonely Bean (the café next to school) was all fugged up with misery and the smell of cough sweets.

'Have you read Tibble's email?' Moss was curled into the seat beside me. She had on three hoodies, layered one on top of the other, because she'd lost her coat and it was freezing.

'Should I?' I wasn't a fan of our Deputy Head's emails. I blew across the top of my coffee to try and dislodge the strange greasy little film that was floating on it.

She shrugged. 'If you want to be really, really depressed.'

It was a week before exams and Archie was about to be summoned back to Transylvania; I was already really, really depressed. I went into Mail. *'"This is not a drill,"'* I read. 'I thought that was exactly what mocks were.' Funny, how that wasn't reassuring any more. I read on, blah, blah blah, *'"rules"'*, blah, blah, blah, *'"regulations"'*, blah, blah, blah, *'"consequences"'* . . . *'"So you can have every evening free for revision, exam week detentions will be moved to the following week. Hope this helps!"'* Not so much. *'"We want you to enjoy your exam experience and with enough EFFORT, you will."'*

I opened the attachments. *Advice*, *Regulations* and *Relaxation*. This was so stressful that I'd have to take them in reverse order:

Mrs Gryll's *Tips on How to Relax Before, During and After Examinations. Dear girls, I am deeply sorry that you have to spend vast chunks of your so-called education being forced to do endless examinations. I hope that my tips on visualization will help: Imagine you are a tree. Perhaps an oak, with broad, relaxed leaves that will drop (as found in deciduous woodland, high rainfall, warm summers, cooler winters).* Mrs Gryll was lovely. She was also a geography teacher and couldn't help herself. *Visualize the waves crashing on the shore (breaking down sediment by attrition) and listen to the soothing sound of the gentle rainfall (frontal rainfall occurring when warm air is forced to rise over cold air . . .).*

Oh God, I hadn't revised rainfall. I'd come back to these. Maybe after I'd checked in with Amber for a quick revision class on yogic alternate nostril breathing. *'Regulations for Mock Examinations . . . Bring bottled water but remove the label.'* I read this one out to Moss. 'Why do we have to remove the label? That makes no sense.' I gulped a mouthful of cold coffee and nearly spat it out. I swear the milk in here was always sour.

'In case it's cheating?' she said, drawing question marks and sad faces in the spilled sugar on the table-top.

'What? Why? The off-chance that filtered water comes up in geography?'

'It must be in case people write stuff on the labels – in tiny, tiny writing? It would probably be easier to do the revision.' And as one, we sighed the deep, deep sigh of Year Elevens who haven't done enough revision.

I read on. '"*Phones, pagers, organisers, music players and any type of electronic communication or storage devices are not allowed in the exam room.*"' 'What even is a pager?' Moss shrugged. 'And we're not allowed to take in "*smart watches (or silly ones)*". Mr Tibble is hilarious.' Neither of us laughed. 'Do you have a transparent pencil case?' She pointed at the yellow fluffy one shaped like a banana poking out of her bag. That wouldn't cut it in the exam hall of doom. 'There's a whole paragraph on the right sort of pens – if we accidentally use a gel pen we'll explode or something. This is so *stressful*.' A leftover piece of tinsel fell from the ceiling and floated onto the table to mock us. 'So many life choices to regret right now.'

'It might be OK.' Moss tried to rally. 'It's very hard to full-on fail. You have to, like, die or something.'

'Tragically, I think the "something" is not knowing the answers. Or, spelling your name wrong on the paper.'

'Maybe we'll get easy papers?'

'We need to distract ourselves so our brains have space for auto-revision. Or something. Carlo?'

Moss ate one of the Jaffa cakes that we'd decided five minutes ago were too stale to be edible. 'I don't think so.'

'But not because you're still worried he's into me, right? Because you get that that's mad now?' Every time we talked about it she said all the right words but ... was it still bothering her? 'Mad? Right?'

'Sure,' she said but without quite enough conviction. 'It's not that.'

'You're still messaging?'

'Yes, *but* ... anyway, I live on a different planet from him.' She gestured at her multiple- hoodie- wrapped- Jaffa- crumb- scattered self.

'But you could have him to look forward to *after exams*, like a really late Christmas present.'

'I appreciate the classic objectification but I don't think it's that simple. Seriously, Elektra, can we just not? Or, at least let's shelve all talk of him until this immediate hell is over.' She picked up a slim volume titled *How to ace exams when you think you've left it too late* and put it straight back down again. 'And then we can have a nice life for about a minute before everyone starts stressing about the next exams. Maybe we could devise a hilarious exam fail video that would go viral, bring us fame and fortune and mean that we never have to do another exam in our lives?' We so had the skills for that. Not. 'What do *you* want?' she asked two Year Sevens who had snuck up on our table. Moss wasn't in a warm and welcoming mood.

It was obvious what they wanted, although they were brave to ask. I held out the biscuits. 'You can take one but they're stale.'

'You're Elektra James, right?' asked Girl One. I nodded. It was in the perfect order of things that Year Sevens knew our names and we didn't know theirs. She'd gone red and was starting to retreat.

'She wants your autograph,' explained Girl Two, pushing Girl One forward again.

I laughed. 'Yeah, right.'

'No, like, she follows you on Insta and everything.'

'Thank you,' I said to Girl One. Now I was blushing. This was a first and it was very ... weird.

'You look different on your Insta.' Girl Two was assessing me closely and I was coming up short.

'Most people do,' said Moss giving it the full withering I-am-in-Year-Eleven-you-are-lucky-I'm-talking-to-you-at-all vibe.

'Have you actually met Cara Delevingne?' Girl One held out the back of an exercise book and offered me a biro.

'Er ...' I said and Moss sniggered. The biro was broken. We were attracting attention. 'Ummm, no ...' Girl One looked disappointed. I back-tracked a bit. I needed to make my only fan happy. 'Sort of?' Moss snorted. 'Not exactly ... as such ...' I trailed off.

'It sounded like you did,' stammered Girl One. 'Harry Styles?'

Moss lost it and sprayed Jaffa Cake crumbs all over the table. 'Don't believe everything you read.'

Girl One passed me a new pen and I scribbled something illegible enough that I could always deny. And then all of sudden she was leaning in close and holding out her phone. 'Smile!' *What?*

And then there was an awkward moment when Girl Two made it quite clear she did not want my autograph. Fair enough. She thought she was way cooler than Girl One – she probably was. '*She*'s got something for you.' She poked her friend forward again.

Chocolate? No. Girl One thrust a single piece of paper at me and they both fled. Giggling.

'Were we like that?' asked Moss in horror. Possibly. I picked some chocolate flakes off her outer hoody. Except less sophisticated and much less cool than Girl Two. 'What is it? Is it a poem? Oh God, it's a poem, isn't it? You've literally got a full-on fan.' I was beginning to feel a bit smug. 'A fan who's writing you poetry. I want one.'

'It's not a poem.'

'What is it?' Advance peek at next week's maths' paper? Tell me there are stem and leaf diagrams.'

'It's a script. All laid out properly and everything. This is so . . .' Amazing? Odd? Freaky? There was a little note scribbled on it.

Dear Elektra, I know you are probably very busy but I like to write plays and films and things. I wrote this about Princess Kate because I think there should be more films about her. I thought maybe you could give it to someone who could make it into a film. P.S. Maybe you could play one of the parts. If you're not too busy. Meena x

'Let me see it.' Moss grabbed it out of my hand and put it down on the sticky table.

'Don't laugh! She's typed it all out properly and it's got directions and everything.' It made me feel quite emotional but maybe that was because I hadn't slept (I'd had a nightmare that the opening credits of the *Raw* premiere were just a long scroll of my Mocks results – turns out the only thing worse than the fear of failure is failure).

'It's quite ... gripping,' said Moss, reading it. 'But why's Kate worried about Prince Charles's bears? Oh, *ears*?' I nodded. Probably. 'I would one hundred per cent watch this.'

'Me too. It's brilliant. But she literally thinks I can just hand this to some director. Like Scorsese or Ridley Scott.' Or, Havelski? Maybe I could just get Eulalie to slip it to him? My phone barked. A notification. I'd been tagged in a photo. Meena's photo. Oh God. There I was – captured grimacing goggle-eyed in all my purple school uniform, unwashed hair, no make-up, period spot glory – signing my very first autograph. I had an odd feeling PPR wouldn't be reposting that one. 'She might have warned me,' I grumbled.

'Stop sounding like a diva,' said Moss. 'Wow, it is *bad* though. You look so ... surprised.' She started giggling. I looked again. Fair, it was so bad it was funny. 'I can't believe she wanted your autograph.'

'She wanted Fake-Elektra's autograph – the one with a wannabe-Cara Insta.' I stopped sniggering and started feeling bad. 'I had to avoid Flissy today because she started asking me about something on my feed and I had no idea what she was talking about.'

'What a hardship,' said Moss, stabbing a pack of sweetener with a plastic spoon.

'She sounded quite impressed.' Flissy would have been good at this. She was never off her media. Why post one bikini selfie when you could post twenty? And all (as Fiona-aa would say) *curated*. No random, enthusiastic or amateur posts for Flissy. She'd go far. She should try acting. She was a terrible actor but she'd be good at the rest of it. 'Moss?'

'What?'

Flissy wasn't the only one posting an illusion. 'I don't really like Fake-Elektra.' I admitted it.

'Yeah. She is seriously pleased with herself.' Moss hadn't even had to think about it. 'But what's the alternative?'

Multiple photos of me curled in the foetal position surrounded by tottering piles of unread text books? Better than Meena's photo but probably not. I looked around the café. Peeling walls, condensation on the windows, a few huddles of miserable Berkeley Academy girls and a **KEEP CALM AND DRINK TEA** poster sagging off its Blu-Tack moorings. There wasn't much here to feed the beast.

'There is no alternative.'

~~WAITING~~
~~WORKING~~
SUFFERING
(EXAMAGGEDON

)

- % of time spent actually doing Mocks: 3% (felt like 300%)
- % of time spent panicking: 82% (felt like 282%)
- % of time spent distracting myself with cute animal videos and/or using Plog as a four-legged comfort blanket: 27%
- % of time spent researching successful actors/entrepreneurs/humans who failed all their GCSEs: 43%
- % of time spent looking up flights to Bhutan and checking whether monasteries would let me join even if I failed RS: 29%
- % of time spent with Archie: 0% because it turns out my mum didn't think waltzing was compatible with exams

TheBizz.com

Bringing you the all the Best
Backstabbing in the Bizz . . .

1 February

We here at Bizz LOVE a leak. Other people love roses or chocolate or diamonds (we'll take those too) but what we really want is GOSSIP.

We didn't think Panda and Sergei Havelski would risk a **test screening** for *Raw* but then if you're brave/stupid enough to cast Sam Gross and Amber Leigh together in an epic of love and adventure then you're probably brave enough for anything. And then there's the *tiny* problem that they haven't even finished filming ... Yep, it's *still* not wrapped, even though they've dropped That Trailer (enough blood, fire and fear to satiate the *Game of Thrones* audience for months – click <u>here</u> to read our piece *Do you have to be a psychopath to enjoy this?*). But there was enough in the can for a rough cut to be tested in front of an audience last night. A *very rough* cut from what we're hearing – *Rough and Raw-dy*, LOL. Because although the audience was small and handpicked for their ability to keep schtum, we found one guy who was happy, out of the kindness of his heart (and in return for the banknotes we slipped him) to give us the lowdown.

And ...

Lowdown is the right word. Our anonymous whistle-blower told us, 'Before we even went in, there was a guy from the production company apologizing.' (God, we love the English. *Sooo cute.*) 'Ten minutes in,' said our snitch, 'we knew why. What is even going on? There's lots of beef, there's plenty of bangs, there's a good amount of blood – the only woman in the audience left after eight minutes – but where is the heart, Sergei Havelski? Where is the love? *And what in the name of the Warrior God is the plot????*'

Not long to wait until we can all decide for ourselves if *Raw* is a dystopian nightmare for real. Scary days for all involved ...

STOP PRESS: How does Georgie Dunn (currently rocking a corset on-set in *Fortuneswell*) do it? We need to know her secret. When we're stumbling out of nightclubs we can't even get an Uber – she managed to get her hands on/all over Rapper Wrong (or someone who looked VERY like him). Some girls have all the luck.

CHAPTER 17

*'I'm not confident about the film. I have no reason
to be confident about the film. We all did our best.'*
Colin Firth

'Elektra! This is shocking.' Carlo came into the Costume Department. It was weirdly empty, just us two and one costume assistant who'd sorted us out and was now disappearing off to have a cigarette.

'*I know.* When did you get your script?' I looked at myself in one of the long mirrors. Bo, my favourite make-up woman, had stuck on some oozing wounds, 'dirtied' me and checked that my hair had been colour-rinsed back to a shade that didn't mess with continuity. Sadly my hessian sack hadn't transformed itself into a glittering gown and no one had washed it since I last wore it. It smelled; lucky Carlo. 'Stella says it's because of the test screening – the audience said *Raw* was a bit low on romance. *Baffling.*'

Today was going to be a weird day. On the upside, I was back on the *Raw* set which was something I'd given up hope on. On the downside, there was the tiny challenge of another love scene with the guy my best friend was seriously into.

'That's shocking too – but this is even *worse.*' He brandished a copy of SweetPop.

'I didn't know you were an avid consumer of SweetPop.' I sat down on a box full of (prop) weapons.

'I didn't know *you* were an avid consumer of body glitter and seventies-style wedges,' he replied.

'What?'

'Your interview.'

'My *interview?*'

'Struggling to keep up with your fame these days,' he scoffed.

'No, Carlo, what?' Something else to have a micro-panic about? 'I have literally no idea what you're talking about.'

He tossed the mag down in front of me, squatted down and flicked it open. '"Five questions with Elektra James,"' he started reading in a ridiculously high voice that I had a bad feeling was meant to be me.

'I can read for myself.' There it was, sandwiched between *Top Tips for Perfecting a Feline Flick* and an advert for spot cream, illustrated with a new super-filtered version of my headshot (liberally jazzed up with Photoshopped stars and hearts).

5 Questions with Elektra James

Up-and-coming young actress, Elektra James (playing Straker in the new soon-to-hit-screens Sam Gross action movie RAW!!) has taken time out from her busy schedule to answer our 5Qs!

Q. 1. Lipstick or Lipgloss?
Lipgloss definitely feels fresher although I lurve a matte lipstick

'This was not me. PPR must have done it.' I was about to be outraged but then I remembered I'd probably said I was OK with it. 'They're masterminding my social media in a close way,' I said, because it sounded a bit better than admitting that they were pretending to be me. 'I told you.'

'Oh yeah, they banned you from it because you kept posting spoilers and revision memes or something?' I nodded sadly. Some of those revision memes had been iconic. 'Well, this is a classy substitute. Good to know you just luuurrrvvveeee a matte lipstick girlllll.'

'Oh God.' I buried my mud-streaked face in my hands. I didn't want to read on. (Also I only liked lipgloss if it wasn't sticky and matte lipstick made me look like a dead forty-year-old woman).

'It gets much, much worse.' Carlo was enjoying this.

Q. 2. What's your favourite thing about being a young actress?

The acting OK, that was true.

And the parties, of course!!!

'With three exclamation marks,' Carlo helpfully pointed out. 'Have you been throwing more parties and forgetting to invite me?

Q. 3. Do you get jealousy from people at school?

No – I get on well with everybody!

'Elektra James, why do I get the feeling these are just straight out lies?'

'Shut up, I'm universally adored.' There was a long pause. 'Let's move on.'

Q. 4. What do you think is the look of the summer?

I'm seriously into body glitter and seventies-style wedges at the moment. Perfect for dancing all night, so number one on my list! So Hot but also CHILL!!!

'That one is my second favourite.' Carlo struck a pose 'Do you think it's a look I could pull off?'

'No.' I replied. Sometimes you have to be cruel to be kind.

5. Who's your celeb crush?
My co-star, Carlo Winn, obviously!!

'Oh Goddddddd,' I wailed.

'It's not that bad.' Carlo was cracking up. 'I totally understand why you'd be *obsessed* with me. Most people are. No need to be embarrassed of your deep and enduring *lurve.*'

'A *showmance.* With *you.* Great. What are they thinking?' I was asking myself that a lot.

'Gossip is good. That's the mantra, #LoveLikes.'

'I'm so confused. I thought they wanted to "leverage my relationship with Archie". Eeeurgh.'

'A love triangle. Brilliant!' He was still laughing.

Archie's reaction wasn't the one I was worried about. 'This isn't funny.'

'It's quite funny.'

'I think Moss might disagree.' And I'd spent literally days calming her paranoia.

'Ohhhhhh.' Carlo clicked. 'Crap.'

'Yeah. I mean, she'll know it's rubbish,' (deep down) 'she'll just be annoyed that I said it. Except. I. Didn't. Say. It. And now I've got to explain.' We set off, walking down Godzilla Avenue to the soundstage. Not *our* Sound Stage A – that was full of crew setting up for 007 – but a different, much smaller one. 'I've been praying for a Straker scene reshoot for months but why this scene? Why not a nice talkey-thinkey scene?' (preferably sitting down). 'Or, a fight scene? Even a *chase* scene? Even a green screen chase scene. *Anything but a love scene.* I promised Moss we were NEVER going to do another love scene.'

'I know. We were messaging when the scripts came through.'

'You're still messaging a lot?'

He nodded. 'I've probably talked more to Moss than any other girl.'

'That you've dated? Got with?'

'Any other girl. Full stop.'

I laughed – that was *shocking*, how had he got away with it so long? 'What do you and Moss talk about? You've only been in the same room twice.' And she cried the first time and ran away the second – but I didn't say that.

'Everything, nothing.' He looked a bit worried. 'I've probably told her too much.'

'What about?'

'Me,' he said and this time we both laughed. 'But yeah, this scene is bad timing. The more I have to get with Straker, the longer it's going to take me to get with Moss. But she can't genuinely think I'm trying to get with you. It's mad.'

'Unthinkable. But it would be better if we didn't have to kiss each other again. Obviously not us – Jan and Straker – and not exactly kiss, but still ...' I trailed off. To be fair to Moss, it was *weird*.

'And it doesn't help that Torr messed her around.'

'She filled you in?'

'Yes.'

Seriously? Moss didn't open up to very many people. '*You* can't mess her around, Carlo. Like, at first I was just thinking you'd be a nice non-Torr distraction—'

'Thanks,' he interrupted.

'You're not still chasing her because she's so hard to get, are you?'

He shook his head. 'We message nearly every day. I want to meet up with her again ... properly.' I waited for him to laugh off the failed meet-up but he didn't. 'So, yeah, we'll need to see how that goes when I can persuade her – but, no, I'm not playing some game.' I looked at him. 'I promise.'

This was the most real conversation I'd ever had with Carlo but we'd arrived at the sound stage. They'd moved some of the set over – some of the 'rocks', some of the weird wood carvings, but it was patchy, with some green screens filling in the gaps between the 'trees' (real trunks, fake leaves) and acres of empty echoing space dotted with ladders and portable heaters and piles of cables. But there was still an *army* of crew rushing around, because that's what it took.

'We, er ... burnt quite a lot of the trees for the trailer,' explained one of the set-builders apologetically.

'Fair play.' Carlo shrugged.

I sat down on a spare 'mossy boulder' (fake moss, polystyrene rock) and re-read my script. I wasn't confident I knew all the lines yet. I said them over and over under my breath. Oh God, I couldn't take this sitting down. I stood up and waved my script in the air. 'There are lines on here no human should be asked to say out loud. Not even in private. "I look into your eyes and I see myself reflected back a hundred times but made complete." *Eeeeugh.* "You are the wind singing in these trees, you are ..." *Vom.* I felt bad for my character.

The electricians who were setting up the lights ignored my little outburst but Carlo nodded sadly. 'I don't see how they expect us not to laugh, and I don't think that's the vibe they're going for.'

Havelski detached himself from the huddle around the monitors and came over (Rhona, his assistant, two paces behind him with an enormous thermos of coffee). 'Correct, Carlo. Nobody came out of that test screening saying "needs more laughs". Actually, one person did, but he left early and was probably high. If the ...' he said something in Hungarian that was almost certainly not complimentary, 'audiences we now seem to be making this movie for want romance, that's what we'll give them. Also, schmaltz, cheese and corn. Except you didn't hear me say that. Ready for today?'

I looked ready. Straker was back in all the glory of her smelly hessian sack. I was *ready*. I just wasn't one hundred per cent *up for it*.

'Meh. Might as well get it over and done with,' said Carlo, swinging his silvery cloak over his shoulders.

'Hey, hey, hey!' said Dan the sound man coming over to join us. 'The Junior A-Team are back together. I'm *Raw*-rring to go,' he said and waggled his eyebrows. We stared back at him 'Come on ... I've read this scene. It's going to be awesome but first you two at least, need to be in the *mood for lurve*.' He sashayed over to the sound control box, fiddled with some buttons and smiled at us smugly as some random beats started to thump through the room. He closed his eyes and raised a hand in musical ecstasy. 'Wait, wait, waaiiittttt for ittttttt ...'

Rousing intro, *And. Did. Those. FEET. IN. ANCIENT. TIMES ...*

'*What* is this?' shouted Havelski. Rhona wordlessly passed him coffee.

Dan opened his eyes. 'The dubstep remix of

"Jerusalem". It's my favourite song at the moment. Possibly for all time.'

'Who does that get in the mood for *lurve?*' asked Carlo.

There was a moment of silence. Everyone looked at Dan. 'Me,' he admitted sheepishly. 'But, fine.' He threw up his hands. 'I'll give you commercial sheep what you want.' Back at his controls, it took only a second for the mood music to take a dive. A deep, deep, dive. 'NEAR,' the speakers blasted out, 'FAR. WHEREEVEEEERRRRRR YOU ARE.'

Carlo looked like he was about to throw up, so did Havelski. I was kind of feeling it. '*I BEELEEEIIIIIVEEEEE THAT MY HEART,*' I joined in. It wasn't putting me in *the* mood but it was putting me in a better mood.

'OFF. OFF!' shouted Havelski, making aggressive cutting motions at his throat. The silence was somehow very loud when the music cut and the focus was back on us. 'So. You two can bring all the trauma that has just been inflicted by Dan here to your performances.' He glared at him and turned back to us with something like sympathy. 'But now we get serious. You have to bring us something that will feel real and true. So. This scene is in the forest clearing.' Or, as this script described it, "Jan and Straker's Special Place". 'So. Elektra. Jan's near-death moment under the ice ...' We all took a moment to get the *Titanic* theme tune out of our heads again. 'This is actually quite a good scene when I watch it back in the edit suite.' Carlo looked smug. I wasn't in that scene. 'This brush with death has given you your, *"Oh no, I just realized – in the nick of time – that I am in love with him!"* moment. It is a classic trope. And so – inevitably – we have The Love Confession. It would seem that much is riding on it. Take a minute. Think love, think American audiences, also think mortal fear and adrenalin. Let's get to work.'

Thirty minutes of blocking and doing walk throughs and setting up and then Bo and her assistant were drenching Carlo from enormous spray-bottles of water and we were ready for shot.

'Quiet on set.' I focused and quickly reread my direction:

Straker takes off her ragged shawl and wraps it around Jan's shoulders. He clasps her hands as she does so and they look deep into each other's eyes. It is a moment. Pure, perfect and yet, charged with painful energy.

'Roll sound.'
'Sound speeds.'
'Roll Camera.'

'Camera speeds.'
'Set.'
'Action!'

STRAKER
No. Oh no. *(Shakes her head, comprehending yet afraid)*

JAN
Yes, Straker *(his voice is low, firm)*. We can't keep fighting this. We need to admit it. To each other, to ourselves.

STRAKER
I can't ... I can't *(she stumbles over the word)* love you. *(This is not what she wants ... or, is it?)*

JAN
You can't not love me *(beat)* and I can't not love you.

'Stop!' shouted Ahmed. 'Nothing you're doing wrong, guys, but we're having some issues with the light levels, the moonlight glow's not right yet. Let's start over.'

Ten awkward minutes (two of which I spent having the wet patches blow-dried out of my costume), another soaking for Carlo, and we started over.

STRAKER
No. Oh no. *(Shakes her head, comprehending yet afraid)* . . . It wasn't a short Love Confession.

STRAKER *(trying to pull away her hand)*
But I don't want you to be The One. This is hard enough already. So hard. *(Her voice breaks)*.

JAN
We are part of each other. Our destinies are bound.

STRAKER *(Almost angry)*
Then every threat is twice agony. My heart is beating *(takes Jan's hand and places it over her heart)*.

'Can we stop for a minute? *Please.*'
'CUT!'
'Sorry, sorry, sorry.' In seconds, everyone was checking me out to see what was wrong. Tangled up costume? Wire in a wrong place? Did I feel unwell? Upset? I looked over to Ahmed and Havelski. 'I'm really sorry but that bit . . . where he puts his hand

on my beating heart … I just … It's going to look like he's putting his hand—'

'I don't want anything grope-y,' said Havelksi. 'Ahmed, what do you think?'

Ahmed mulled it over. 'I'm not sure. Amber and Sam keep *adding* that direction into their love scenes – their improv is getting out of control. I'd be happy to cut? We don't want to look like we're repeating ourselves or relying on tropes.'

Havelski snorted. 'No, we wouldn't want to do that. Shame no one told the writers. So? We go straight to the first kiss? Or rewrite that exchange? But we don't have any writers here today.' He didn't sound that sorry.

'We could go with "My heart is beating" and drop the *feels* bit?' suggested Ahmed. Carlo sniggered.

Havelski glared at him. 'Well, first some more deep eye-gazing and then the kiss. OK?' Great. I'd accelerated the worst bit. 'So pick it up at "every threat is twice agony." But hold the eye contact this time. Let's rehearse it and see how it's working before we roll.'

'Don't blink, Elektra,' said Carlo under his breath as we got into position. 'Whatever you do, don't blink. Winner gets to drive the buggy.'

'Look deep into each other's eyes,' intoned Ahmed like a hypnotist.

'Carlo, stop laughing,' said Havelski a few minutes

later. 'What is wrong with you two today? Somebody get me a coffee. Ten minutes, then we get on with this for real.' On the downside, we hadn't got through the scene yet. On the upside, it was one-all on the Don't Blink Challenge.

There was more milling around. Someone was towelling Carlo down at the same time as Bo was refilling the water sprays for the next take. One of the crew was manhandling out a (fake) tree that had dropped all its (fake) leaves. Two of the grips were tussling over an old copy of *Closer*. A whole team of people were doing all the things they needed to do to reset so we'd be ready to go again. Dan was leaving the work to his assistant and was playing a little medley of ABBA hits and Havelski was drinking strong black coffee like his life depended on it. No moonlight lighting. No tense vibe. No perfect moment. No (real) 'Special Place'. Nobody could see this and think of romance.

Nobody.

Not even Moss. I was an actual genius. 'Carlo,' I said when he emerged from his rub-down, 'we need to snap her.'

'What??' Pretty sure he blinked. It was the element of surprise.

WAITING

- % of time spent dreading *Raw* being released/being a massive fail: 112%
- % of time owning hashtag #RawGlamour 0%; % of time spent watching Fake Elektra owning #RawGlamour 1% (too weird)
- % of time spent listening to Moss trying to be cool about Carlo: 16%

43

Days to Go . . .

Subject: Stop worrying Elektra (and get ready to **Party!**)

Dear Elektra,

We got all the messages! Yes, I am aware of the Open Casting for the new J.K. Rowling project but I really don't think that's the way to go – not least because you won't get away with playing a thirteen-year-old! I'm sensing you're a bit *panicky* and you really mustn't be! I know things feel slow to you right now and I know that being back on the *Raw* set reminded you how much you love it, but you need to be patient. I promise you that we're always looking out for projects to put you forward for but they have to be the *right* projects. We've only had two enquiries in the last month that were playing-age appropriate for you. One for an actor who was comfortable with being in a bikini for the duration of the shoot (all the other characters wearing suits and ties) and the other one, well, the casting brief sounded like it had been written by a serial killer. Not every job is a good job. And it is worth *waiting* for the good jobs.

In the meantime, enjoy school. Trust us, you don't want to be an actor without an education, you really don't.

On a happier note, the *Raw* Wrap party is *finally* happening (and I don't think they'll postpone it this time!) You need to bring a parent because it's being held at licensed premises and you can bring one other guest. *Please* keep all these details 'under wraps' because there's a no Press, no paparazzi rule. Havelski has laid down the law that it's to be a night of *real life* fun!

Date: 21 February
Venue: Urban House East, London, EC2
Time: 8.30 p.m. (speeches at 9.30) *until late!*
Dress: *Keep it Raw . . .*

Stella x

P.S. That reminds me. I looked you up on media last night. I know that PPR are running your accounts now – that happens, but are you OK with the direction it's taking?

CHAPTER 18

'I can think I'm the only thing in the room.'
Kit Harrington

'It's *nearly* right,' said Moss diplomatically. It was two hours before the *Raw* Wrap party and I was wearing a black lace Topshop off-the-shoulder crop top and an A-line black skirt that hovered indecisively around my knees. It was all right for her. She was curled up on my bed wearing a silver wrap-y mini dress that shimmered every time she moved, like a short version of one of the Warri tribe costumes that I'd lusted after the whole way through filming.

'I look ridiculous. I swear I looked sophisticated and glamorous in the shop, like an actual proper person.'

'You *are* an actual proper person.' It was a bit worrying that that was the bit she chose to confirm.

'I feel stupid.' I got into my wardrobe. Right into it. It wasn't very big but there had to be an outside chance that The Absolutely Perfect Party Dress was concealed *somewhere*.

'Will the whole cast be there?' Moss shouted at me from the bed.

'I think so. Amber is flying Kale home early from his doggy-yoga retreat in the Maldives so he can support her and ... I'm pretty sure you already know Carlo's going to be there.' I emerged from the wardrobe with a pile of clothes and a perfectly straight face. 'This one?' I held up a red dress that had looked good on me when I was thirteen. She shook her head. 'How's it going?' I was asking about Carlo, not my doomed fashion quest.

'It's going well.' Moss tried to look coy for the first time in her life. She failed.

'Very well? Like, on a scale of "I'm enjoying the attention" to "get with me NOW".'

'You're very annoying. No! Not that skirt, it's *hideous*!'

'Would you get with him tonight?' I chucked the offending skirt onto the growing discards mountain on the carpet. Plog was leaping around like I'd made him a personal canine ball pit.

'You know I would ... if he tried.' *Finally,*

she'd accepted that Carlo was about as much romantically into me as I was into physics revision. Who knew that the best way to reassure Moss on that particular madness was a) to film another love scene, b) to borrow Ed's phone and snap her stories from set (quality material, my personal favourite being a shot of Dan and Carlo doing the Titanic pose) – and c) to tell her every detail (not a single one of which was romantic) until she was begging us to stop. We'd worn her down.

'Are you actually crazy? He's been trying to get with you for almost as long as Havelski's been trying to finish off *Raw*. Just don't run away this time.'

She cringed. 'But is it too *weird*? I can't have a thing with a *real actor*.'

'Er, Mossy. You are best friends with a *real* actor. OK, with an actor ... with someone who has acted.'

'That's *ridiculous* too.'

Fair. 'Carlo likes that you're not obsessed with what he does. He's definitely going to try tonight.' She buried herself in the pillows and made a muffled sound that I was going to interpret as positive. 'This?' I held up a short yellow skirt. Did it have a *Clueless* vibe? No, judging from the look on Moss's face when she emerged from her freak-out, it didn't. I was running out of options.

'Honestly, what you've got on is the best.' She got off the bed and came over. 'Let's *make* that outfit you.' She had a worrying glint in her eyes. 'The problem is, it's too long, look.' She made me look in the mirror and folded up the hem. It was a definite improvement. 'Your legs are definitely your best feature.' Which made me feel good and yet, looking at my face, quite bad.

'I haven't got time to take it up.' I barely had time to brush my mismatched hair.

'Easy.' She picked up a pair of scissors. 'Stand very still.'

'Are you mad? My mum will kill me.' But Moss was still holding up the hem and my legs did look quite good. It was *tempting*.

'Are you going to let your mum make all your fashion decisions?' Well, no. If I did that I'd be going to this party in knee-high white socks (and not in an ironic way). 'It will only be a couple of centimetres, she won't notice. And it will be a Moss Sato Original. Cutting edge design.' She waggled her eyebrows. 'See what I did there? Come on, don't you trust me?'

'Not always,' I answered truthfully.

'Am I or am I not your fashion guru?' She was standing behind me wielding the scissors in a way that made me nervous about giving the wrong answer.

'Except for the time you made me wear my knickers over my jeans.'

'We were six and it was experimental. Also, we were hoping for superpowers. You should have got over that by now.'

I stared at my reflection, then at Moss and the very large scissors, then back at the mirror. 'Fine. Let's do it. No! Wait! Wait!'

'OK, take a moment. Take a deep breath. Close your eyes. Seek spiritual guidance.' This was so un-Moss. I shut my eyes.

There was a little crunching noise. '*Moss!*'

'Somebody had to make a decision.' She shrugged. Half my skirt was hanging off. 'I'm not going to miss the start of the most glamorous night of my life because you're scared of losing a bit of fabric.' A bit? She was creeping round to the front now. 'Ah. I think it might be a little lopsided.' We both looked. It was at least four centimetres shorter on one side than the other. 'Stop hyperventilating, I'll just go round again and even it up … Ah. Actually I think uneven is probably more "Keeping it *Raw*"?' One painful minute of scissoring later. 'Maybe put on nicer knickers?'

Urban House East was a nondescript black building squashed between a butcher's shop and a hardware store in a narrow side street in Shoreditch.

'Elektra James! Don't you dare pretend you haven't seen me. Come here and give me a hug.'

Sam was waving from the lobby. 'Do you like my scar? And my leg?' Oh God, he was on crutches. 'Dashing? Rugged? I feel like a pirate, you know?' I actually didn't know. The closest I'd come to piracy was stealing biscuits from the sixth-form common room. Terrifying.

'Was it a stunt? Was it the scene where you single-handedly fight off twenty-three Terra tribe members from halfway up the Cliff of Dreams?' I'd always wondered how they'd pull off that scene without a trip to A&E. 'Or the scene where you fight off thirty-six Terra tribe members from the rope bridge strung between the highest trees in the Dark Forest?' I was not only at my first industry party; I was literally *burbling* at an A-Lister. 'No? The scene where you jump from your wild but loyal steed onto the back of a wolf-like thing and strangle it—' I could have gone on for some time. Had Kale attacked him? How much damage could a small but very fierce Pomeranian do?

'Drag racing,' he said happily. 'Didn't hurt a bit. Well, not until the opiates wore off. Hahaha.'

A pretty girl in black ticked us off on a list and secured some frayed hessian bands printed with *Raw* onto our wrists. I would never take mine off. Another ridiculously pretty girl whisked away our coats. Moss tugged down my skirt and stood very close to me for cover.

There were too many people in this lift – but then, there is no lift in the world large enough comfortably to accommodate me, Moss, my mum and Sam Gross on crutches, especially as Sam smelled quite strongly of whisky and neither Moss nor Mum could look him in the eye. I looked at all the buttons. We were headed for the Penthouse. Oooh, I could stop off at the fourth floor Potting Shed Spa and have a little massage to relax me en route. Or maybe visit the Pure Oxygen Cloud Room on the fifth floor? The lift was lined with mirrors. Mirrors recording that three people were too nervous are to look the fourth in the eye and woah, that my skirt was *short*. I hoiked it down a bit, two seconds later and it pinged back up to just under bum level.

'You look great,' whispered Moss reassuringly and just a bit too loudly. Mum stared at the skirt and gave a little anxious whimper. She tugged; it pinged back again.

'Big improvement on your Straker look, Elektra,' said Sam, who was plainly far too important to worry about any dress codes and was wearing a dark suit, a white shirt and his signature red loafers (the rumours about concealed heels were true). He looked like he'd stepped out of an advert – which now I came to think of it he probably had. He turned to my mum before she could start worrying that he was creepy. 'You all look great. I see where

Elektra gets her good looks from.' A sentence both ridiculous and yet oddly predictable. Moss lost it. 'And what a charming girl Elektra is. You must be a brilliant parent.' He gave Mum the Sam-Gross-guaranteed-to-make-you–swoon smile. Was this how old people flirted? Handed out compliments on parenting?

The lift doors opened to an explosion of noise and laughter and lights – and a huge guy with an earpiece barring us from going any further.

'Phones,' he said and held out a beefy hand, like an upsized version of my deputy headmaster.

'Come on, mate,' said Sam in his best A-lister-talking-to-civilian-man-to-man. 'That doesn't apply to me, does it?'

'I'm sorry, Mr Gross, but the rule applies to everyone. No press have been invited and nobody is taking photos.' When *finally*, I'd made it to a VIP event? *The irony*. 'Mr Havelski wants no images released other than the approved group shot that is happening at midnight.'

'Oh, I don't think we'll still be here at midnight,' said my mum.

'Elektra's got form on leaving our productions too early,' said Sam, putting his arm around me. 'She's got to stay for the group shot.'

My mother was torn; she was either going to have to fall short of her parenting standards or disappoint a Hollywood star. 'We'll leave straight after that, then,' she said. I was impressed. All I needed was an A-lister around 24/7 and she'd be manageable.

'I still need the phones.' We handed them over; big-scary-guy stuck labels on them and dropped them into a barrel. I looked around the room. There was a high vaulted ceiling with industrial metal beams. The room was dotted with mismatched velvet sofas and high winged armchairs grouped around low marble tables. A long bar of beaten copper snaked down one side of the room reflecting the cut crystal lightbulbs hanging above it. On the other side of the room, a wall of glass doors opening onto a terrace lit only by candles and fire pits. *So Instagrammable.*

A waiter wearing something that looked a bit like a Warri tribe costume (i.e. not very much) handed me a cocktail menu.

I scanned it. *Drink to remember, drink to forget.* I could have the **RAW CLASSIC**, **THE DREADS**, **THE BUGS** or **A NEW DAWN** – except I couldn't because they all seemed to be three parts Sam Gross's own brand whisky.

'Ah, sorry,' said the waiter. 'Wrong one. You need the *Mocktail* Menu.' He handed it over.

'I'm going **DEAD TOO SOON** because this is the one and only time I will have a drink named after me, even if that recipe is unnecessarily aggressive.' "Violently crushed", "Torn too young", this bar needed to calm down.

'I'm not risking fermented barberries,' said Moss. 'I'm definitely going **JAN THE HERO** tonight.' What a surprise.

'Is Carlo here yet? Text him?'

'Except we don't have phones.'

'Then let's go find him.' I dropped my voice. 'Just let me offload Mum.' She was looking terrified, not least because someone had handed her a BUGS. I'd read the ingredients, there was a high chance it would exterminate her.

'Elektra!' I spun round to see Bo. I practically jumped on her.

'Mum, meet Bo – I told you about her? One of the make-up artists.'

'Oh, yes! Thank you so much for sorting out Elektra's spots,' she bellowed.

'Elektra has lovely skin.' Bo whipped out a tiny tub of concealer and 'improved me' on the spot (literally) and then launched into the intricacies of creating my dying wounds. Once Bo started talking about wounds she was quite hard to stop. Moss and I started slowly backing away.

We made it out onto the terrace. It was lit by huge stone firepits surrounded by benches, light-bulb fairy lights strung between the trees. There was a second bar out here made of distressed wooden planks like one of the huts in *Raw* and a DJ booth. And, right in the centre was a huge pool, lit from beneath, gleaming blue. 'We are one hundred per cent not swimming,' I said once I'd recovered the power of speech.

'Bit early in the night to rule it out.' It was Carlo. Obviously. He gave me the briefest of hugs without once taking his eyes off Moss and then went over to kiss her hello. Which was a very awkward-in-a-too-much-tension kind of moment. I was optimistic. 'Where's Archie tonight?' asked Carlo. 'Is he with the bats?'

'Yeah. And I wanted to bring Moss.'

'Except that *I* wanted to bring her, that was definitely the right call. You look stunning, Moss.'

'Unusually charming, Carlo.' I joked.

'But I *am* charming. That's my greatest flaw.' He turned to Moss. 'My *only* flaw.'

'Carlo!' shouted a leggy blonde from the other side of the terrace. 'Carlo Winn! What a *coincidence*.' It was the wrap party for the film he'd starred in and she'd interned on, so not that much of a coincidence. Carlo waved vaguely in her direction. 'Hey, Carlo!' She was persistent.

'Thank you all for coming.' A voice boomed out and a spotlight was trained on Pete-the-Producer. Carlo was saved. 'Can I have everyone's attention for a minute?' The party noise calmed down. '*Raw* is going to be the movie that everyone is talking about next year—'

'But God knows what they'll be saying,' said someone behind me just a bit too loudly. Oh God, couldn't we just ignore all the trolling for one night and pretend that *Raw* was one hundred per cent going to be the cinema hit of the year?

'An epic exploration of love at the edge ...'

'*Push audiences over the edge*', roared a dozen voices and half the room started singing the theme tune to the trailer (which was possibly or possibly not also the theme tune to the movie).

'S-Amber, S-Amber, S-Amber,' chanted someone who'd definitely enjoyed one too many **NAMELESS DREADS**. Amber smiled tightly from one edge of the room; Sam grimaced from the other. They were obviously having an 'off' night. There was more. So much more. Talk of post-production and plans for distribution and promotion and generally, world domination. I didn't understand very much of what Pete was saying and not just because everyone else had got bored and started talking over him. 'We're still working on the edit ... but enjoy the clips we're going to be showing later this evening on the screens.' He gestured around and for the first time I noticed the huge flat screens on every wall. 'You're our very first audience. And now a big hand for our director, Sergei Havelski.' There was loud cheering.

Sergei hauled himself onto a small table. It jiggled worryingly.

At that exact moment the lift doors opened to reveal Eulalie. She was wearing a skinny little dress entirely covered in black feathers, she'd embellished her Chanel bag with bug-shaped brooches and her hair was swept up into a dishevelled silver beehive. She looked amazing.

Havelski stared, everyone turned. Eulalie smiled, grabbed a cocktail from a passing waiter and made her way through the crowd – which had parted like the Red Sea – to the front.

Sergei beamed at her. 'So, I'm going to keep this short. It's been … tough. We've got through it. There are lots of people in this room I hope I'm going to work with again … on other projects.' He raised his arms and the table wobbled. 'Fill your glasses and let's pray for kinder audiences than the one in this room tonight.' Nearly everyone laughed (but then, the drinks were strong).

'Elektra James!' Eddie staggered up to me. He was being held up (barely) by my babe of an on-set tutor, Naomi.

I gave them a joint cuddle. 'Eeurgh, you're all wet, Eddie.'

'They're playing the *Raw* theme tune,' he said. 'Under the water in the pool. How cool is that?'

'You've been in?' He'd obviously been in. 'You need to change.'

'I so do.' He reached for his shirt.

'Don't get your abs out again, Eddie.' Naomi sighed. 'We'll find you another shirt.'

'No, no, no, I'm going swimming again. But first a drink. Another drink. Have you got a drink, Elektra?' I held up my **DEAD TOO SOON**. 'This is good. All good. This situation ... is indeed ... beneficial.'

'OK,' laughed Naomi. 'Let's get you some water. To drink.' She hauled Eddie off to the bar.

'Silence!' called out Amber. She motioned wildly. Someone hit the spotlight. 'Thank you!' she shouted over the noise, 'for your SILENCE!' The hubbub calmed. 'I'd just like to thank everyone who has supported me and made this project so special. I'd like to thank my talented daughter.' Was she talking about me? 'I hope I have taught you something about – acting, yoga ... about men.' She shared a conspiratorial smile with my mum who she was standing next to – she was definitely talking about me. It was a beautiful moment until Carlo and Moss sniggered. 'And Carlo Winn, such a charming young man, such a future ahead of him. Is there anyone else in the cast I need to single out?' She stared around the room. Everyone looked at her, and at Sam, and back to her like this was the Wimbledon final. Sam downed his drink. 'No. I can't think of anyone.' Sam downed the drink of the person standing next to him. 'Now onto the crew ...'

*

'Elektra!' said Moss grabbing me ten minutes later.

'What? What? Is the Carlo sitch progressing?'

'What? No! Well, yes.' She blushed. 'But that wasn't what I was going to say. It's you!'

'I know I'm me,' I said. Was she on the cocktails? Carlo came over and slung his arm around her shoulders, not so awkward now.

'On the screen.'

What? I looked around. On the screen in front of me, Sam/Raw scaling a cliff. On the screen to my right, Raw and Amber/Winona in hand-to-hand combat.

'*That screen.*' Moss pointed.

Oh God. She was right.

It was me.

In a hessian sack.

Just one three-second clip being played over and over like some rogue Boomerang. '*Eat the Bugs, Eat the Bugs.*'

Too. Much. To. Process. I shut my eyes.

When I opened them the clip was still playing but now Moss and Carlo were getting off passionately – silhouetted romantically against my *massive* bug-filled screen face.

I smiled and backed happily away to the bar.

TheBizz.com

Bringing you the all the Best
Backstabbing in the Bizz . . .

22 February

Wait! Is that the sound of our waters breaking? Cause we are heavily pregnant ...

With GOSSIP.

Which we are about to birth. Have we taken this metaphor too far?
Last night was the night of the *Raw* launch party and we here at *The Bizz* may or may not have engaged in some low-key illegal stalking *action* (Becky took one for the team and got with the bouncer). We pushed ourselves to the limits of investigative journalism and boy did we learn a lot.

And we even remembered some of it this morning.
So, without further ado, here is a condensed list of the things we witnessed (even *we* couldn't get photos):

S-Amber *totally* not getting on. Sam downed whiskies at the bar, we didn't see them actually speak to each other once and Sam was the only person that Amber didn't thank in her speech.

Sergei Havelski's mystery woman *killing* it. She wore fringe, arrived two hours late, stole people's drinks, danced on a table and kissed Sergei Havelski. And she's like ... Old. YASSSS QUEEN SLAY.

Carlo Winn's jump in the pool to save some random hot girl who fell in. He practically saved her life. So what if she just swam to the side and he had to get rescued by life-guards? The *sentiment* was there. We're not sure if he wanted to save her or just wanted a Mr Darcy-in-a-wet-shirt moment. Either way we're not complaining. Just discussing the incident meant we had to turn up the air con in the *Bizz* office.

And how does that fit in with the rumours that Elektra James, the other young actor with a decent part (total unknown but beginning to rack up the Insta followers), is into her co-star??? She wasn't weeping into her mocktail but then she wasn't getting with anyone else either. Time will tell ...

From: Fiona at Personality PR
Date: 24 February 09.15
To: Elektra James, Carlo Winn
Cc: Edward Dell at Panda, Peter at Panda, Stella at The Haden Agency

Subject: Release Promo!
Attachments: Press Schedule (CW & EOJ; Sample Interview Questions etc.)

Dear Carlo and Elektra,

RELEASE really is *looming*! *So exciting!!!* Sergei has had a quick word with us about making sure you're not over-scheduled and that you have lots of support. You do! We're here with you every step of the way!

Elektra – we're ALL OVER your social media – the figures are looking great!! We've applied for your BLUE TICK!!! Carlo – you're doing a great job, you're a natural (!!!) but shout if you need help. There are some full interview requests for you both from journalists (the kind we can't 'step in' for) and, most excitingly, we've managed to set up the TV slots that we wanted (yay!!!) (see schedule attached).

I'm attaching a little list of handy hints and sample questions. If you've got any concerns just shout!! We're going to get you through this *unscathed*.

We'll be in touch soon about arrangements for the PREMIERE –
so *exciting*!!!

What a time to be alive!

Fiona x

*** PPR * ON FIRE in Soho since 2010**
⭐ Currently promoting RAW the Movie A Panda Productions
feature, directed by Sergei Havelski, starring Sam Gross and
Amber Leigh COMING SOON! ⭐
Follow us on Twitter @Personality Facebook: PersonalityPR
Insta @PersonalityonFire

★
CHAPTER 19

'It's all smoke and mirrors and I often feel a horrible fraudster.'

Benedict Cumberbatch

I was curled up next to Archie in the biggest armchair in our sitting room. It was a squash but Moss and Carlo had claimed the sofa. My phone barked at the same time as Carlo's buzzed. 'Fiona from PPR,' he said.

'Is it about outfits? For the premiere?' I asked hopefully. It was only weeks away. *It was only weeks away* (the FEAR) – on the upside, it was time to start talking clothes. 'Will you definitely be able to be there?' I asked Archie for the hundredth time.

He nodded. 'Seriously, I'm at home loads for the next few weeks. They're filming all the episodes I'm not in.' Because Tibor Snolosky was locked up in an ivy-covered tower with only a slim volume of poetry and romantic dreams for company while everyone else rushed around slaying vampires and trying to rescue him. (I might skip those episodes.)

'Will they really send you stuff to wear?' Moss asked me. 'Sometimes it's quite hard being your friend.'

'You'll look beautiful whatever you wear.' Had Carlo forgotten Archie and I were in the room? What had she done to him?

'Fiona-aa said we could get lent stuff.' It was unreal – even if I had a bad feeling PPR would choose something that would make me look like a rich thirty-year-old with a thing for matte lipstick. 'I dreamt last night that I was walking the red carpet in my hessian sack and skates.' I'd pay back all – no, half – my *Raw* money for just one night of dreamless sleep.

'What was I wearing?' asked Carlo predictably.

'There wasn't room in my dream for your ego.' Moss laughed and he just grinned at her. 'But Havelski was there. He was directing me on my physics GCSE paper. He wasn't happy with my performance on radiation exposure risk.'

'That's not a dream,' said Moss. 'That's a nightmare.'

'No, a nightmare would have been if I hadn't

woken up before we got into the cinema. I am *terrified.*'

'It'll be OK,' said Carlo, but with less of his usual swagger. He'd been in a few episodes of a TV series in America before *Raw* but he'd never had to worry about a movie premiere before. *Anyone* would be scared.

'It won't be OK if *The Bizz* is right,' I said. 'Last week they posted three borderline dodgy behind-the-scenes shirtless photos of you—'

'I need to see those,' interrupted Moss with no dignity.

'And,' I went on, ignoring her, 'the happy news from "a source" that the whole thing was a nightmare from beginning to end and that everyone was hoping that the wolf-like things had eaten all the footage.'

'They couldn't actually do that,' said Carlo. 'They're *green screen* wolf-like things.' Seriously? Who knew? He was making a fuss of Plog who'd pushed open the door and come to join us. 'This dog is way bigger and dottier than I remember.' Yeah, that happened.

'When has *The Bizz* ever been right?' said Archie.

'They called S-Amber,' I reminded him. 'I can't believe those two are still together.'

'The trauma of filming *Raw* brought them together,' said Carlo.

'But will the trauma of release keep them together?' Havelski had told Eulalie who told me that they'd made up after the *Raw* party. Even the tabloids were struggling to keep up. 'So, what's the email about?'

'Sadly, it's not about the premiere. It's briefing notes on how to handle the press,' said Carlo.

'Like how-to-wrestle-a-crocodile or how-to-handle-an-anaconda,' said Moss. 'If my costume design plan doesn't pan out I might train to be a journalist. I quite like the whole fear vibe.'

'You can interview me any time,' said Carlo. Tragic.

'It won't be meant for me, then,' I said. 'They're not going to risk me saying something that sounds like my real life.'

'Did you see your interview in *Teen Tantrum?*' asked Moss. I shook my head. 'OK, it wasn't a proper interview – I don't suppose they could pretend to be you for one of those,' (I wasn't sure), 'it was yet another of those "ten things you didn't know about X" ones. I'm learning so much about you, Elektra. I didn't know you had "a signature smart-but-casual look" and had overcome "teen trauma and stress about your appearance" by mastering the five-step cleanse.'

'Deep,' said Carlo.

'What was the photo like?' I asked.

'Amazing. Except so tuned you'd probably have fallen over in real life.'

'Legs too thin or boobs too big this time?' I asked.

'Both, also really big head but it kind of worked.'

'It's getting a bit sinister.' Archie could say that, he'd never been asked to write about his complexion woes for a teen magazine.

'I'm not ... loving it,' I admitted. 'Like, I really appreciate that they're doing it all for me but it is a bit weird. People at school keeping asking me about stuff I've posted and I don't know what to say.'

'Do you explain?'

I shook my head. 'It's quite hard to explain – if you're not in the industry.' Moss rolled her eyes. 'It's just easier not to talk to anyone.' They all laughed but it wasn't that funny. It was easier not to think about it – which would be easier if I didn't look at it. And not looking at it was the plan.

I was going to take a little social media break.

From myself.

Carlo was still reading the PPR email. 'This is for both of us,' he said. 'But mostly for me. There's a bit here, Elektra, that says you "won't be overburdened with press obligations" because they're going to "prioritize" me over you.'

'That's sexist!' Moss and I complained as one (ignoring the fact that he had a bigger part).

'Do you *want* to be overburdened with interviews?'

Fair point. It's not like the school were being nice about letting me skip classes. Mum was literally going to have to promise them they could auction Sam Gross's first-born child to fund their new music room if I was going to get the release day off. 'But we've both got to do some TV stuff. Look.' Carlo passed me his phone and I scanned down the long attachment until I found the bit he was talking about.

The Lunch Show	...	ITV	Amber Leigh, Sam Gross, Carlo Winn, Elektra James	*Emphasize . . .* ✳ Funny set anecdotes ✳ Quick 'family' banter ✳ Discussion of how well you bonded ✳ Excitement!	*Avoid . . .* ✳ Funny set anecdotes that reflect poorly on the production quality ✳ Pessimism!
The Lateish show	...	BBC	Carlo Winn, Elektra James	*Emphasize . . .* ✳ Flirt! ✳ Witty banter	*Avoid . . .* ✳ Talking about school (nobody cares)
Women who Brunch	...	...	Carlo Winn, Elektra James	*Emphasize . . .* ✳ Mother-daughter bonding ✳ Mentoring ✳ Female role models in Hollywood ✳ Sharing clothes!	*Avoid . . .* ✳ Boring with gender politics and/or pay disparities

'Who do you think I'm meant to flirt *with* on the *Lateish Show?*' asked Carlo.

'Anyone you need to?' suggested Archie.

Moss rolled her eyes. 'It's a tough life.'

Carlo had taken back control of his phone and was reading out extracts. '"*Helpful hints. Number one – if you're being interviewed with a co-star, don't a) fight with them, b) ignore them or,*" Big one for you here, Elektra, "*c) talk over—*"'

'It doesn't say that,' I interrupted, opening the attachment on my own phone. Oh, it did say that. They were our very own tailor-made guidelines. '"*Remember that you're a professional performer,*"' I read. '"*If you can eat bugs, climb cliff faces and wrestle rapacious wolf-like creatures in* Raw *you can act your way through a ten-minute interview (!!!)*".' That slightly begged the question whether we *had* pulled off all these things but everyone was going to find out the answer to that pretty soon. 'OK, so we just act being proficient interviewees. Got it.'

'But then two lines down it says we have to "*be authentic*",' said Carlo.

'No, it says we have to "*come over as authentic*",' I said. If Fiona-aa had taught me anything, it was that there was a difference.

'Just be yourself,' said Archie. I don't think that was *exactly* what they were after, anyway, I'd forgotten how.

'But not too much yourself,' said Moss, looking worried. 'I mean, don't tell them about that time in Year Seven when you ...'

'Stop!' I said at the same time as Archie and Carlo said, 'What?'

'I really don't think they're going to be asking about *that*,' I said.

'It might come under *"offer up short genuine anecdotes like golden nuggets",* said Carlo. 'And now we're all thinking about chicken, aren't we?' Yep. 'And then there's a list of sample questions.'

'Hand them over,' said Archie. 'I'll give you guys a mock interview.'

'Don't we have to have a publicist glued to our sides?' Or possibly speaking for us.

'That's me,' said Moss. 'I'm your publicist; the first thing I'm going to say is that there are to be no questions about that time in Year Seven when you—'

I stopped her with the kind offer to swap Year Seven stories.

'Elektra James,' said Archie a minute later. 'Can I just start off by saying what a *thrill* it is to be here talking to you?'

'No, you can't, get on with it,' I said. 'I'm a very busy film star with twenty interviews lined up behind this one. You've got five minutes before I turf you out to talk to *The Times.*'

He ignored me. My diva vibe needed work. 'What attracted you to this project?'

I'd have been attracted to any project. *Obviously.* 'Er ... it was the first offer I'd ever had? Except for the one to voice the second-most-important squirrel in a local nuts' commercial?' Yep, it definitely needed work.

'Try again,' he said, looking at me sternly over the top of his glasses.

'I was excited at the thought of working with Sergei Havelski?' I ventured.

'Because you were a fan of his work?'

'No, I hadn't seen any of his work.'

'There's a problem here, Elektra. Honesty. You've got to rein that in.'

'But I thought we were meant to sound real.'

'But not stupid,' said Moss/my publicist helpfully.

'I'm sure our readers would love to know what preparation you did for this role?'

I sighed. 'I worked *very hard* with a personal trainer to *master* all the required physical skills demanded by the role.'

'I think you should totally ask her what physical skills she's now the master of,' suggested Carlo. 'Perhaps a little video clip of her running to accompany the article?' Hilarious.

'What was it like working with Sam Gross and Amber Leigh?'

'It was ... interesting.'

'You must have learned a lot from working with stars of that calibre?'

'Yes,' I said.

'It says here,' said Carlo, skimming down the briefing document, 'that we're to avoid monosyllabic answers unless we're facing hostile questioning. You're not being hostile to Elektra, are you, Archie?'

'Never,' he said. 'Yeah, give us a bit more. What did you learn from Amber Leigh?'

'How to dump someone for cheating without bothering to check whether they actually are?' suggested Moss (who was the only person in the world that I would have let get away with saying that).

'She taught me ... how to do the Camel Pose.'

'And once again would you like to demonstrate?'

'Not funny.' And yet maybe it was.

'This is a good one,' said Archie. 'And tell us, Elektra, what was it like working with your young co-star Carlo Winn?'

'It was hell,' I said simply. 'Sheer hell.'

'And at what point did you realize this movie was going to suck?' That was Carlo, not Archie.

'*That's not funny.*'

'But what would you do – what would *we* do – if someone asks that – I mean, not like that exactly, but I don't know, talked about the *rumours* or something?' Carlo looked as worried as I felt, which weirdly made me feel a bit better.

'You'd say, "This movie is a classic in the making",' suggested Moss – she would definitely make a good publicist.

TheBizz.com

6 March

Has Georgie Dunn been having too much fun? Turned up late to set ten too many times? Been too distracted by Rapper Wrong to learn her lines? Rumour has it that they're placing bets on the *Fortuneswell* set about how long she's going to last before the Director, Amrita Sharma, calls 'Cut' on her character. How brutal will it be?

Death by carriage collision?

Nasty complication in childbirth (tricky plot twist there)

Consumption? Always good for ratings.

Or, our personal favourite, and suggested by absolutely nobody, execution at the hands of Napoleon himself – possibly for spying but maybe just for I-hate-les rosbifs – LOL.

So is Georgie crying into her gin sours?

Maaaaybe, but she seemed happy enough when we spotted her lunching with the (hot young) producer of *Celebrity Island* …

From: Stella at Haden Agency
Date: 7 March 09.58
To: Elektra James
Cc: Charlie at Haden Agency; Julia James

Subject: Extra Day *Fortuneswell*?

Hi Elektra,

I know you've got a lot on with promo for *Raw* (less than three weeks to go!) and school but do you fancy spending Wednesday **16 March** doing an extra scene's filming? It's been a while since we booked you a day off school! Aphrodite Productions have been in touch and they know it's last minute but there's another London scene that has 'come up' for Clemency. It was all a bit vague. Vague but good.

It's one day with a respectable number of lines. The script's attached. Have you got time to get that off-book? Let me know ASAP!

Stella x

From: Jonathan Tibble, Deputy Head at Berkeley Academy
Date: 7 March 15.16
To: Julia James
Cc: Mrs Haroun, Head Teacher, Berkeley Academy; Mrs Green, Head of Year 11
Subject: Elektra James's absence from school
Attachments: Memorandum.doc

Dear Mrs James,

Further to our recent conversations (and after consultation with Mrs Haroun and with Elektra's Head of Year, Mrs Green) I confirm that I will grant Elektra permission to be absent from classes on the dates listed on the attached memorandum (only for the hours specified) so that she can fulfil publicity obligations arising in connection with the upcoming release of the movie in which she has a role (*Raw*). I also (with some reluctance) grant permission for her to be absent from school for *one day only* for filming on a project in which she was involved over the Christmas vacation (*Fortuneswell*).

While we are happy to support Elektra – and we do take your point that at this stage her acting is somewhat more than an extra-curricular and may even be something she pursues as a career! – this is GCSE year and if she is to complete this year as expected, she cannot be allowed to disrupt class schedules. I am pleased to hear that she will be making up any missed work.

We are thrilled that the staff and ten lucky girls from the sixth form are to receive complimentary tickets to the Premiere of *Raw*!

We are also thrilled by the offer of a copy of the Film poster signed by members of the cast to be included in the auction to raise funds for the School netball exchange trip.

Jonathan Tibble

Berkeley Academy, Believing and Achieving since 1964

CHAPTER 20

*'I don't like talking about myself. I don't like
attention. Which is weird in this career.'*

Riley Keough

'Well, hello!' Phil Nelson got up to shake my hand.
'You must be Elektra.' Not a tough deduction. I
was the last one out to join his little line up of *Raw*
actors and I couldn't possibly be mistaken for any
of the others.

'So good to meet you.' Ivy Epson didn't look up
from her phone.

'Where should I sit?' Amber was trying out
various positions on the sofa, being raised and
lowered by two assistants so as not to crush her
dress. To be fair, it was Dior. I was dressed like I
was going for a job interview as an accountant. This
was my mum's fault – also, my fault for not putting

up better resistance. This would be way easier if I'd been being socially confident Clemency in my Clemency gown or, even action hero Straker in my Straker sack.

'If you could just cosy up to Carlo on the end there,' directed someone with an earpiece. 'That would *be perfect.*'

I squished on and hissed at Carlo to budge up. Everyone edged along a bit until Amber got stressy about needing space for her skirts and everyone nudged back again. Great. I had one buttock on the nation's most famous sofa. They hadn't dropped the lights so we could see the 'studio audience' clearly. Too clearly. It was a small audience, mostly production members but supplemented today by Moss and Archie (he'd been right about his shooting schedule, he was back in London). No one else had brought an entourage. No one else had been stupid enough to take that invitation seriously. I'd thought they'd make me less nervous. Wrong.

'Live in three minutes.' A producer bustled past with a clipboard.

'If you could actually follow the autocue today, Ivy, that would be *fabulous.*' Phil lounged back on the presenters' sofa. There was so much space on that sofa.

'Scared of a little originality, are we?' Ivy spat. I looked at Carlo. He was already trying not to laugh.

He had a very infectious laugh – a major problem sitting next to him in any exposed situation.

'No, it just makes it very hard for everyone else here.' Phil gestured to us. I was so not up for being the human shield in whatever weird beef/sexual tension was going on here.

'Sometimes you have to be selfish to get ahead.' Ivy smirked and looked down at her phone.

'And how's that going for you?' Phil snorted.

'Pretty well.' She didn't look up from the screen. 'I've just applied for your job on the Ten O'clock show.'

'Positions, please,' shouted a producer.

'You what?'

'Roll Camera.'

'I applied for your job,' said Ivy slipping the phone down between the seat cushions. 'To replace you.'

'What THE—'

'AND WE'RE LIVE!' A red 'On Air' sign lit up at the same time as the lights dipped dramatically – everywhere but on us. We were literally in the spotlight. Also hot seat. A small trickle of sweat ran down between my shoulder blades.

'Good evening, I'm Phil Nelson.'

'And I'm Ivy Epson.' They smiled warmly at each other. And *we* were meant to be the actors.

'We have such a packed programme for you coming up today on *The Lunch Show*. Don't we, Ivy?'

'Yes we do, Phil!' A loving pat on his arm. 'Are you up to it?'

'Oh, yes, I'm up to it'

'So am I.'

'Good.' Tight smile.

'Good.' Slipped smile.

The producer was gesticulating wildly for them to move it on.

'Anyway,' Ivy was back on it. 'We'll be meeting the man making James Bond themed ice-cream sculptures in Devon; the woman who has decided to dedicate her life to educating teens on the possible dangers of eating too much hummus.' That one got a big 'oooh' from the audience, but then hummus always gets a strong reaction. 'And the family who've chosen to live as pigs in North Wales.'

'I'm particularly excited about that last one, Ivy.'

'That doesn't surprise me Phil!' She laughed sarcastically. 'But first we're here with the stars of the upcoming film *Raw*! Let's have a lovely *The Lunch Show* welcome for our studio guests!'

I could just make out someone holding up a card, CLAP.

'Of course, Sam Gross and Amber Leigh need no introduction, they've been household names for decades.' Amber glared at Ivy. '*Fabulous* dress Amber!' Damage limitation. 'But we also have two newcomers sharing the sofa – Carlo Winn and

Elektra James!' There was an odd little burst of applause coming very much from the bit of the room where my 'entourage' were sitting.

'And now for an epic introduction to the film itself, we've got the trailer to play for you.' We'd watched it too many times even to flinch at the severed limbs bit. 'Wow! Amazing!' said Ivy taking her hands off her ears. 'But er ... what is the film *about*? Sam?'

'Well. I play ...' And he was off. A potted description of the roles we all played in one well-practised minute.

'But what's it about?' pressed Phil.

Sam gave an *almost* imperceptible shrug. 'Good art asks questions, you know?' Nope, nobody knew. 'It doesn't always provide answers.' It was a sound attempt. Phil leaned forward, he wanted more. Sam took a gulp from his glass and looked disappointed to discover it was water. 'Er ... the creators of this movie are presenting their ... *creation*?' Inspired.

'Mmmm, yes.' Amber nodded sagely. 'Sam's right. We want the viewers to have their own take on it and then the story will grow, taken in multiple directions by a million imaginations.'

'But what's it *about*?' Phil said again. I'd had a dream last night two hundred Sylvanians dressed in combat uniforms had asked me the same question – over and over. Or, maybe a premonition.

'Well ...' Amber looked to the 'heavens' and finally found inspiration. 'I think it's really, at its heart, about the human soul. The soul's *tenacity*. You know? In the face of real hardship. Like love and faith and spirituality.' Sam had moved onto rolling his eyes. 'Even after the apocalypse, these things, they live on,' she tapped her heart, 'within us.'

Sam straightened up. 'You could say that. Or you could also say it's a testament to how quickly even a small group of people will break down into warring factions. Prepared to kill each other over the pettiest things.' Amber had been having a go at him about smoking in the Green Room.

'Warring factions that *love* can bring together.'

'Love and warring factions – what a *fun* mixture,' interjected Ivy.

'Oh, really?' Phil turned to her. 'Do you think so?'

She shuffled her papers awkwardly and Phil smugly took back control. 'Talking of love, the off-screen rekindling of the relationship between you both,' he looked at Sam and Amber, 'is really beautiful.'

'*Beautiful*,' echoed Ivy.

'Is there anything you want to tell us about that?'

'I'm pretty sure the tabloids have it all covered,' said Sam but he took Amber's hand. I relaxed a *tiny* bit. S-Amber would do most of the work.

'We do have ...' She hesitated and looked at Sam

questioningly; he nodded. 'We do have a teeny announcement to make.'

Ivy clapped her hands in glee. 'Well, *The Lunch Show* is the best place to make announcements. An unexpected exclusive for us!'

'Well,' began Amber. The presenters leaned forward, Carlo and I leaned forward too. There hadn't been any hints of this to come in the Green Room. 'We – Sam and I,' she looked lovingly at him, 'we think it's time to add to our little family!' A chorus of 'aaaws' came from the studio audience. 'We're getting ... a dog! Yes, a little canine brother or sister for our adored Kale.' Sam, who'd been doing very well, sniggered again.

'Oh. Well, that's very nice.' There was a cold wind of disappointment blowing from the open spaces of the presenters' sofa. 'Lovely.' Ivy got a grip. 'What kind of dog?'

'Oooh, I think it has to be another Pomeranian.'

'WHAT!' Sam jerked upright so fast that there was a domino effect and we all rocked around perilously. 'I am NOT having another of these ... handbag things. I want a Real Dog.'

'Kale's a real dog.' Kale was more like a very angry rat than any dog I'd ever known but I wasn't getting involved. I was quite surprised he wasn't making his Lunch Show debut with his mummy.

'I want a Great Dane or a Ridgeback or, if I have

to compromise, a German Shepherd.' Sam was losing his cool.

'Those aren't dogs. Those are small horses.' They weren't holding hands any longer. 'They'd probably *eat* Kale.'

'Hopefully,' said Sam.

'Hahahaha.' Phil let out a nervous laugh. 'And we can't wait to hear what breed you choose. *Later. After the show.*' If Phil had let it run, he might have had a break-up-on-air exclusive. 'But let's find out a bit about you, Carlo and Elektra. Could you each describe yourself in three words?'

Impossible question. I'd let Carlo go first. He could hog the limelight. I was good with that.

'Chill, energetic and ...' Even he was struggling.

'Hot?' suggested Ivy.

Carlo grinned. 'I couldn't possibly say.' Laughter from the audience (possibly not from Moss). Carlo turned to me. 'What are your three words, E?'

'Um ... nervous?' My voice sounded all squeaky. I forced it lower. 'I mean excited,' (too low, I was out-growling Sam) 'no, I mean excited *and* nervous.' Did that count as three words?

'Of course, you must be dying to see yourselves on the big screen!' said Phil. It did risk being a near-death experience.

'I'm really looking forward to the premiere.' Carlo jumped in to save me.

'And do you have a date for that?' Ivy leaned forward.

'I don't know.' He smirked. 'Depends if you're free.'

Sam laughed. Amber calmly stamped on his toes with her stiletto.

'I meant,' Ivy raised a single, deadly eyebrow, 'has the *date of the premiere* been confirmed yet?'

Carlo blushed, possibly for the first time in his life.

'Anyyyywayyyy,' Phil continued gamely, 'I assume you'll be taking each other,' he gestured to Amber and Sam.

'Only if Ivy isn't free,' Sam snorted with laughter. Amber subtly shifted her stiletto, probably crushing another toe.

'Elektra, you must be looking forward to the premiere as well? You say you'll be nervous, which is so cute.' Phil paused while the audience were roused into a couple of 'aaaaws'. 'But judging by your Instagram that kind of glamorous event is right up your street.'

'Um … yes.' I tried to overcome the trainee-accountant-vibe and look more glamorous. Body language – how did glamorous people sit? I shoved Carlo hard and he moved by, at most, two millimetres.

'It must be so exciting to be your age and to have a voice in the virtual conversation?' I was going to take that as more of a hypothetical statement than a question. 'And you want to use your youth as a force for social change?' That time Phil was definitely asking a question. Did I? Who wouldn't? I nodded and smiled awkwardly. Why wasn't he asking Carlo this? 'So you're going to be a social media warrior of sorts?'

'Of sorts,' I echoed back uncomfortably. I kind of hoped I was going to be an actor.

'But let's talk about you going to lots of glamorous places!' Ivy joined in.

'Yes,' I mumbled, wishing I could get out of this real conversation.

'And juggling everything with school,' she went on. 'It must be so weird mastering maths in the morning and hitting hip restaurants and events in the evenings?'

'Yes!' Because that *would* be weird. Not least because I'd never mastered maths.

'And out of the fun happenings you've attended, which would you say has been the most fun?' Ivy leaned forward. What? That hadn't been in our 'likely questions' briefing paper.

'Oh …' I stretched it into a long pause. My smile was starting to ache. 'That's too hard to choose.' Definitely tipped into full-on lying now. On camera. Not in an acting-y way.

'But if you had to?' She pushed.

'Um …' My mind was (not surprisingly)

completely blank. 'That one.' I was pretty sure the lights had got brighter. I'd definitely got hotter.

'Which one?'

'Emmm.' The pressure wasn't helping. I was seriously regretting my brilliant idea of a social media break (from my social media). Ivy started helpfully making suggestions, listing 'happenings' for me, pointing out that we didn't have much time. We had too much time. I was panicking, nothing she was saying was making any sense. 'The ... um ... the one you just said?' Make it stop.

I felt Carlo stiffen beside me. He started to say something but Ivy didn't let him in. 'The awareness raising event? For the Space-Seed charity? That was the most ... fun?'

'I mean ...' I could feel myself going bright red. 'Not, *fun* fun.'

Carlo was staring at the floor. Amber and Sam were staring at me. Phil and Ivy were staring at me. Most of England was staring at me.

'Of course, that's a charity you've recently posted about supporting. Do you want to tell us a little about it?' No. No, I didn't. 'So, Space-Seed is a charity supporting ... ?' Ivy waited for me to fill the gap.

Seeds? Had to be something environmental. Seeds *in* space? That couldn't be right? Or could it?

The gap lengthened.

Carlo hissed two words at me.

'Boneless children,' I repeated them loudly. *So intense.* 'Supporting bonele—'

'*Homeless* children,' Carlo cut in over me. 'She means *homeless* children.'

'Yes! *Homeless* children, that's what I said.' I really wanted to go home now.

Ivy narrowed her eyes and stared at me.

'OK ... *lovely*, wonderful,' said Phil, who might have been trying to help. 'And how much did they manage to raise that night?'

'Um.'

'I suppose the charity side of these things is easily forgettable.' Now Ivy smiled snidely.

'Oh no ... I ...' I hadn't stuttered this much since my French oral. I heard a little moan. It could have been me or it could have come from my 'entourage'. 'I actually ... I mean, I actually left before they ... announced it?' Was that credible? I had no idea how these things worked.

'Just there for the canapes?' asked Ivy.

'No, definitely not. I ... er ... I missed them as well?'

'Sounds like you weren't even there,' Ivy continued.

'Maybe a poodle?' broke in Amber desperately.

'Were you there?'

'Or a Labrador,' said Sam really loudly. 'Let's talk about dogs.'

'Elektra? The event?' Ivy wasn't asking about dogs.

'I ... er ...' My throat had gone completely dry. My brain had shrivelled up with mortification. I had no excuses, none. And what was even the point? A bit late in the day but the truth was the only thing I could come up with. 'I wasn't actually there.'

'So easy to muddle up these things,' said Amber quickly. 'I'm always forgetting if I've supported the NSPCC or the RSPB. Easily done.'

But Ivy didn't let any of my *Raw* family in. It took her thirty seconds tops to get me to confess to another handful of no-shows and dozens of mystery endorsements.

This was exposure.

★ CHAPTER 21

'Don't make acting a blood sport because it will destroy you.'

Billie Piper

'Elektra!' Somehow Archie was there as I rushed off the set. I shook him off. Moss was just behind him, her eyes wide and worried. I pushed past them, I didn't want to speak to anyone. I especially didn't want to speak to anyone that would be nice to me. And nobody could say anything that would make the shame go away.

If I could have teleported myself out of there to somewhere far, far away I would have done, but instead I ran the short corridor to the dressing room they'd given us to use and locked the door. I'd left my phone in there and it was vibrating wildly on the table. The lock screen kept flashing up with new little white blobs of text. Mostly notifications, *so many tweets* and I couldn't not look. Hundreds of them, saying the same thing in increasingly inventive ways: *You're tragic/a user/fake/outed* ... How could there be so many of them? Most of 'my' followers weren't even real. And now – because I wouldn't speak to them In Real Life (hated that phrase) – texts were coming in from Archie and Moss. I didn't read them. I had ten missed calls from Mum. People were knocking at the door, calling my name in voices I knew and didn't know. I ignored them all.

I lay down on the floor for a bit. Like a starfish. It felt sort of comforting even though the carpet was prickly.

'Elektra?' This time it was Carlo's voice at the door. He knocked again. 'She's still not answering,' I heard him report back to what I assumed was a small crowd of angry witch-hunting peasants baying for my blood. I didn't want to speak to Carlo. It was easy for him. The hot but chill Instagrams. The witty but not pretentious tweets. The casual turning up to things because he didn't have to get up in the morning and wrestle with chemical synthesis and fronted adverbials.

I stared at the ceiling, tracing the outline of those weird plastic ceiling panels. Maybe I'd stay on this floor for ever. Eventually, my phone would die and if I kept the door locked I would be completely isolated from the rest of the world. True, the fruit bowl would go off but there were bowls of *Lunch Show* branded mints and tiny squares of chocolate. They could last me at least a month if I developed some self-control. After that, I could maybe go on midnight food-collecting quests – hunt foxes in the urban wilderness or, because I was a realist, steal from the other dressing rooms. My phone battery was on eighteen per cent. I might as well keep torturing myself until it gave out. I started to scroll.

Seven emails from Fiona. One email from Jonathan. One from Havelski. One from Stella. No, wait, two from Stella, eight from Fiona. I didn't open them.

Forty-two texts – at least half from the crowd outside the locked door.

Loads more unanswered calls, mostly from Mum and Eulalie. I was surprised Plog hadn't got in touch.

But that was still nothing compared to the tweets.

I was trending. Me. Or was it me? Who knew? I (we?) had a hashtag. One that Fiona-aa hadn't come up with.

#ElektraWozHere

I grimly flicked through some of the offerings.

Me Photoshopped between Kim and Kanye at the Met Gala #EleKtraWozHere

Me Photoshopped into the peace negotiations

at Versailles after the end of World War 1 #ElektraWozHere

Me Photoshopped into the Victoria's Secret show #ElektraWozHere

Oh my God. Loads of them.

There was another knock at the door. Distracted by a montage of me standing in for not just George Washington but also Jefferson, Roosevelt and Abraham Lincoln on Mount Rushmore, I forgot my live-as-the-ITV-hermit-plan and wrenched it open. '*What?*' It was Archie. He put his foot in the door. 'I can't talk,' I said.

'That's OK. Just let me in, anyway. We can "not talk" together.'

'*The tweets.*' It came out as a wail and he dodged my defences and came in. I slammed the door shut. 'Have you seen them?' Of course he'd seen them. The whole world had seen them.

'Are you OK?' he asked, making an odd coughing, snorting sound.

I looked at him. 'Are. You. Laughing?' He shook his head. He nearly got away with it and then another strangled snort escaped him.

'Do you think this is *funny*?' I shouted. I'd just humiliated myself and probably the entire production as well.

'Well, no. Obviously not. What happened out there wasn't funny. It was sort of cruel.' He tried to hold me but I pushed him away. 'But ... some of the tweets, the hashtag ... Did you see the one where you were beating Usain Bolt in the hundred metres?'

'What is WRONG with you? This is *hideous* and you're *laughing* at me.' I paced up and down the tiny room. Half the emergency chocolates seemed to have 'disappeared'. '*They screwed me over* and you think it's funny.'

He stopped laughing. 'They did and I don't – but also *you* messed up a bit and people are taking the piss.'

'*I* didn't do anything! *This*,' I brandished my phone 'This was all PPR. They did this. It's Fiona-aa's fault.' The last bit came out as a scream. Because when you're in the wrong, attack is the best form of defence.

'Sure, but you knew it was getting a bit dodgy.'

'You don't get it. You DON'T GET IT.'

'Why don't I get it?' He calmly helped himself to a handful of emergency mints.

'Because,' I said slowly, 'because you've never been a sixteen-year-old *girl*. You think they're going to listen to me? The producers? PPR? They don't give a HELL what I think.' I sped up. 'They just want me to post pretty pictures on Instagram and sit on a sofa and talk about outfits I didn't choose and hand out tips to apply make-up I'd never wear. Nobody's pressuring Carlo to post this stuff. *And you're safe in Transylvania when nobody can get to you for years.* You're just doing acting and I'm meant to be doing acting *and* school *and* this stuff – and I have to do it EXACTLY THE WAY THEY WANT ME TO – except I CAN'T so now I'm not allowed to do it but somehow it's STILL MY PROBLEM.' I took a gulpy breath. 'I don't know anything—'

'Oh, just stop it, Elektra.'

'What?'

'Stop it. Don't say you don't know anything. *Make* them listen to you. You're talented, and you're smart. If you want to do something your way, then DO IT.'

I sat back down on the floor with the last of the hospitality chocolates. Mutely, I offered him one. He came and sat beside me and I put my head on his shoulder and started to cry.

'It's OK,' he said over and over until I got to the sob-hiccough stage and started eating chocolate again. 'You'll be fine,' he whispered in my ear. 'You've modelled for *Victoria's Secret*, you can do anything.'

Now I laugh-sobbed. 'You're such a classic guy. I've brokered peace deals after world wars and outrun Usain Bolt and you only focus on my modelling.' I wiped my eyes on his jumper.

'The door?' We'd been ignoring all the knocking

and calling for ages. I nodded and he got up and opened it.

Moss practically jumped on me. 'Are you OK? That was *carnage*. I will kill Ivy Epsom, if I see her again.'

'Plan B, assassinate Ivy,' said Archie. What was Plan A?

Moss scooped up the last chocolate square and then remembered my peril and handed it to me. 'I'm ready. With violence.'

There was another knock at the door. I'd given up on my isolated hermit cave dream so I opened straight away.

'Thanks, Elektra.' Sam came in and made a beeline for a minibar I (fortunately) hadn't known was there. Moss sort of shrank into the corner and stared at him. 'Thank you for taking the attention off the fact I couldn't describe what my own film is about and clearly have ... compatibility issues with my long-term girlfriend.' He poured himself a large glass of brandy. 'Anyone else?' We shook our heads with varying degrees of reluctance. He seated himself regally on the only swivelly chair and spun around. 'And, obviously, I wanted to check you were OK,' he added awkwardly when the chair had stopped moving. 'Don't panic. Lots of actors get help with their social media. I've done it when I've been really busy. Amber too. It frees up time to do this stuff that kind of makes you a celebrity in the first place. You know, like *acting*. Everyone makes it look like they're in three places at once when they're probably either on-set or watching Netflix and getting their assistant to post.'

'Except I'm not a celebrity and I wasn't busy being one.' I'd mostly been busy *not* revising for exams. It wasn't a good enough excuse. 'It's the charity stuff that's the worst.' Nobody contradicted me. I was a morally horrible person. 'I didn't even know what Space-Seed did.' Everyone cringed. 'Worse than the fake events – they didn't full-on lie about *that* many.'

'Yeah,' agreed Carlo. 'Just enough to kick off #ElektraWozHere.' Everyone looked at their phones and then at the ceiling or each other. Nobody looked at me.

'You just need some sort of damage limitation,' said Archie.

'We should plot,' said Carlo.

'Brilliant.' Sam rubbed his hands together. 'I love plotting. I was once in this movie about a plot to overthrow Hitler.' He stared at the ceiling for a minute. 'Come to think of it though, we failed and really bad stuff happened and we all died – so maybe don't ask my advice.' He looked quite upset.

'Right, team.' Carlo jumped up. 'Let's do this.' He looked around the room. 'Where's the whiteboard? We can't plan without a white board.' He wheeled around desperately. 'Ah-hah. The mirror.' He grabbed a Sharpie (probably originally intended for me to sign autographs for all my *adoring* fans), and wrote **THE PLAN** in big letters in the middle of the glass. He took a step back to consider his handiwork and added a cloud shape around the title. 'So,' he made a little bow, 'now we just need the ideas.'

I knew everyone was just trying to distract me but I went with it. 'I'm taking back my social media,' I declared. Never had I more needed an alter ego to take the heat and never had I been more sure that was a really poor idea. There was a wave of approval and Carlo wrote, **E IN CONTROL**. Very misleading.

'I still think we should assassinate Ivy Epsom.' Moss had forgotten that she was too scared to speak in the presence of Sam Gross.

'No, no, no, don't put that.' I *almost* laughed.

Carlo looked aggrieved. 'But I've already written ~~Assassin~~—'

'Maybe stop there.' Things were bad enough. 'Rub it off.'

'It'll *ruin* the look of my mind map.' Carlo was invested.

'Just put "assassinate Kale",' suggested Sam.

'No!' we chorused.

'Sam Gross,' said a cool voice from the doorway, 'you are on your final warning.' We'd left HQ unlocked. Amber went over to Sam and they hugged so long we all felt uncomfortable. I'd never understand them. 'I was just having a little chat with Ivy,' she explained when Sam half-released her. That sounded terrifying.

'We're plotting.' Carlo filled her in. 'Elektra's taking back her social media. She's going to be real.'

'Real.' Amber said the word slowly like it was new to her. 'It sounds quite modern. Lots of no make-up selfies in *really* flattering light? With primer ... and concealer. That kind of thing?'

'Sort of ...' I said. 'Except with less effort.' So, not really.

'Warts and all,' said Carlo. 'Except no actual warts because, well, warts aren't going to work for anyone.'

Amber came over and gave me a hug. 'Hang in, Elektra. This is what it's like – but only sometimes. *You* need to start looking out for *you*.' And on that cryptic advice, she collected Sam and her coat and they went off to be proper stars that knew what they were doing.

'Thank God they've gone.' Moss breathed out. 'Sorry, but I find them stressful.' Fair. 'But you should have done lots of hot selfies with them before they left. Like pouty ones.' Yes, because only I could be in the Green Room of a TV studio with a couple of A-listers and still manage to be a social media fail.

My phone made a little dying gasp, battery running-out noise and I looked at the lock screen. A text from Mum **I should have known about all this. I'm so so sorry xxxx** I was totally not going to cry again. I was *fine*. I sniffed, the hospitality flowers were giving me hay fever. 'I need to write something,' I said. 'Not on the mirror but for out there – something explaining – no, apologizing for – what happened.' It was my fault.

'Do you think that will stop all the Twitter jokes?' asked Moss. She'd been nervously checking her phone again.

'Probably not,' said Carlo. 'What? I'm just being honest. It'll pass ... eventually.' So comforting.

'Just quit it all,' said Moss. 'Except not acting because that's the bit you like, right?' Right. 'Just become a media refusenik. It's a thing.' Tempting ... so, so tempting. But then being the ITV-hermit had been tempting too. 'I mean, you hate social media now, right?'

Hate social media?

Did I? What? Who could hate a world that gave them *stalking* and dancing pugs? On one rogue occasion, Moss *as* a dancing pug. No. I shook my head. 'I don't hate it. I just can't do it the way they want me to.'

'Yes. Do it the way you want to,' said Archie (managing not to add, 'like I already told you').

'That's the plan. E in control.' He made it sound easy. 'Although,' he paused, 'you could also ... no, too mad. The hashtag ...'

'What about it?' From where I was sitting I could see one up on Carlo's screen, 'Me' kissing Prince William on the balcony of Buckingham Palace. Terrifying.

'You could join them?' Er ... *sorry?*

'Why would I do that? Are you mad? I. Just. Want. Them. To. Stop.'

'You want control?' I really did. 'Then make them laugh *with* you. Not *at* you.' He left a little pause for us all to think about how much everyone was laughing *at* me. 'We could get stuck into a bit of Photoshopping ourselves.' Archie looked at the others for support. 'Elektra announcing the wrong winner at the Oscars #ElektraWozHere? Elektra stepping off a yacht at the Cannes Film Festival?' Better, stepping off a yacht and falling into the Med? #ElektraWozHere. Elektra falling over on the red carpet behind Jennifer Lawrence? #ElektraWozHere ...'

Another pause, everyone looking at me nervously,

'You know what?' I said and now they looked at me expectantly. 'I like it.' Was I sure? Maybe not *sure* but ... 'I'm up for it. Let's do it.' If I couldn't make it stop, maybe I could make it hurt less.

By the time we left the dressing room/Command

Control HQ every bit of the mirror was covered in #ElektraWozHere inspiration graffiti.

And I'd already posted one photo.

Me, lying in my fave starfish pose on the prickly dressing room carpet #ElektraWozActuallyHere.

From: Fiona at Personality PR
Date: 11 March 15.37
To: Elektra James

Subject: FOLLOWER NUMBERS UP!

Dear Elektra,

OOOOOPS!!! You should have asked if there were posts you needed to be briefed on. You need to keep on top of @ElektraJames – set aside a block of time every day (or even better a.m. and p.m.). Remember this is about *you*!!!

But follower numbers are significantly UP, which is great!!! (And we haven't even had to pay for them!!!) I suggest Retweeting/ Re-posting adding the hashtag, *#Raw* because we always have to remember this is about promoting the movie, not just Elektra James!!! We'll try to keep you trending as long as possible (I'm worried that you're going to lose attention because of that *earthquake* – poor timing – but we'll do our best). I have no objection to your posting some content of your own deploying the ElektraWozHere hashtag (surprisingly clever idea!!!) but *only if* you use *flattering shots* and avoid self-deprecating humour – Elektra should be flying high, not falling over!!! SUCCESS SELLS. FAILURE IS NOT FUNNY.

The ElektraWozActuallyHere hashtag is a terrible idea. Please delete those posts.

Love etc.

Fiona

* PPR * ON FIRE in Soho since 2010
⭐ Currently promoting RAW the Movie A Panda Productions
feature, directed by Sergei Havelski, starring Sam Gross and
Amber Leigh COMING SOON! ⭐
**Follow us on Twitter @Personality Facebook: PersonalityPR
Insta @PersonalityonFire**

From: Fiona at Personality PR
Date: 11 March 16.03
To: Elektra James
Subject: STRATEGY!!!

Dear Elektra,

I've just seen your message asking to take back control over your media.

Of course you've always had control over your media. We have only been here to help!!! But, is this wise? What we'd suggest is more of a sideways shift in strategy. We've been BRAINSTORMING in house and we think there are real opportunities in presenting you as a spokesperson for REAL and we're already coming up with content ideas to make that happen! Did you see the Guardian Opinion piece on *Pressures on Young Actors to Sell Themselves?* It didn't make a great deal of sense to me BUT it's opened a door for us to push to get you some more press and media attention!!! We can probably even get you some more TV time!!! We're going to add the hashtags #RawandReal and #Rawlateable to all your posts!!! We hope you love them as much as we do!

Love and hugs,

Fiona

From: Fiona at Personality PR
Date: 11 March 16.37
To: Elektra James
Subject: Strategy (2)

Dear Elektra,

We got your message saying you didn't want us to post on your behalf any more. Is that across ALL MEDIA?!! And are you SURE?! If you work really hard and post every day at key times – you could position yourself as THE FACE OF REAL. We're drawing up some fresh advice for you now. Lots of inspirational quotes by other people about being yourself!!!

Love etc.

Fiona

* PPR * ON FIRE in Soho since 2010
⭐ Currently promoting RAW the Movie A Panda Productions feature, directed by Sergei Havelski, starring Sam Gross and Amber Leigh COMING SOON! ⭐
Follow us on Twitter @Personality Facebook: PersonalityPR
Insta @PersonalityonFire

From: Fiona at Personality PR
Date: 11 March 17.22
To: Elektra James
Subject: Strategy (3)

Dear Elektra,

We got your further message thanking us for everything we'd done on your media accounts. As asked, I confirm we will cease posting on your behalf. *Can I urge you not to forget hashtags going forward?*

Good luck.

Fiona

* PPR * ON FIRE in Soho since 2010
⭐ Currently promoting RAW the Movie A Panda Productions feature, directed by Sergei Havelski, starring Sam Gross and Amber Leigh COMING SOON! ⭐
Follow us on Twitter @Personality Facebook: PersonalityPR
Insta @PersonalityonFire

From: Jonathan Martin at Panda Productions
Date: 11 March 17.58
To: Elektra James
Subject: *Raw*

Dear Elektra,

Thank you for your email.

I'm not aware of the interview incident you're referring to. I'm not sure I understood your email but whatever happened no, this is not the sort of scandal that concerns me. To answer your question clearly: you will *not be erased* from *Raw*.

Yours,

JM

14

Days to Go . . .

CHAPTER 22

'I'm going to try to be me, which is not as easy as it sounds.'

Elektra James

My – OK, Clemency's Barton-Wood's – drawing room was beautiful. There was a fire burning in a huge fireplace and two tiny mustard-yellow silk sofas with gold feet that looked like they belonged in dolls' houses. There were also two camera men (with cameras, obviously), one guy untangling lighting cables, a sound guy doing something technical to the furry boom, an old man in a white wig, dressed in what I presumed was servants' livery, Lucy Morton dressed in something pink and ravishing and our director. I could just curl up and hide in this world for the next few months. Even this one day felt like a gift from the gods – and not just because they dyed my roots; Clemency Barton didn't have much more to worry about than her love life and her wardrobe, bliss.

'Nice to have you back, Elektra.' Amrita smiled. 'Great that you're not too busy with *Raw* promo to help us out.' I shuddered. She was far too busy to be a fan of *The Lunch Show*, wasn't she? 'Today should be quite straightforward; there's no dancing and there's no food to worry about.' She definitely looked at my boobs when she said that. Today (real and fake) they were neatly and safely contained in a pistachio coloured dress with a *much* higher neckline. 'The only prop we have to worry about today is the monkey.'

The monkey? 'A *real* monkey?'

She looked at my face and laughed. 'I know! Mad.' *Awesome.* 'Sorry, I know he's not mentioned in the script – it's very much a last-minute addition. We thought Clemency would definitely have a pet, don't you think?' Yes! I thought, yes! Things might have been a bit *tricky* recently but I was getting to hang out with a monkey. I was good with this addition. 'It's literally *two seconds* of screen time and not much handling.'

'Where is it?' I asked, looking around excitedly in case it was hidden behind one of the sofas.

'Outside with the trainer. We're going to get completely set up and ready for it before it comes in. We don't want to make it wait around too long on-set in case it gets anxious.'

'Animal rights trump actor rights,' said Lucy, just loud enough for me to hear her. I had a feeling Fake-Elektra had campaigned for performing animal rights or maybe that had just been Real Me stressing about Plog. I shook it away and concentrated on Amrita.

'Elektra, I want you/Clemency here, sitting by the fire. You're embroidering – well, trying to – but the monkey keeps playing with the threads until he settles on your knee. It will be a lovely little period vignette. Then the butler announces Belle. The minute Clemency sees the state she is in, she knows she needs to give her all her attention, so she hands the monkey to the butler who withdraws.' Amrita was walking all around the room, showing us in turn where we needed to be. 'And then it's just Belle and Clemency, sharing confidences – you've had the script. We'll take it in stages. Everyone happy?' We all nodded and she turned to John. 'Do you want to bring them in?'

The monkey was small, with a long tail and skinny arms, dark-haired except for a golden fluff all around its little, weird, scrunched face. It looked like a very clever, very angry, very ugly baby wearing a parka with a furry hood. Except for the tail obviously. I felt a tiny twinge of doubt. I wasn't great with babies.

'Does it have a name?' I asked the trainer, an old-ish woman with bright white hair. It probably had a cute personality.

'Of course *he* does.' She stroked his little head protectively. 'Justin ... Justin Bieber.'

What was it with people giving acting animals these names? 'Does he mind the collar?' It was a little black velvet thing, like a choker. I would totally have worn it but Justin didn't seem keen, he kept tugging at it.

'He looks beautiful, doesn't he?' The trainer wasn't quite answering me. 'We weren't going to put him in a little red jacket though, not for any money.'

'Am I meant to hold him?' I put out my hand tentatively. He drew back and bared sharp little teeth. 'I don't think he likes me.'

'Animals pick up fear,' said the trainer dourly. 'You're making it harder for him.'

Lucy came over and stroked the monkey gently. He made a little high-pitched chattering noise and the trainer looked pleased. I summoned up some courage and stroked him the same way; his back arched and his fur stood up all over. Justin Bieber was brutally rejecting my advances.

'Don't worry, Elektra,' said Amrita. There was only one animal expert in the room but I think we were all picking up the signals loud and clear. 'He doesn't *need* to be on your knee. He can just stay playing at your feet. You can get him to do that, can't you?' She was asking the trainer, not me. It was obvious I wasn't going to be able to get Justin to do anything.

'If that's all you want, sure.'

'You can wait outside for this bit if you want, Lucy? I think it might take some time.' If it took much longer, she'd have the baby (her bump was huge now).

'That's OK,' said Lucy, trying not to laugh. 'I'll stay and watch.'

A couple of minutes later, I was sitting on a damask sofa wearing a muslin gown and 'embroidering', with a monkey playing at my feet. The way you do. Except he wasn't playing. What he was doing was investigating the ribbons on my shoes. Very closely. 'Justin,' I whispered. 'Could you maybe not do that?'

He looked at me and very deliberately undid one ribbon. I tucked my feet under the hem of my dress, Justin came too. I did not want a monkey under my skirt.

'Help,' I said. And again, a bit louder, 'Help.'

Six takes to get two seconds footage of nobody saying anything at all. I had sweat patches under my arms. Monkeys were no longer my second favourite animal.

'The *plan*,' said Amrita, 'was that at this point

you'd scoop up Justin in your arms.' So often things sound better than they turn out to be. 'But I think it might be better if the Butler just takes matters into his own hands and leads the monkey out of the room. That way we can avoid contact.' Justin and I looked at each other – we were both good with that. 'Let's just get the Belle-in-monkey-out bit filmed and then we'll take a break.'

'Did you know this – something like this – was Georgie's scene in the last version of the script?' said Lucy. We'd been taken into another sitting room and left alone to perch on dust-sheet covered mini-sofas with mugs of coffee and a selection of Catering's finest shortbread. I shook my head. 'I probably shouldn't have told you.' She looked guilty.

'I won't tell anyone. Is she ill?'

Lucy looked awkward. 'Maybe.'

'She's not pregnant, is she?!' Sometimes *The Bizz* got it right.

Lucy shrugged. 'I don't think so. She's just not here.'

'Do you know why?'

'Not officially.'

'Unofficially?' She didn't say anything. Whatever Lucy knew or thought she knew she was going to keep to herself. 'Will she mind not doing this scene?'

Lucy shrugged. 'It's always hard to know with

Georgie.' She stirred sugar into her coffee. 'Amrita likes you.'

'I can't dance, can't wrangle monkeys,' (can't keep my boobs in my dress, can't run starry social media), 'so I'm not sure why. I like her too. She's very warm.' Havelski was warm too (Eulalie certainly thought so) but in his very own – much harder to spot – way. 'I was so happy to get another day. *Fortuneswell's* the only thing I've got since *Raw*.' I started to explain about *Raw* but she cut me off.

'I know about *Raw*. Of course I do, it's got *Sam Gross* in it.' She gave a Belle-like love-sigh. 'What's he like? I mean, in real life?'

'He's ... interesting,' I said and told her only the bits that everyone already knew about him and Amber.

'Are you nervous about the premiere?'

Nine days to go now. 'I'm so nervous. I should be, the pre-buzz is horrible.' I was off-message again.

'It'll be *brilliant*,' said Lucy with too much enthusiasm. The buzz was very loud. 'Nobody'll judge you,' she added. People *were* going to judge me. There were probably people buying tickets just for the fun of that. People were already judging me but that was my own fault. 'I was in a film that got trashed.' She was trying to reassure me. 'I got over it.' She looked pained. 'Eventually. I was ten. I got another part ... when I was thirteen.'

Brutal. 'I bet there were other actors in it that didn't work again.'

There was a long pause and then she said, 'It's vicious out there.' We both clutched our mugs a little closer. 'It's like *Project Runway.* *"One day you're in. And the next day you're out".'*

'*Fortuneswell* could run for years.' A long series was the way to go, that was the dream.

Lucy nodded. 'So long as I don't get edited out or replaced by CGI or something.' She shuddered. 'I don't want to be out there again. It's worse than dating. Fewer eligible roles and even more competition.' I nearly asked her if she was having a thing with James Moore but I wasn't brave enough. 'Er ...' she looked a bit awkward. 'How's all the promo stuff going?'

I cringed. 'You saw all that.'

'I'm not on Twitter but I saw an #ElektraWoz ...' She trailed off.

'Was it a good one?' I said, because to be fair, some of them were quite impressive. I'd lost my dignity, I was desperately trying to cling on to my sense of humour.

'You were wearing sequins and holding the glitter ball. I think that's a win. And then I stalked you for a bit. Cool move, posting some of your own.' Lucy looked impressed and I cringed. I hadn't felt cool for a long time. 'I liked the one where you were clapping like a seal at the Oscars.' She hesitated. 'Seriously, is it all OK?' I didn't know how to answer. I'd posted an apology and I hadn't looked at what anyone had written about it. I'd posted our 'own' #ElektraWozHere offerings and I hadn't looked at what anyone had said about them either. And I'd survived the next few interviews (mostly because all the interviewers had been warned off asking me anything that wasn't super bland and easy) but it was way too early to call the damage. If Stella was right, I wouldn't really know what that was until *Raw* came out. The worse the film, the harder a kicking I'd get. I'd made the stakes even higher. 'Are the publicity people still posting for you?'

I shook my head. 'No. I'm doing it. I'm going to be me.' I gulped my lukewarm coffee and added, 'which is not as easy as it sounds.' But I had to try, it was either that or move to the highlands of Chile and live as an alpaca. 'I'm not trending any more,' I added. That was a good thing.

'You should have got a loved-up selfie with Justin Bieber,' said Lucy. 'That would have got you trending again.'

I laughed. The Real me and the Real Justin Bieber. What a missed opportunity.

'This scene is all about the emotion,' said Amrita when they were ready for us again. Justin was nowhere to be seen (he was probably already at home, reclining at the side of his swimming pool, skimming scripts and choosing his next role). 'Secrets that shouldn't be found out.' On-screen was the best place for that sort of emotion. 'There's a lot going on under the surface.' Amrita focused on Lucy. 'Belle, you're the one telling the story – you've had a declaration – *A Love Declaration*! This is the first time in your young life someone has told you that they love you – and it's the man you love. You are bursting with excitement and happiness and, yes, nerves. Clemency, you are listening to all this – it's like one of your romance novels coming to life. You are thrilled and a little shocked and remember too that you have your own – slightly ridiculous – crush on Luddington.' Harsh. 'Belle doesn't know you've harboured those hopes so you have to *hide* those feelings of hurt and disappointment and yet make them real to the viewers. We have to see something that she can't or won't see.'

I stopped trying to be me and started to be Clemency again.

The cousins sit close together, clasping hands, Belle is agitated)

333

BELLE

Oh, Clemency! I never imagined *(breaks off)* well, I did dream but I never dared hope . . .

CLEMENCY *(she knows at once that this concerns Viscount Luddington)*

He gave you . . . hope?

BELLE *(shakes her head happily)*

More than hope. He spoke . . .

CLEMENCY *(desperate to know and yet afraid to hear)*

Of his regard?

BELLE

His regard . . . yes.

CLEMENCY

And you spoke to him of your . . . regard? *(Tries to compose herself and not give away her cocktail of emotions)* Then it is understood between you? He spoke in such a way that left no room for doubt?

BELLE

None. He said . . . he said, that he

```
esteemed me ardently. Oh Clemency,
"ardently" (tears of happiness in her eyes)
and I said to him ... I said, "I too
esteem you ... deeply.'
```

That was my sort of Love Declaration.

'And ... cut! Good job.' Everyone was smiling. It had been a long take and it had gone well. 'Take ten and back for angles.'

I caught Lucy's eye and we grinned at each other. We knew it was good. Everyone was happy and we were borderline smug. This was what it was all about.

WAITING
(FOR THE
PREMIERE OF RAW)

- % of time spent googling red-carpet disasters: 76%
- % of time spent googling actors whose careers were destroyed by a single movie: 69%
- % of time spent googling 'when doomsayers get it wrong and movies turn out to be surprise hits': 2%
- % of time spent googling 'when critics get it right and actors set up a commune on the last place on the globe with no internet': 89%
- % of time spent posting Real Me posts: 0.5% (because Real Me was distracted)
- % of time spent dreading Raw being a massive fail: 1000000%

★
CHAPTER 23

'I'm fine.'
Elektra James

01.56 Awake. Check that dress for premiere (not chosen by Fiona-aa, chosen by me and Eulalie and – a silky slip of raspberry loveliness – the most beautiful thing in the world) is still hanging on the back of the wardrobe. Cuddle Plog. *All good.* Will get to sleep soon.

02.13 Awake. Get up for fourth visit to loo.

02.31 Still awake. Pretty sure there's a spot growing on my chin.

03.12 This spot has potential to be *huge.* Get up and generously apply toothpaste because it's all I can find in the bathroom. Maybe it will just *lurk* for a few days.

03.14 Go down to kitchen. Get biscuits for me and Plog.

03.21 Go to loo *again* for another nervy micro-wee. Go back down to kitchen and stare in fridge. Not sure what I'm looking for but eat some cheese.

03.27 Can't sleep. Regretting the cheese. Shadow of premiere dress hanging on back of wardrobe is now freaking me out. It's *moving*. Is it *possessed*? Also, Plog keeps going around in circles on the bed. Think he's nervous.

03.41 Check phone. Resist temptation to wake Archie and/or Moss.

04.11 Hear Mum go down to kitchen. Decide against joining her. She'll be stressed.

04.35 Check again, spot is bored of lurking and has erupted. My life is over. I am going to the premiere of *Raw* with a bag over my head. Decide against posting #candid pic because I don't want to be THE FACE OF REAL.

04.55 Might as well go to the loo again for something to do. Also, need to reapply toothpaste. Google how to hide eye bags.

05.19 Will this night last for ever?

05.55 Yes, yes, it will . . .

18.30 Odeon, Leicester Square #ElektraWozActuallyHere

'Put your head between your legs.' I heard Mum's voice; it seemed to come from a long way away.

'Someone find her a paper bag to breathe into,' said a voice I didn't recognize.

'Has anyone got a paper bag? *Anyone?*' That was Moss. I heard Carlo check that *she* was OK.

'Paper bag, paper bag, paper bag ...' It echoed away.

'Visualize a sun-dappled meadow,' said someone else who might possibly have been Amber. 'A *calm* meadow!' she screamed. Yep, Amber.

'Well, that's unhelpful. Get her a strong drink.' Definitely Sam.

'Just breathe,' said Dad calmly. 'We're all proud of you whatever happens ... and if you want to go home, I'll take you.'

'Breathe in ... breathe out ...' Amber wasn't giving up.

'Pah, she is not needing to breathe.' Eulalie cut her off. 'She is needing le champagne.'

'Has anyone got any champagne?'

'Champagne, champagne, champagne ...'

'Maybe have a few sips of this first.' Archie held out some water.

'Oh my God, calm down everyone!' I said. 'I'm *fine!*'

Everyone stared at me. Amber looked positively disappointed.

'Then why are you slumped on the ground?' asked Carlo. So sensitive.

I pointed to the casualty. My shoe. My beautiful, beautiful shoe.

Eulalie gasped. 'But that is being worse than le panic.' To be fair, she'd paid for it. I'd never need a stylist with Eulalie and Moss on call. 'Heel or strap?' she demanded like a TV doctor trying to diagnose a patient.

'Heel,' I said, lifting my foot up like a hoof needing to be shod – and possibly flashing some lucky onlookers. So many pounds' worth of loveliness *wrecked* because I couldn't walk on heels. The shame. S-Amber, reassured that I wasn't dying and didn't need their magical gifts of whisky and yoga, walked off arm in arm to look doubly fabulous for the photographers.

'I've got one,' panted somebody I'd never seen before, holding out a brown paper bag so big I could have fitted my whole head in it – my back-up plan.

'Merci,' said Eulalie, pulling off my shoe, grabbing the bag, dropping it in and handing it back to my unknown rescuer. A very large diamond was flashing on her finger. What? *Wait.* What?

'Eulalie? That *ring?*'

'The *dress*, Elektra,' she scanned me from head to toe. 'It is looking like perfection.'

It *was* perfect and I loved it and I loved her for it but she totally wasn't getting away with it as a distraction. 'The *ring?*' It was weighing down her left hand.

'I am telling you *everything*.' Brilliant. The movie

could wait. 'But not now, *after*.' Oh. And she and her rock disappeared at speed.

'You can borrow *my* shoes,' offered Mum, which was a kind sacrifice – except that her shoes were hideous and my feet are at least two sizes bigger than hers. I took off the other shoe and Mum squished it into her handbag.

'You OK?' Archie put his arm around me, which made it a lot easier to stay upright. Sort of OK. The dress was good, the legs were OK, my feet were, well, they were just big, bare feet. This was 'keeping it *Raw*'.

'What are you all doing hiding around here?' It was Fiona-aa wrapped in a cloak of many colours, with a clipboard, ear-piece and look of panic on her face. She was trailed by her assistant, nervy-Freddy.

'Just sorting out a problem,' said Mum.

'Who's got a problem?' Fiona demanded to know.

'Me ... I've got a problem.' I whispered, craning around to check that I hadn't got any dirt on the back of my dress.

'Surprise period?' she whispered back (loudly).

'Sorry? What? No.'

'It happens all the time. I put it down to excitement. So, what is it?'

'Look at me.'

'Actually ... you look really good.' Fiona sounded surprised, like only Fake Elektra could pull that off.

'Tiny spot but nobody will notice that.' Which was what I'd persuaded myself until she pointed it out.

'Keep looking,' I suggested.

Her eyes scanned me up and down. 'Shoes. Or rather, no shoes.'

'I'm going to try and style it out.'

'Or,' she said wearily, 'I could just get the back-up pair walked over.'

'You have a back-up pair of shoes with you?'

'Many pairs. You don't think you're the first actor to break a heel on the red carpet, do you?'

Five minutes later, I was slipping on the shoes Freddy was handing me. Did they have a back-up *me* in case of malfunction? Oh ... *wait*, they did.

'Wow!' Archie tugged me aside. 'Elektra!' He was grinning. 'You made the poster!'

The poster was double-decker bus sized. It was *intense*. There was Sam Gross with no shirt. There was Amber Leigh with hardly any clothes at all. There were scary wolf-like creatures. There was blood. There was fire.

And there was me.

My face – a huge blurry photocopy of my headshot, cut out and stuck somehow on the head of the biggest wolf-like creature. Under it someone had scribbled *#Elektra WozHere* ...

'You guys all need to be walking down that carpet about now, yah?' Fiona interrupted the moment (and it was a moment). 'There's a big crowd. A couple of A-listers have turned up! And some B-listers. Lots of C-listers.' She dropped her voice. 'We're not even *paying* most of them.'

'So what are they doing here?'

'They're getting photographed, Elektra.' Ah. I should have guessed that. 'Some of the cast of *Fortuneswell* are here,' she added.

'*Lohan Winter is here?*' Mum sounded like she was going to need to breathe into that paper bag.

'Not Lohan, because he's in LA accepting some award.' And possibly also because I'd never spoken to him and/or he hadn't forgiven me for the cranberry-boobie incident. 'But Ally Sheer and Lucy Morton are over there.' She pointed. They were standing in a little group laughing with James Moore and Mike.

'Elektra, I want that dress!' Rhona (Havelski's assistant) came over and gave me a careful hug so as not to crush it. There were lots of people around us now, mostly with earpieces and clipboards. People with tickets that weren't in the cast were all being ushered away to take their seats. My parents were dragged off by someone wearing a lanyard – Mum walking backwards, mouthing an anguished 'good luck' to me like it was the last time she'd ever see me alive.

'Where's Carlo?' asked Rhona. 'We need to get you guys ready to walk.' I pointed him out. He was standing, head dipped, forehead to forehead with Moss. 'Trust Carlo to have picked someone up practically on the red carpet.'

'She's his girlfriend.'

'Seriously? Well, that's a first.' Rhona looked impressed. 'I'll go and peel him away.'

'If I'm going to get into that cinema, I need to go now,' said Archie. I didn't want him to go. 'You'll be great.' Would I be great? This was work. I had to be great. At least I had to be OK. I didn't feel great, or suddenly, even OK, I felt sick. Throw up sick. I was telegraphing panic, he pulled me close. 'I was so scared before my first scene on *The Curse*,' he whispered, 'I vommed on Poppy Leadley's cloak.' I have no idea why that was comforting, but it was. 'But I do need to go in now.' There were at least three people, including Fiona, trying to get my attention. This was happening. 'I'll catch up with you the very first second I can. I promise. Enjoy every moment.' Archie leaned close and whispered in my ear. 'I love you, Elektra James.'

And he was gone almost before I clocked that he'd said it at all. I ignored Fiona and watched him. Now he was chatting to Carlo, no doubt wishing him luck, and now he was hugging Moss. He looked back at me and grinned.

He *had* said it.

And the first chance I got, I'd say it right back.

*

344

'Elektra? Elektra?' Carlo was waving his hands in front of my face. 'Are you OK? You look sort of ... spaced out. You're not going to fall over again, are you?'

I came back to earth and smiled at him. 'No. All good. So *good*.'

Carlo looked a bit wavy; he was trying and failing to tie his bow tie. 'I've got a bad feeling it's too late to make a run for it,' I said, helping him. Fiona-aa and Rhona and lots of other people were giving us instructions. Where to walk to, where to pause, how long to pause, who to talk to first, who not to talk to at all, how to get away ... So many instructions, only some of which we'd been told ten times already. We looked at each other and gulped.

'Catch up to Sam and Amber,' said Rhona, giving us gentle nudges onto the carpet. 'They'll help you. We're all right behind you.'

S-Amber had accessorized since I last saw them – Amber with Kale; Sam with a new miniature Pom puppy (both dogs on matching glittery Swarovski leads). They were already talking to journalists a few feet away. I could hear bits of the conversation. 'He's called Krispin, he's our new baby and isn't he *adorable* ... It had to start with a K' (Amber). 'I wanted Kauliflower – with a K ...' (Sam). So chill.

'Over here, Elektra!' A flashbulb went off in my face.

345

'Who are you wearing?'

'Sign this!' Aaaaagh. What was my name?

'Sign this!' How did I spell it? Was I meant to put Elektra or Straker?

'This way!' Which way?

'This way!' What way?

'How do you feel about being "Actually Here"?'

And then Sam's arm was around my shoulder and I could smell the aftershave he advertised and he was answering questions easily for both of us and I said some words and nobody laughed except at the bits they were meant to laugh at and anyway Krispin was taking half the attention. Amber had linked her arm in Carlo's and she and Kale were helping him show off. Turns out he was a natural at it.

It was too fast to worry about whether I was doing it right. Even inside there was no time to stop, Producer Pete was already standing in front of the curtained screen (a real red velvet curtain) giving the same sort of speech he'd given at the Wrap party, and people were paying the same amount of attention. It was like any night at the movies – except for the clothes and the jewels and the drinks and the special branded popcorn and – in the front few rows – the tension, *so much tension*.

I was shown to a seat right at the front. Carlo was next to me.

I located my parents, two rows behind me; they looked like they were going to throw up. Eulalie was easy to find because she kept leaping up in her seat. Moss and Archie were right at the end of that row.

The lights went down.

'I'll be back at the end,' said Carlo quietly and he got up and half crouched, half ran from the row. Had he gone to be sick? Should I follow him? Should I tell someone?

Was it too late?

PANDA PRODUCTIONS PRESENTS ...
A FILM BY SERGEI HAVELSKI

I stopped breathing. The theme tune was loud. It was also quite distressing.

There was movement at the end of the row. Some people getting up. Some whispered 'sorry's. Were they walking out? *Already?!*

And then he was sliding into the empty seat next to me. 'We thought we'd change seats,' he whispered. 'Is that OK? Archie held out his hand and I took it and clung on.

RAW

I looked up at the huge screen and waited for it all to begin.

THE CULTURE
Raw: The Movie

By Faye Carramore

A dystopian insight into the future of the film industry?

Raw has been billed (by its own publicity team) as the big blockbuster hit of the summer, telling the story of two rival tribes emerging after the annihilation of most of the human race.

This film has everything . . . if you've got a crush on Amber Leigh, some serious blood lust and no intelligence. The makers have certainly thrown a lot at it – big set, some expensive actors, crazy effects and endless explosions. I'd have been wholly unsurprised if the kitchen sink had come winging over the Cliff of Dreams.

This film leaves you asking questions.
Unfortunately, the questions it leaves you asking are: Why did this film ever get made? Why did I spent an hour and a half of my life watching it? Why did the script make me want to vomit the whole way through? Why does this have to be the future of the capitalist Gomorrah in which we live? Why did they waste these actors on this?

This film is a bleak, one might even say dystopian, model for the future of a film industry dominated by commercial, capitalist, shallow concerns.

We're giving it **one star** only because we're impressed by the green screen wolf-like creatures.

THE LONDON
Raw: The Movie

By G. Macintyre (Press Association Film Reviewer of the year)

My God, how badly I wanted to savage this film. I'd read the pre-press, I knew there were issues, I was sharpening my metaphoric pencil.

I wanted to tell you that it was poorly plotted, saccharine and gratuitously violent. *And it was all those things.*

But the truth is: I DON'T REMEMBER THE LAST TIME I ENJOYED A FILM THIS MUCH SINCE *Mean Girls*.

It was fast paced (possibly because it didn't have a plot to hold it back, but whatever), it was action packed (I love gratuitous violence) and it was hot – mostly because of the explosions, but let's not forget the (ahem) passionate scenes featuring real-life couple, Amber Leigh and Sam Gross. Sam and Amber are convincing as the post-apocalyptic couple whose love crosses boundaries, but the young stars Carlo Winn and Elektra James deserve a mention. They were impressively in control, handling demanding material and some clunky lines. I was moved to tears by one scene featuring the young actors but I won't reveal more for fear of spoilers!

Forget what you've heard. This film has everything: a fine cast of established and break-out talent and it's fast, fun and truly entertaining.

I have a feeling audiences will love it . . .

Make. It. Stop

Review

Carlo Strong
Hot. Talented

Elektra James
Break out
How did she
eat those
bugs?

Sam Gross
We thought
was past it b
he ruled tha
lake scene .

HOLLYWOOD SPEAKS

SERGEI HAVELSKI HAS ALREADY COMMITED TO HIS NEXT PROJECT:

SISTERS IN ARMS but first he's taking a two month sabbatical! Rumour has it he's got a personal project to take care of . . .

BUZZFEED

Top Ten Movies We Can't Help But Love . . .

New entry! Number One: Raw the Movie! Intoxicatingly bad. We loved it.

Radio Review

By R Rand

I'd complain about the script but I'm not sure they had one. Had its moments though and some good performances . . .

Culture Chronicle

The naysayers are intellectual snobs. This is enormous fun. Loved it!

LA TIM
BUSIN

Better than ex
opening week
Raw the Movi

HOLLYWOO
CHRONICL

Are Raw the
Movie high gros
enough to get Pa
Productions out
trouble? Jonatha
says . . .

odzilla Reviews

The Greatest action Movie this year. NO IRONY . . .

From: Stella at the Haden Agency
Date: 1 April 10.01
To: Elektra James
Cc: Julia James, Charlie at Haden Agency

Subject: You!

Dear Elektra,

Can you come in and see us ASAP?

Aphrodite Productions (*Fortuneswell*) have been in touch. They're considering developing the role of Clemency in new directions and they'd love to have a conversation. Exciting.

But you have choices, *your* choices – although we're going to make sure you've got the support to make the right ones. We have *a lot* to talk about!

Stella x

P.S. Just telling you one more time, #ElektraWozGood

Acknowledgments

It is a truth universally acknowledged that writers that get to the end of a trilogy are in need of a lie down and some serious grooming – oh, and that they owe heartfelt thanks to an army of people. But we'll try to keep this one as short as a Regency Love Declaration.

The first thank you is to our readers – we hope you enjoy this one too! We love hearing from you and coming to visit your schools – get in touch anytime, we promise we'll get back to you.

Huge thanks go again to the wonderful team at Simon & Schuster (swelled for *It's A Wrap* by Jenny Glencross and Catherine Alport). You've looked after our books – and us – splendidly. You've spoiled us with cake and the *best* covers (virtual flowers to Jenny Richards & Lisa Brewster) and all the endless less visible things that get our books to our readers – and especially, thank you to Jane Griffiths, our editor, you are simply brilliant at what you do and we appreciate it. And thank you lovely Hannah Sheppard at DHH Literary for all that you've done and especially for finding Elektra her home.

We have been so touched by the support these books have had from bloggers and fellow authors and librarians and other book enthusiasts. Special thanks must go to those who've hosted our blog tours: Jo (BookLover Jo); Jim (YAYeahYeah); Chelley (Tales of Yesterday); Viv (Serendipity Reviews); Alix (Delightful Book Reviews); Beth (The Reader's Book Corner), Amber (Mile Long Bookshelf); Emma (Never Judge a Book By its Cover); and Zoe (No Safer Place). And to the authors who have offered us kind and generous words for our book covers Katy Birchall, Abi Elphinstone, Emma Carroll, Beth Garrod, Jenny McLachlan, Sarra Manning and Chloe Seager – thank you! But so many others have helped us in lots of ways – not least by taking the time in busy lives to post lovely reviews. If we were to try and name everyone the list would be as long as one of Torr's self-important text threads (and we'd miss someone out and feel BAD) but we hope you know how grateful we are. Twitter (which gets a bit of a kicking in this book) can be brutal – but in the corner that is book world we've found generosity, enthusiasm and real friendship too. You are brilliant.

Thank you to our lovely experts. James Barriscale who sent us helpful emails from the set of *The Hurricane Heist* (on such pressing points as water sprays between takes!) and to Immy Wilkinson for 'reminding' us how to dissect a frog (good luck at Uni!). Once again, we haven't let reality hold us back too much … you bear ZERO responsibility.

And as ever thanks and love to our hugely supportive non-book-world friends and family.

And finally, to our characters – good luck, we'll *miss* writing you!

Permissions

Quotation Anna Kendrick Chapter 1, pg. 1 from The Guardian 14 May 2015 (Mary Barnes); quotations Colin Firth, Chapter 3, pg. 32 and Chapter 17, pg. 238 from The Guardian 31 March 2001 (Susie Steiner) and Chapter 13, pg. 185 from The Guardian 1 January 2011 (Kate Kellaway); quotation Eddie Redmayne Chapter 5, pg.67 from The Guardian 6 November 2016 (Tim Lewis); quotation Sienna Miller Chapter 7, pg. 102, from The Guardian 16 March 2017 (Decca Aitkenhead); quotation Ruth Negga Chapter 8, pg.120 from The Observor 29 January 2017 (Tim Lewis); quotation Amy Adams Chapter 12, pg.172 from The Guardian 5 November 2016 (Hadley Freeman); quotations Billy Piper Chapter 15, pg.211 and Chapter 21, pg.304 from The Guardian 13 July 2016 (Live Chat); quotation Benedict Cumberbatch Chapter 19, pg. 276 from The Guardian 24 October 2016 (Live Chat); quotation Riley Keough Chapter 20, pg.291 from The Guardian 20 August 2017 (Sanjiv Bhattacharya)

Quotations Ryan Gosling Chapter 2, pg.13, Chapter 6, pg 87, from The Times 7 January 2017 (Polly Vernon); quotations Hailey Baldwin Chapter 4, pg.46 and Chapter 14, pg.199 from The Times Magazine, 11 March 2017 (Harriet Walker); quotation Idris Elba Chapter 9, pg.137, The Sunday Times 13 August 2017 (Chrissy Iley); quotation Robert Pattinson Chapter 10, pg.148, from The Times 11 November 2017 (Kevin Maher); quotation Emma Stone Chapter 11, pg.161 from The Sunday Times 26 February 2017 (Jonah Weiner); quotation Daniel Radcliffe Chapter 16, pg.226 from The Times 24 September 2016 (Charlotte Edwardes); quotation Kit Harrington Chapter 18, pg.257 from The Times 4 November 2017 (Hattie Crisell).

FIND US ONLINE

 website: waitingforcallback.com

@honorcargill Waiting for Callback
@perditact @perditawriter